MW00386678

Designed For Love

Yellow Pine Series

Charlene Amsden

Published by Quilldancer Publishing, 2020.

This is a work of fiction. Similarities to real people, places, or events are entirely coincidental.

DESIGNED FOR LOVE

First edition. September 30, 2020.

Copyright © 2020 Charlene Amsden.

Written by Charlene Amsden.

This book is dedicated to those who made it possible:

My beloved, Charles J. O'Kelly,

As well as my family & friends

Ramona Fowler,
Jessie Gussman,
Julia Gussman,
Melli Lantz,
Brooke Limesand,
Kelly McCullough,
Lucie Ulrich,
Jill Urbach,
Lisa Vazquez,
Caryl Walker,
and
editor extraordinaire,
Shelby Bolton

Chapter One

Arabella watched the Spitfire Ranch truck roll to a stop in her driveway. She pulled her hands from the dishwater and dried them on a towel while walking toward the back door. There was no way this cowboy would come to the front door like a civilized visitor. Why would he? He wasn't civilized.

She draped the kitchen towel over the back of a chair and glanced around, making certain Scheherazade, her pedigreed Shih Tzu, snoozed on a cushion in the dining room bay window. Whatever Grif-fin Blake wanted today, he wouldn't be snarling at her about her "nine-pound nuisance" riling up his precious cattle.

She crossed the kitchen, opened the back door, and stood on the threshold with her arms crossed. Blake emerged from his truck looking like everything Hollywood led one to believe a cowboy should —long-legged, slim-hipped, broad-shouldered, and dark-haired. He even had bedroom blue eyes. The man was gorgeous. Too bad, unlike most of Hollywood's movie screen cowboys, he was also the world's biggest jerk.

She infused her voice with false cheer, calculated to irritate. "Good-morning, Mr. Blake. What can I do for you?" Every time she had encountered Griffin Blake in the ten months since her uncle willed her his home, Blake had been less than cordial. She didn't know why he was standing on her lawn, but whatever his reason, she was pretty sure she wasn't going to like it.

Since he couldn't possibly be here about Scheherazade, he must have come with another list of reasons she wasn't welcome in Montana. This time she planned to stay calm. She wasn't going to be the one feeling like an idiot when he left.

Arabella took a long, slow breath, exhaling through her nose. Squaring her shoulders, she watched him climb the stairs and stride across the back deck. When he stopped in front of her, legs planted wide, hands jammed in the back pockets of his Wrangler's, she gave him an insolent once-over, just like he'd once given her. She started at the squared toes of his battered, brown cowboy boots. Her gaze traveled up his long legs, noting the Professional Bull Rider's buckle on his belt, the snap-front, western-cut denim shirt, the curly dusting of dark hair peeking out from under his collar, the ticking of his clenched jaw, and his midnight blue eyes shaded by the brim of his brown Stetson. Ara-bella lifted her chin and asked, "So, what do I owe the—" her lip curled, "—pleasure ... of your visit?"

She watched his chest heave as he took a long, slow breath. His denim shirt grew taut across his chest. For one weird moment, she wanted to reach out and test his muscles to see if he was as solid as he looked, or just full of hot air.

She fisted her hands and planted them on her hips. *Touch him? Where had that thought even come from?* She raised her eyebrows and tilted her head to let him know she was waiting for his reply.

"Your dog ... " he started, only to be interrupted by an excited series of yips and the clattering sound of toenails scrambling across ceramic tile. Scheherazade popped out of the house, shooting between Arabella's blue jean-clad legs, a fluffy peach and cream blur wiggling frantically from toe to tail the way she did whenever she saw someone she loved. Arabella couldn't imagine why that included this particular cowboy, but apparently, it did, even though he appeared to be immune to the little dog's sweet, puppy charms.

Griff looked from the dog at his feet, to his monstrous, black, one-ton truck, and back to the dog at his feet. His gaze snapped to Arabella, and his baritone voice rumbled. "You have two of them now?"

Arabella glanced toward his rig, where a white and gray Shih Tzu stood with its paws pressed to the driver's side window. Everything was suddenly clear. She turned back to Griff. "No, I don't." She really did try to fight the grin that curved her lips. "Please tell me you haven't stolen someone's dog? You know there are laws against that, right?" As she spoke, he looked more and more horrified. She bit her lip to keep from out-right laughing.

Griff jerked his Stetson off of his head and pointed it at his truck. "She was running down the highway!"

Arabella stepped onto the deck and closed the kitchen door behind her. If the little dog in his truck had truly been on the highway, she was glad Griffin Blake had stopped and picked it up, not that she was going to tell him that. Walking around the odious man, she marched across the deck and down the steps. When Arabella opened the driver's side door of his truck, the wiggling Shih Tzu inside jumped eagerly into her outstretched arms. She patted the squirming dog down, expertly avoiding licks while checking for injuries. Finding none, Arabella gave the pup a scratch behind the ears and a kiss on top of its head. She turned back toward Griff with the dog still in her arms.

Hat still in his hand and hanging at his side, Griff stood on the deck. His gaze bounced from the dog in her arms to Scheherazade, sitting with her little butt on his right boot, her favorite place to be whenever he was around.

"So, you're a cattle rancher?" Arabella asked as she sauntered toward him.

GRIFF eyed her warily. She dang well knew he was a cattle rancher. He nodded in answer to her question but kept his mouth shut. She was gorgeous, golden-haired and green-eyed, but everything about her screamed city girl, especially her terminally prickly attitude. Even though he was at least a half-foot taller—and standing four steps above her to boot—she still managed to look down her elegant, little nose at him.

"You breed cattle?" Her blonde eyebrows arched higher, and her pink lips curved into a smirk.

Griff sensed a trap. She kept asking questions when she already knew the answers. Again, he remained silent and just nodded. He shifted his feet and turned sideways, providing a smaller target for whatever words she planned to hurl at him. Her ridiculous, little dust mop dog scrambled to stay on his boot.

"From all I've heard, you also raise some of the best rodeo stock on the circuit." Arabella ascended the steps and stopped directly in front of him. Griff was still trying to process his surprise that she knew anything at all about rodeo stock when she added, "Seems to me, that should take some attention to ...hmm ..." she shrugged, and her grin grew even more gleeful, "... detail?"

Every instinct he possessed screamed for him to back away. Griff stood his ground but stared at her forehead instead of meeting her sparkling, green gaze. So what if her dog was tan and the new dog was gray? Big deal. A dust mop was a dust mop. He'd had more than enough of her attitude and snapped, "Whatever your point is, make it!"

No sooner had the words left his mouth than realization punched him. Griff's gaze jerked from Arabella's raised eyebrows to the dog in her arms, then rebounded to the dog on his boot and back up to that questioning golden brow. One look at the blatant laughter shining from her eyes cinched it. Heat climbed the back of his neck and burned his face.

He locked his jaw, lifted his chin, and slid his Stetson onto his head. A gentle ankle shake nudged the dust mop off his boot. With a careful sliding, sideways step, he passed Arabella, then cleared the deck stairs in two bounds. Five steps later, he was safely at his truck.

Griff stopped beside the driver's door but didn't look around. His voice came out in a low-pitched rumble, "You want me to try and find his owner?"

"I think I should do it," Arabella answered, clearly still amused. "They probably want him back sooner rather than later, and look how long it just took you to figure out that he's male."

Griff opened the cab door, climbed into his truck, and wheeled away without looking back.

ARABELLA watched him drive away. She knew she should probably be ashamed of herself, but she wasn't. That fancy etiquette course her Uncle Tom had insisted she take had taught her how to be pleasant and cordial even when she felt otherwise. Of course, that's also where she'd learned to be haughty and condescending. As a general rule, that side of her personality didn't come naturally, but Griffin Blake pulled it out of her without any trouble at all.

The man was arrogance personified. She'd first met him the after-noon her uncle died. She'd been standing in Tom's kitchen in a state of shock, staring at the assorted car parts on a make-shift sawhorse-and-plywood table. Blake barged into the house demanding to know who she was and what she was doing there. Her uncle's lawyer, Harlan Mas-tery, had warned her that the five acres she'd inherited were surrounded by Spitfire Ranch and that she'd find the living conditions hostile. Un-til she'd met Griffin Blake, the owner of Spitfire Ranch, she'd thought he was referring to her uncle's nonexistent housekeeping skills.

Over one hundred twenty years had managed to pass without any-one stressing over the fact that the Harper homestead nestled inside Spitfire Ranch. Then Tom Harper died. Within five hours of his pass-ing, Griffin Blake ordered Arabella out of the house and initiated a ver-bal battle they'd been fighting ever since.

In the last several months, she'd poured a lot of elbow grease and money into transforming her uncle's cottage from a greasy auto shop into a livable home. Besides, having never known her birth family or having anywhere permanent to grow roots, Arabella was none too keen to sever her connection to her family's one-hundred-twenty-year-old heritage simply because the neighbors weren't neighborly.

She decided to start her search for the little Shih Tzu's owner in the local veterinary clinic.

Arabella parked near the clinic door and stepped from her pickup, intending to walk around to the passenger side and retrieve the dog carrier. A tall, denim-clad cowboy beat her there.

"Mr. Blake." She eyed him over the bed of her rig. He nodded toward the cab. She supposed he was asking permission to get the dog, so she nodded back. If he wasn't going to talk, neither would she.

Arabella snickered. Maybe they'd get along better if they kept it that way. He hefted the dog carrier out of the cab. "Is something funny, Miss Harper?"

She turned to lead the way to the glass door of the small animal clinic. "A little." She shrugged. "I was thinking that if we stuck to just nodding our heads at each other, we might actually manage to stay civil."

His mouth quirked as he reached past her to catch the door she'd opened. His chuckle sounded over her head as she passed his outstretched arm. The rich sound spiraled around her. He smelled good, too, like leather, pine, and tangy citrus. She couldn't help but notice a dimple creased his right cheek near the edge of his mouth. That one little indention almost made him seem human.

"Hey, Junie!" She greeted the receptionist behind the counter as Griff set the dog carrier down.

"Oh, no!" Junie, the auburn-haired receptionist, hurried over. "Has something happened to Scheherazade?"

"It's not Scheherazade. Mr. Blake found this little guy alongside the highway. We were wondering if you knew anything about a missing Shih Tzu?"

"Hey, Griff," Junie greeted, then answered Arabella, "I haven't heard anything, but let's check him out. Maybe he has a chip. We aren't busy today. I'll go see which one of our docs can take him." She grabbed a clipboard from under the counter, "In the meantime, one of you needs to fill out this new patient paperwork." Junie shoved the clipboard toward them, then hurried through a door marked "staff only."

Griff and Arabella both reached for the forms. Their right hands tangled. Griff captured her fingers then reached in with his left hand to take the clipboard away. "It has occurred to me that this is actually my responsibility."

"I suppose that's true." Arabella stared at her hand engulfed in his and hoped her voice didn't sound as startled as she felt. The jolt that went through her at his touch almost felt like recognition. Rightness. She gently twisted her fingers free of his calloused hand. "But between the two of us, I have more free time. My interior design business hasn't exactly taken off." Inexplicably breathless and weak-kneed, she moved to a plastic chair and sat.

Griff followed, sinking into a seat across from her after placing the dog carrier at her feet. "I told you before, there's not much call for all that fancy stuff here. Let me buy your land. You can go back to Seattle."

Arabella closed her eyes and sighed. "No." Same argument, different day. She didn't really want to have this fight again. She braced herself for a litany of why she didn't belong and how much better off she'd be ... *gone.*

He sat perched on the chair, clipboard on his knees, and started the paperwork even as he asked, "Why?" No anger. No censorship. Just *curiosity*?

That was new. Arabella lifted her gaze in surprise.

He looked up at her. The right side of his mouth quirked. "Believe it or not, I don't want to fight, either."

Arabella arched a skeptical brow, and his grin grew even wider. He put the clipboard on the seat beside him and reached out, taking her hand. "Let's talk."

The low timbre of his voice sent another flare of heat through her, as did the rough tenderness of his grip. So, if he couldn't buy her out, he'd charm her out? She turned her wrist, freeing her hand from his. "Well, this is a new tactic."

The staff door popped open, and Junie emerged. "Dr. Turner said she'll meet you three in exam room two."

Room two was all stainless steel and linoleum. Griff put the dog carrier down on the table, and Arabella opened the cage door. Their new little friend seemed to know where he was and refused her attempts to coax him out. She looked at Griff. "Would you hold the cage? Then I'll just go ahead and pull him out."

Griff said, "Here, let me try." He lifted the carrier and tuned it so the door faced him. He held out his hand. "Come here, little fella. No one is going to hurt you."

Arabella opened her mouth to tell Griff those were the exact same words she just used, and they obviously weren't going to work, except the little dog inched closer to the opening. Griff kept murmuring softly. Before long, the frightened animal eased his head out of the cage and sniffed Griff's fingers.

"That's it, little guy. Come on." Griff scratched the dog under the chin, coaxing him all the way out of the cage. Arabella closed the cage door behind him. The frightened dog trembled on the table. Griff picked him up and cradled the small animal against his broad chest.

Arabella plunked down in a cold plastic chair. She knew Griff didn't deserve her glare but couldn't seem to help it. She should have realized he'd be good with animals. Scheherazade loved him, plus, he ran a vast cattle ranch and ran it well, but she didn't want to find anything likable about him.

Griff looked up, saw her face, and grinned.

By the end of their visit, Nadine Turner, the vet, informed them, "The dog is chipped. His name is Fauntleroy. He's probably four years old and he appears to be healthy. I didn't find any signs of neglect or abuse.

"Fauntleroy," Griff muttered. "Of course."

"His owners," Nadine continued, "are Alan and Dana Bellamy. They have apparently disconnected their telephone. On Monday, we'll call the veterinary clinic on record to see if we can track the Bellamys down. In the meantime, there is no charge for this visit, but we do need someone to foster Fauntleroy. Would one of you like to volunteer? If we don't hear from the Bellamys within 30 days, we'll look at a more permanent placement."

"I'll keep him," Arabella offered.

"Wait," Griff said. "This is a male. Your dog is—."

"Spayed." Arabella smirked at him. "I'm relieved you remember their genders."

He gave her a withering look for the jab and lifted the dog carrier. "I'll carry Roy out to your rig."

"Fauntleroy," Arabella said as she left the room.

Griff gave an exaggerated shudder. "Ain't gonna happen."

Arabella almost laughed as she led the way outside. If he kept this up, she'd mistake him for a human being. She needed a distraction. "Oh, come on," she said. "What kind of names do you give your cattle?"

He shook his head. "They aren't pets. We don't name them."

She stopped. Griff almost tripped over her. "Seriously?" She rounded on him. "All those animals and none of them have names?"

"The dogs, the horses, and the bulls have names."

They stood face-to-face in the parking lot. "But not the cows?"

Griff shrugged. "They have numbers."

Arabella's lips thinned. "I see. The females have no value."

"Not true." Griff countered. "The dogs have names because they come when you call them. The horses have names so we can identify which one is which when we talk about them. The bulls have names for the rodeo fliers. The surplus heifers and the steers don't have names because it makes it easier to cull them—sell or butcher them. Believe it or not, I don't really want to sit down and eat a steak named Rosie or Pete. Besides, there are thousands of them. We'd never remember them all. Easier to keep track of them with an ear tag and a scanner. Now," he motioned with the carrier, "can we go?"

Arabella huffed and turned away.

Griff secured Fauntleroy in the passenger seat, then glanced at Arabella as she buckled her seatbelt. "I'll see you at home."

She arched her brow.

His lips thinned. "You know what I mean."

She nodded. Of course, she knew what he meant. He meant his home, where she was the interloper.

Griff pulled into her driveway right behind her. He opened her passenger door and lifted Fauntleroy's cage from the seat almost before she got her key out of the ignition. "*Deja vu*," she said, then her eyes widened, and her voice rose. "Wait. Did you follow me into town?"

"No," Griff nodded toward the pallet filled with feed sacks strapped onto his flatbed truck. "I was on my way to town when I found Roy. I brought him to your place, then finished my errands. You passed by Walther's Feed-n-Seed as I finished loading. I saw you turn into the veterinary clinic, so I walked across the street. I didn't know there wouldn't be a bill, and I didn't want to stick you with it if there was."

Arabella pondered that as stepped out of her car. She was relieved that he hadn't followed her into town yet felt pleased he'd followed her into the veterinary clinic and had worried about possible bills. The contradiction was discomforting, and she wasn't sure why.

Griff followed her up the stairs and across the deck. She stopped outside her back door and faced him, arms crossed. "But you did just follow me home?"

"Uh." A shocked look crossed his face and he shook his head. "Yeah. Uhm, manners?" He shrugged, glanced down at the cage in his hand, then back up at her. "I didn't think. I mean, it never occurred to me *not* to see you home."

Arabella arched her brow, but unlocked the kitchen door and swung it open, motioning for him to enter.

Griff stood as if frozen, two steps from the threshold.

"What?" she asked.

"You're actually inviting me in?"

She understood his surprise. After the first time he'd invaded the cottage, she'd made it very clear he wasn't welcome. Just like she's done earlier that day. Whenever Blake stopped by, she made a point of blocking the doorway or shutting the door behind her, and she'd likely do so again if he resumed being a jerk, but for now ... she considered his jean-clad legs and cowboy boots. "You seem clean enough and you're minding your manners," she said, turning to go inside. "Wait!" She swung back toward him. "You are housebroken, aren't you?"

He grinned at her. "Mostly."

"Okay, then. Come on in."

Scheherazade danced in the doorway. Griff scooped her up with his free hand and carried her inside. She leaned into his chest without protest while he cleaned his boots on the welcome mat and hung his hat on a peg by the door.

Chapter Two

Arabella's house was not at all what he'd expected. Griff had visited the cottage many times while Tom was alive, but he barely recognized the place now. Tom's house had smelled of woodsmoke, dirt, grease, and motor oil. Heavy draperies had smothered the windows. Two sawhorses and a piece of plywood had served as Tom's kitchen table—an identical match to Tom's, dining room table. And both of them were usually cluttered with bits of whatever car he'd been rebuilding.

Arabella's home was light and airy. She'd tiled the kitchen floor and painted the woodwork white. The walls were buttery-yellow, and her sheer, frilly curtains allowed the bright mid-May sunshine to spill in freely. A vase of purple lilacs, probably from one of the bushes in her yard, sat in the middle of her old-fashioned, green-topped, chrome and linoleum table. Her house smelled like flowers, cinnamon, and sunshine.

She'd installed all new, stainless steel appliances. Through the dining room archway, Griff spotted a cherrywood table with matching chairs. And had she replaced the hardwood flooring? Surely, she couldn't have gotten the grease stains out of the original?

"Well?" Arabella's voice made him realize he'd stalled in the doorway, stunned. He didn't try to hide his admiration. "Wow!"

Arabella smiled and motioned him further into the room. He stepped aside so she could close the door, then put Sherry-what's-her-name down. As he set the pet carrier on the floor in front of her, he knelt and said, "This is Roy." The two dogs sniffed at each other through the cage vents but showed no signs of animosity. "Should I let him out?"

"They got along earlier. Go ahead." The dogs greeted each other in typical dog fashion, then Sherry bolted out of the kitchen. Fauntleroy chased her in a happy game of puppy tag.

Griff and Arabella stood. She motioned toward the kitchen table. "Coffee?"

Surprise jolted through him. He'd expected to be ushered right back out the door. "Black, please."

Her kitchen table was a small, four-seater. Griff pulled out the chair closest to the door and sat, not wanting to wander too far with his boots on. He continued to survey the room. He didn't know what he'd been expecting, but this wasn't it. Plants hung from the ceiling and crowded the windowsills. A crystal hummingbird dangled from the curtain rod over the kitchen sink. A row of cookbooks sat on a wooden rack atop the refrigerator. Red ceramic salt and pepper shakers adorned the stove, and a red hand towel draped the oven door handle. Matching braided rag rugs covered the floor in front of the kitchen sink and the back door. She hadn't just moved into Tom's house; she had refashioned it into a welcoming home.

As Arabella lifted a ceramic strawberry-shaped cookie jar from beside the now gurgling coffeemaker, Griff noticed the gold-shot, white, granite countertops. He stood as she approached the table and slid the cookie jar toward him.

"Snickerdoodles. Homemade." She looked up at him. He saw a hint of uncertainty in her green eyes. She bit her lip and backed away, flapping her hand toward the coffee pot. "It'll be just a minute yet."

Griff realized he was making her nervous and sat back down. He knew he'd been quiet way too long but had no idea what to say. Then the dogs charged back into the room and under the kitchen table. He looked down at his foot and grinned. "So, what is this dog's fascination with my boot?"

He smiled at Arabella. She looked at Scheherazade sitting on his right boot and shook her head. "I have no idea. She doesn't do that to anyone else. I could move her, but she'd probably come right back." Arabella shrugged. "I'm afraid she isn't as well-trained as your dogs."

"I have working cattle dogs, not pets. I'm sure the rules are different." He widened his eyes. "She is housebroken, right?"

Arabella's laugh was light and musical. Her lips turned up in a smile and the tension left her shoulders. "Scheherazade is. I don't know about Fauntleroy."

Griff looked at his boots in mock concern.

Arabella laughed again. "Don't even try to tell me your boots haven't been in worse things." She set two small ceramic plates next to the cookie jar.

That little bit of silliness had chased the tension from the room. Griff leaned back in his chair. He had work to do elsewhere, but Arabella intrigued him. Until she'd chewed him up so thoroughly that morning, obviously enjoying every minute of it, he hadn't thought of her as a person. Labeling her "city girl," he'd considered her a pampered, self-centered, opportunist. Griff supposed that didn't paint him in a very good light. When he'd encountered her that first day in Tom's filthy kitchen, he'd followed his knee jerk reaction, and in all the times he'd seen her since, he'd never bothered to reassess his opinion.

Arabella carried two red ceramic mugs filled with black coffee to the table. She slid one to Griff and slipped into the chair at his left. He'd expected her to sit at the other end of the table, as far from him as possible. When she didn't, he relaxed even more.

Arabella handed him a plate and reached for the top of the cookie jar. "How many? One? Two?" She assessed the width of his shoulders. "Seven?"

Griff smiled. "Better only have three." He patted his stomach. "Gotta watch my girlish figure."

Arabella snorted. "I live in the middle of a cattle ranch. I know how hard you work." She went still and the smile faded from her face. Griff figured it was because she realized she'd just broached a sore subject. He really wanted to talk about it, but he didn't want to fight.

He watched as she carefully placed three cookies on his plate, rearranging them as if getting them just right was of vital importance. The room seemed to shrink.

ARABELLA couldn't bring herself to look at Griff. How could she have forgotten he wanted her land? Why did she bring up the one subject she didn't want to discuss? They'd just end up fighting again. She sighed.

Griff gently touched his index finger to the back of her hand. She jerked away and looked up warily. "I understand now why you don't want to sell," he said, waving to encompass the house around him, "But what I don't understand is why you stayed in the first place."

Arabella sighed. She'd let the enemy in. Might as well go ahead and start the fight. She glared. "I suppose it's because you made me feel so welcome."

His face registered shock. His laughter, when it came, was unexpected and uninhibited. Both dogs scrambled away from his feet, and Arabella scooted away from the table. She'd braced for an argument and received genuine, baritone joy.

"I'm sorry," he gasped as his chuckles came to an end. "I've always been a sucker for understatement."

He grinned at her, not looking sorry at all. "Ah, city-girl," he said, "I did want you gone." He reached over and patted her hand. "But consider it from my point of view. Tom never mentioned you. Never. So, from my perspective—a message came through on my cell phone that Tom had passed. I went down to the hospital, and they told me his next of kin had already released his body to the mortuary. I didn't know he had a next-of-kin anywhere near Montana. While I'm still reeling from that, I return home, and there's this flashy, red SUV in Tom's driveway. Then

I walk into his house to find an expensive-looking little blond standing in the middle of his shoddy kitchen, where she's noticeably out of place." He stopped and spread his fingers.

"Expensive?" Arabella parroted. She'd been driving a discount rental car and wearing costume jewelry. Plus, she purchased her clothing from a department store chain.

Griff shrugged. "You were wearing high heels and a little gray skirt. Your hair was all twisted up on top of your head with little sparkling pin things. You had on a pink shirt that was nothing but ruffles, and your designer jacket showcased your assets better than it kept you warm."

He shook his head. "Sweetheart, this is a cattle ranch. You had on stockings and pink high heels. You looked like New York's 5th Avenue and couldn't have seemed more out of place if you'd tried."

Arabella blinked. He remembered exactly how she looked. She had no idea what he'd worn, but she remembered exactly how he'd made her feel. Heat climbed her face. She hunched her shoulders and tucked her hands beneath her thighs, hoping to contain her rebounding humiliation.

"So, you thought you'd call me a few choice names and throw me out?" Her voice came out too thick. She stared at the table. It wasn't the things he'd called her; it was his contempt. Like right now. He'd described her clothes as though they were her. He'd walked into Tom's kitchen that day, taken one look, and instantly dismissed her value.

"I am sorry." He reached toward her but stopped when she flinched away. "I saw a city girl and a lot of heartache. I know you didn't deserve the things I said, and I'm done chasing you away, but—."

"But—" she prompted softly, knowing she should just leave well-enough alone. What flaw rendered her inconsequential? Why was it everybody recognized it instantly but her?

He sighed. "But I'm still not sure you belong here."

She nodded her head. *Story of her life.*

Even her great uncle and guardian, Thomas Harper, hadn't invested much of his time in Arabella's life. She had no idea why he'd listed her on his hospital records as next-of-kin, or why he'd left her his estate, but he had, and that was something.

"Why can't I belong here?" she whispered through clenched teeth. She hadn't meant to ask the question out loud. Shouldn't have, because the bitter sting of tears followed it.

"Oh, crap. Honey—" Griff half rose from his chair and started to reach for her.

Arabella raised her right hand to stop him and turned her head away. "Don't!" She wasn't a crier. She'd learned a long time ago it did no good. She knuckled away the few tears that escaped her control. "This really doesn't have anything to do with you. You just tripped over some old history." She was proud of how strong her voice sounded despite the tightness in her throat. "I'll be all right in a minute." Or never. She'd probably never be all right, but she was usually pretty good at faking it. Arabella excelled at self-sufficiency and independence.

Griff handed her the handkerchief from his pocket. She looked at the snowy white square of linen in his hand and thought it seemed as out of place on his ranch as a city girl. Rather than accepting it, she squared her shoulders and drew in a steadying breath. That was enough weakness for one day. She raised her chin and swiveled to face him. "For the record," she said, her voice was a little husky, but steady, "when a girl starts to cry, sympathy often makes it worse, not better."

"No. I know for a fact that is bad advice." Griff waved both his hands as if to erase her words. "For a guy, when a girl cries, it's a no-win situation. Not offering comfort is a death wish, so we have to try. Most of the time, we don't know what we did or how to fix it. Plus, no matter what we do, we're just gonna make it worse. But even that's still not as bad as doing nothing at all."

Arabella looked up at him. His voice had been light, but his indigo eyes were somber and filled with remorse. As she met his gaze, something deep in her heart moved and shook. Fresh tears threatened. She wrenched her gaze away.

"See," he said, dropping his hands to the table. "Told you so."

That earned him an inelegant snort and a rueful smile. Arabella reached for her coffee cup. They sat quietly, each of them eating a cookie. The silence around them served as an emotional truce while they re-centered. Arabella was thankful and just a little bit surprised to find the quiet wasn't discomforting.

Once she felt confident her emotions were under control, she picked up her second cookie and pointed it at Griff, "So, who goes first? You want to tell me why you hate city girls?"

Griff shrugged. He picked up his coffee cup and stared into it. "I was married to one for a while. It didn't work out."

He didn't say anymore, and Arabella wasn't sure she wanted to ask. Okay, she was certain she wanted to ask; she just wasn't certain she wanted to hear. She'd taken enough hits for one day.

"I guess that brings us back to my original question," Griff said. "Why do you want to stay?"

SHE sat quietly for so long, Griff didn't think Arabella was going to answer. He wasn't sure he wanted her to answer. She was nothing like his ex-wife, Melanie. For one thing, Melanie had turned her nose up at his home. She probably would have refused to set foot in Tom Harper's grime encrusted cottage at all. But the most significant difference was that Arabella had stayed. He wanted to know why.

She shifted away, but answered, "You said that my great uncle never mentioned me. Did he ever mention any other family?"

Griff shrugged. "There was someone he'd go off to visit a couple of times a year. I didn't know if they were family or not."

"Me," Arabella said. "At the beginning of every school year, he'd come to meet with my teachers. Then at the end of the year, he'd arrange for my transfer to whatever summer program he'd chosen. Tom is the only member of my family I ever met."

Before Griff had time to process that shock, she continued, "My birth certificate doesn't list a father. My mother was fourteen when I was born. She skipped out of the hospital without me. My grandmother wanted to put me up for adoption, but Tom bought me."

"Bought you?" Griff's eyes blazed. He reached for her hand. "What do you mean, he bought you?"

Arabella crossed her arms and stared at her coffee cup. "He bought me. He paid my mother and grandmother each five thousand dollars to assign him legal guardianship."

"Why would he do that?" Griff shook his head. "If he was your legal guardian, why didn't you live with him?"

She hunched her shoulders. "I've spent my whole life wondering that. I guess I'll never know. He hired people to foster me until I was old enough to attend boarding school. I lived with six different families before kindergarten. I must have been a difficult child, right? Or why so many?"

Griff had never wanted to touch anybody so badly in his life. She hadn't looked at him since she started her story. Pain emanated from her stiff body. She needed gentleness and compassion but shied away from his touch. And why wouldn't she? What had he given her but grief and judgment? "I thought I knew Tom. This is unbelievable."

Her breathing hitched. She jerked her gaze to Griff, wary, watchful, ready to bolt.

"I'm not doubting your word." He held his breath, hoping she'd trust him more than he deserved. After several moments, some of the tension leached from her body. She exhaled.

He sighed, too. "Tom was a loner. He didn't talk about himself much, but he seemed like a decent guy. The fact that he bought you is bad enough, but how could he explain all the details without telling you why? That just seems cruel."

"He didn't *explain* anything. I found the details. When I cleaned this place out, I discovered a set of dated financial ledgers all labeled with my name. Every detail, every place I stayed, and every penny he spent is recorded in black and white, from paying my mother's hospital bill to the last check he sent me in college."

"So, you just found out your life story a few months ago?" How on earth was she even sane?

"Not everything. The nuns had told me some of it—I attended a Catholic, all-girls boarding school. They cautioned me against the sins of the flesh, visited upon me by my unholy mother." Arabella actually smiled at that. "It seems that my mother attended there while pregnant with me. They told me she was quite head-strong, willful, and disobedient. The nuns assured me that I did not have to make her choices. As a deterrent, they encouraged Bible reading, gardening, school studies, and rational thought."

Griff couldn't decide what prompted her smile and wasn't sure how to ask. "So ...." He eased the words out. "Your mother? You've met her?"

"No." She shook her head and scooted closer to the table, reaching for her coffee cup. "I have no idea where my mother might be. Or my grandmother. And thanks to Tom's ledgers, I am at peace with that."

"Yet there is something in your mother that you appreciate. I heard it in your voice."

"Yes." Arabella smiled again. "Learning about her probably saved my life. My mother wasn't a wonderful person, and I don't want to emulate her, but she wasn't all bad. One of her paintings still hangs in the school library. Sister Paula Francis showed it to me. She said the art room was the only place my mother was happy. We'd just had a lesson on honoring our parents, and I was outraged. Why and how was I sup-posed to obey that commandment? Sister March said the easiest way to honor my parents was to respect myself and do nothing shameful. Sister Paula told me to use the talents I'd inherited for good. I yelled, 'What talents?' and she took me to the painting."

"So, you had something of value to anchor you?"

Arabella's eyes reflected surprise. "Yes. Exactly. I had something to build toward."

"How old were you then?"

She shrugged. "Eight? Nine? Somewhere in there."

"You lived in the school year-round?"

"That, and a variety of summer camps, followed by four years in the college dorms. The last time I saw Tom alive was on the first day of college, my freshman year. He paid my tuition every year and mailed me quarterly support checks until I graduated. He didn't attend graduation, but he sent a congratulatory card and a final, generous check. I didn't hear from him again until a few months ago when his lawyer called. He said Tom was dying and wanted me to come. I didn't get here in time. The rest, you know."

Griff sat with his hands pressed flat on his thighs to keep from reaching for her again. She'd told that entire horrific story almost dispassionately, as if such things were commonplace.

His feelings must have shown on his face. Arabella glanced up and her eyes went wide. "Hey," she said. "It's okay. I survived." Then she reached out to comfort him. He turned his hand under hers to hold her. Again, she pulled away.

She held her own hands and tried to smile. "Nobody beat me. I received a good education. I've had friends. My life could have been worse."

"It also could have been better." Griff looked around her cheerful yellow kitchen, realizing she'd forged this house into a place to belong. He wanted her to know he understood. "I thought I was neglected. My parents were always wrapped up in each other, and sometimes I had to remind them I existed, but they were there when I needed them." He made a rough sound in his throat. "I thought not having siblings was lonely, but I have a home and a heritage." He leaned across the table. "I get why you stayed here. This is your home. I'm done trying to chase you away." It was a promise. Griff thought about offering to pray with her, but he hadn't been to church in so long he wasn't sure he remembered how to pray out loud for anything other than meals.

Arabella spoke to the tabletop. "But I'm right in the middle of your ranch. You still want the land."

Griff sighed. "It is five acres in the middle of three thousand plus. I don't need it."

"Then, why—?" She looked up, waving her hand in the air and indicating all the history between them. "If it doesn't matter?"

"It was never the land." He owed her his story; she'd given him hers. "It was another city girl. Melanie, my ex-wife. I met her in Laramie when I was on the rodeo circuit. I didn't know she wanted a cowboy romance, not a real cowboy, until it was too late. I was twenty-two. She loved the flash and fun of the rodeo: live bands, partying every night, and the excitement of being seen with a professional bull rider." He shrugged. "I did okay, but I was never going to be a top contender. A few days after we got married, I busted my leg, and we came back to the ranch. She hated it here. Hated the remoteness, the fact that Yellow Pine has no nightlife to speak of, and in no time flat, she hated me. Our marriage didn't even last three months."

"I'm sorry. That's incredibly sad."

"I took one look at your fancy fingernails a nd s parkly jewelry, and—." He waved his hand. "I'm sorry."

Griff studied Arabella. She'd lived on his ranch for the better part of a year, and he knew nothing about her. He knew Tom left her some money, and that she'd rented out Tom's Auto Garage in town rather than selling it. He also knew she had a job, but not precisely what she did. Had she made friends? Did she have anyone who cared? Was her life any better in Yellow Pine than it had been in Seattle?

He opened his mouth to ask when his cell phone rang. It was so unexpected and far from his thoughts that he looked down at his shirt pocket in confusion. The phone rang three times before he reached for it. "My foreman." He swiped to take the call, hitting the speaker button out of habit. "Yeah, Tank?"

"Hey, boss, you coming home with that chicken feed?"

Griff spent the remainder of the afternoon mending fences and trying not to think about Arabella, which resulted in an argument with himself.

She's a city girl.

But she's a city girl with grit. Her resilience is phenomenal.

Even so, she's a city girl.

Her head isn't easily turned by cowboys. She's never fraternized with my ranch hands. Plus, she moved here by herself. And she'd stayed.

She stayed even knowing she wasn't wanted.

He wasn't encouraged by the fact that he couldn't find a counter argument for that thought.

He'd been such an ass. Griff knew he shouldn't be thinking about Arabella anyway. Given their history, she had to despise him.

He rode his ATV in from the range at dusk and put his tools away. He had an excellent foreman and competent employees and didn't need to physically work the ranch, but Spitfire was his home. His heritage. It wasn't in him to pay someone else to maintain his life while he sat idle.

He stepped out of the equipment shed and looked toward Arabella's cottage, a quarter mile to the west. Soft light glowed from her kitchen windows. She'd put considerable effort into her own home, building a place she would always be welcome.

His own house was closer, but it was dark. The lights would come on with a flip of a switch, but no one waited for him. Leira, the wife of his accountant and personnel manager, kept the place clean. She also occasionally left covered dishes in the fridge for his dinner. He'd heat the food in the mi-crowave and eat alone, usually at his desk in the office, sometimes in the family room in front of the TV. His house wasn't a home. It was just a place he went to eat and sleep. Arabella's cottage was clearly a home, yet she lived even more alone than he did. What made the difference?

He crossed his yard and climbed the steps to his back porch even though he wanted to walk down the driveway to Arabella's and ask why her house felt like a home when his didn't. She'd think he was nuts.

Chapter Three

After Griff left her house on Sunday, Arabella had a hard time getting him out of her head. He'd been kind, compassionate, and understanding—and she'd been surprisingly forthcoming because of it. Considering their history, she shouldn't have felt comfortable sharing her family rubbish. They'd managed a lengthy, civil conversation. That boded well for the future.

First thing Monday morning, he cantered into her yard on a broad-chested Appaloosa gelding. The horse was magnificent. The strong-jawed, rugged man astride it even more so. Griff sat tall in the saddle and moved with fluid grace.

He dismounted as Arabella descended the deck stairs, her high heels clicking on the wooden steps. She kept her eyes on the horse, trying not to notice how Griff's blue-plaid shirt hugged his shoulders and curved over his biceps. "What a beautiful horse."

The Appaloosa turned his head and watched her approach. Griff took a step back, giving her room. Arabella held her hand out, fingers together, palm up.

The gelding sniffed her hand, then huffed. Arabella laughed softly. "Sorry, boy, no apples." She ran her hand up his nose and scratched gently around the halter straps.

"You're comfortable around horses?" Griff sounded surprised.

Arabella tipped her head in a one-shouldered shrug. "I ride. Uncle Tom was pretty thorough with my education." She ran her hand along the shoulder of the Appaloosa. "What's his name?"

"Ap."

Arabella swiveled and looked at him. "You're kidding, right?"

Griff shrugged. "I'm sure we've got papers with his real name on them somewhere, but we all just call him, 'The Ap."

She shook her head.

"What?" he said. "You think we should call him Lord Pranceleroy or something?"

"Look at him. He's exquisite, and you've reduced him to a generic description." She stepped closer and looked up at Griff. "How would you like it if I just called you cowboy?"

He grinned, "I think I might like that just fine, city girl."

Arabella blinked and looked away. So much for optimism; she was still just a label. She moved toward her pickup. "Not to be rude, but I was headed for work." *So why are you here?* was implied rather than spoken.

Griff tapped his shirt just where the phone stuck out of his pocket. "The vet called."

Arabella turned back toward him, pushing her pride aside to focus on what was important. "What did she say?"

"Apparently Roy—."

"Fauntleroy."

"Whatever." He waved his hand and continued as though she hadn't interrupted. "—is from Boise, Idaho. His family moved away, and the next info anyone has on them is when Roy turned up here."

"So, we're still waiting?"

"Seems that way. Plus, there's another dog. A pregnant female. She ended up across the highway on Bryce Tyner's horse ranch."

Arabella smiled. "Oh, good. I'll get to meet her tomorrow afternoon when I stop by there after work."

Griff tossed the Ap's reins across the saddle and took a step toward Arabella. "Stay away from Tyner," he demanded.

Stay away from Ty? Stunned, Arabella rounded to face him. "Excuse me? What gives you the right—."

Griff raised both his hands, palm out, in a placating gesture, but his baritone voice remained hard and unyielding. "Bryce Tyner is an ex-con who served time for murder."

More labels and judgments. Arabella's lips thinned. Anger sparked in her eyes. "Bryce Tyner is one of the most sedate people I've ever met. If he got angry enough to kill somebody, they probably needed killing."

Griff stared at her with his mouth agape.

Okay, maybe that was a little much, but the man and his labels infuriated her. She marched over to him. "Do you even know Ty? Have you ever spoken to him or spent any time with him at all?" Arabella stood on her tiptoes and glared. "He's one heck of a lot less scary than you are!"

"Are you dating him?" Griff demanded.

"No," Arabella snapped. "I stop by his outfit a couple of times a week, and he lets me ride one of the horses, but what business is it of yours?"

Griff grabbed her shoulders and yelled, "He's dangerous!"

She expelled an exasperated grunt. "Seriously? Ty has never been rude to me." Arabella poked her finger into Griff's hard chest as punctuation. "He's never raised his voice to me." Another poke. "And he's never manhandled me!" Poke.

Their gazes locked. Griff blinked. She felt a shock wave roll through him. He carefully released her shoulders and stepped back. "I'm sorry." His voice was thick. He closed his eyes and took a shuddering breath.

Unappeased, Arabella clenched her fists and raged, "Apology not accepted!"

His eyes snapped open. Fists clenched, he answered, "Are you even listening? I'm afraid for you!"

"And I'm afraid of you!" Arabella snapped right back.

He jerked as though he'd been sucker-punched. His face paled.

Arabella almost felt guilty. It wasn't true. She wasn't afraid of him. He'd yelled, and he'd clasped her shoulders, but he hadn't bruised or shaken her. His hold was commanding, but not hurtful. She'd known she wasn't in danger, which is why she'd felt safe enough to shout at him and thump on his chest. The man just made her so darned mad. She pressed her lips together and glared.

"Right," he said. The Appaloosa, well-trained, had stayed where Griff left him. Griff backed away, jaw clenched, his face pale except for two spots of color burning across his cheekbones. He gathered the Appaloosa's reins and swung into the saddle.

Arabella didn't climb into her pickup until the retreating hoofbeats faded.

That evening, Arabella pulled up to the mailboxes along the highway at the end of the private drive shared by Spitfire Ranch and her own home. An ancient green Subaru rolled in behind her on a floppy tire. She recognized the car as one belonging to Spitfire Ranch and knew an older woman usually drove it. Dawdling at the mailbox and sorting through her typical collection of junk mail, Arabella considered approaching the car and offering aid, but couldn't see the driver. Besides, help was probably already on the way.

About the time Arabella started feeling awkward just standing around, the passenger door on the Subaru opened, and an ebony-haired woman emerged. She called out, "I am Leira, from the ranch. I have a car full of groceries, and neither Hale or Griff answer their phones. You're Ms. Harper, *si*? You live in the little house?" The woman waved her hand vaguely toward the east.

Arabella confirmed her identity, offered her first name, and whatever assistance was needed, including help changing the car tire.

Leira opened the back of the Subaru. "I live on a ranch full of macho men. I am happy to let them be macho. We are not changing the tire. I will take a ride to the house, though." She bent into the car and emerged with a bulging grocery sack. Arabella assisted with the transfer, boggled by the numerous food sacks until Leira explained that she'd purchased groceries for Griff's house, the bunkhouse, and her own home. They stacked the groceries in the bed of Arabella's pickup, then climbed into the cab.

"There are nails all over the road about two miles back," Leira said as Arabella drove. "I was in the middle of them before I noticed. I've already called Highway Patrol."

"Nails? Who would do something like that?"

"It was probably an accident," Leira answered. "They fell off a truck or something."

"Of course." Arabella pointed toward the ranch house. "I just realized; I've never driven past my own driveway."

"I'm not surprised. It was my Hale that fixed your fences after you first moved in. He said you are good people, but the boss ...." She shook her head. "Sometimes, he gets an idea in his head and just won't let go."

Shortly after Arabella moved in, Scheherazade had escaped from her enclosure twice. Both times Griff had brought the little dog home and chewed Arabella out. The second time he'd sent an older cowboy down to fix her fences.

Arabella tried to think of something positive to say. "Well, it was kind of Griff to send your husband to mend my fences, even if he was just protecting his cattle from my minuscule dog."

Leira turned in her seat to face Arabella. "Oh, no. No matter what the boss said, he wasn't worried about your dog hurting his cattle. He was worried about what the cattle would do to your dog. An angry cow protecting her calf, or an irritated bull guarding his territory—." She shook her head. "The boss acts all growly and mean, but he's not so tough. It would break him up if something happened to your little dog."

Considering Scheherazade's adoration for Griff, and Fauntleroy's trust in him, Arabella had no trouble believing Leira's observation as far as animals were concerned, but she still had reservations. "It wouldn't hurt him to save a little bit of that compassion for people."

"*Justo*," Leira agreed. "Be patient. He'll come around once he gets to know you. Wait and see."

Arabella didn't hold out a lot of hope. Besides, she had no interest in getting to know Griffin Blake any better than she already had.

When they arrived at the ranch, a cattle hauler jutted out into the access road. Arabella maneuvered slowly around the front end of the semi. As they pulled into the ranch yard, both women gasped. Arabella tromped on the brakes.

The gate to the corral stood ajar. Cowboys formed a broad semi-circle of sorts around a massive, black and white bull. Most of the men stood near fences, machinery, or some other form of cover. One young ranch hand clung to the grating halfway up the side of the cattle hauler above the sharp horns of the watching bull. The massive animal turned his gaze to the new threat, Arabella's pickup.

"Don't move," Leira whispered.

The passenger side of the pickup, where Leira sat, broadsided the bull. He walked his front end around to face them. Leira freed her seatbelt but remained trapped in the bucket seat with nowhere to go.

"Will he charge?" Arabella whispered. She shifted to park but didn't turn the engine off.

"Not while his head is up," Leira said. "If he puts his head down, I'm trying for the jump seat behind you, but may end up in your lap."

"Understood." Arabella released her own seatbelt.

The bull moved two steps closer. The kid dangling from the cattle hauler yelled and banged his foot against the side of the trailer. The bull's head swiveled at the sound. Leira reclined her seat. As the back lowered, she launched herself into the extended cab behind Arabella. The cab rocked, and the bull trotted forward. Both ladies sucked in air.

The bull continued right past the door and stopped at the pickup bed. He nosed through the grocery sacks and came up with a carrot. Arabella emitted a sound somewhere between a giggle and a sob.

Focused intently on the passenger side of the rig, neither of them noticed Griff approach the truck. They both gasped when the driver's door jerked open. Griff pushed on Arabella's shoulder. "Move over. Let me in."

Arabella shifted away from him and onto the console. Griff levered the seat backward and slid in beneath her legs, claiming the steering wheel. He filled the cab, bringing the scents of man and citrus and pine with him. Arabella tried to slide into the passenger seat. He shook his head and rested his arm across her thighs. "I don't want you any closer to that door." He kept his voice low.

Struggling to maintain her awkward, bent-neck position, Arabella clutched the driver's seat head-rest on her left and braced against the dashboard on her right. Her skirt protected her dignity, but neither it nor her pantyhose blocked the heat shimmering from her every point of contact with Griff.

He kept his bare arm pressed across her knees and shifted the pick-up into drive. They slowly rolled forward.

"It's working," Leira whispered. Arabella didn't know what was working since, hunched the way she was, she could no longer see anything on the passenger side of the truck.

Griff eased the rig forward. Slow-inch by slow-inch, they crossed the barnyard and rolled into the corral. A red-headed cowboy closed the gate behind them.

"That was brilliant." Leira did not sound impressed. "You've got the bull in the corral. Now how do you plan to get us out?"

Pointing across the enclosure, Griff indicated a gate on the other side. Hale, already there, lifted the latch while keeping the fence between himself and the bull. Griff said, "That's easy. His new brides are right out there in the field, and a couple of them are already in season. As soon as *Muerte Manchado* finishes polishing off his veggies, he'll move out on his own."

Manchado wasn't a word Arabella knew, but *muerte* meant death. She looked at Leira.

"Spotted Death." Leira translated. "The PRCA, Professional Rodeo Cowboys Association, billed him as the bull no man could ride."

Griff added, "Ninety-six outs and only two rides. I bought him to sire my next round of calves. Let's hope his sons inherit his fire."

Several more long, slow minutes ticked by. Arabella's stomach muscles protested her hunched position. She tried to shift. Griff noted her posture and slid his right arm around her waist to support her back. "Better?"

Yeah, except now her lungs wouldn't function. Arabella gave him a head-shaking nod. He seemed to recognize her distress. His left hand landed on her thigh, and his arm tightened, pulling her toward him. She shifted her right arm from the dashboard to the steering wheel and braced herself. She wasn't uncomfortable enough to make his lap seem like a better choice.

Leira let out a cheer. Arabella twisted toward the windshield in time to see the bull trot into the paddock. Hale closed the gate behind him. Bracing her left hand on Griff's shoulder, Arabella pushed. He let her slide back into the passenger seat.

As she sorted out her legs, Griff signaled someone to open the gate behind them. He smoothly reversed the pickup out of the corral and across the barnyard to the house. Cowboys seemed to come out of the woodwork. Leira orchestrated the grocery disbursement and told Hale where to find her car. She also thanked Arabella for her help.

Within moments only Griff and Arabella remained in the deserted ranch yard. Even the cattle hauler had pulled out. Arabella climbed into her pickup and reached for the ignition. No keys. She turned toward Griff.

He stepped into the small triangle of space between her open door and the side of the pickup. "I wanted to thank you for helping Leira today, and for letting me commandeer your rig."

Arabella pressed herself as far from his bulk as the driver's seat allowed. Conflicting sensations washed over her. His scent crowded the small space, conscripting what little oxygen she'd recouped after their earlier contact. She straightened her spine and tried to breathe. Griff planted his right hand on the door frame and smiled at her.

Five o'clock shadow shaded his jaw. Thick, dark lashes provided a striking contrast to his dazzling, indigo eyes, and that flirty little dimple to the right of his mouth drew her gaze. Arabella fought the insane urge to lift her hand to touch it and struggled for composure. She should say something, but what? She managed to squeak out, "No problem," but the breathless quality of her voice must have signaled otherwise.

"Are you all right?" Griff leaned closer.

She thrust her arm out and shouted, "Stop!"

He froze. His face paled, and he stepped back, letting his arms fall to his side. "Sorry. I didn't mean to frighten you. I forgot."

She opened her mouth to tell him she wasn't frightened, but what was she supposed to say? *I hate you, but for some reason, my body goes into meltdown whenever you're around?* Yeah, probably not. "My keys?" she answered.

He looked surprised and jammed his hand in his pocket, extracting a tangle of metal. "Habit," he said, separating one set of keys and a jackknife from the knot. Those he returned to his pocket. Her keys, he hooked on the end of his index finger, extending his arm so she could take them without touching him.

Fist closed around the keys, Arabella said, "Thank you." Griff touched his hand to his hat in salute and strode toward the corral.

She didn't breathe freely until she was out of the Spitfire barnyard and several yards down the access lane, at which point something more immediate caught her attention. The young cowboy who'd been hanging off the side of the cattle hauler walked along the road. He didn't glance around as she approached, but he shifted closer to the edge. The curve of his shoulders and the shuffle in his walk telegraphed dejection. As Arabella drew abreast of him, he swiped his sleeve across his eyes.

She pressed a button and lowered her window. "Hey, you all right? You need a ride?"

He glanced up; his brown eyes shiny with unshed tears. "I'm okay."

He was just a kid who had yet to shave for the first time. Arabella flipped the switch to unlock the passenger door and said, "Yeah, I see you're okay. Come on, get in and tell me what's wrong."

He angled his head so his white-straw cowboy hat hid his face. "I suppose you think I'm a sissy."

"No, I don't," Arabella said with conviction. "Trying not to cry hurts like the dickens, and it's certainly not for sissies." She put the pickup in park, levered herself across the console, and opened the passenger door. "Come on, get in. Nothing seems quite as bad after you talk about it."

The kid climbed into the passenger seat.

"My name is Arabella," she said. "Where am I taking you?"

"I'm Johnny, and I don't guess it matters where you take me. Hale said for me to get Ms. Leira's car. I'm supposed to change the tire and drive it back to the house, but I don't know how."

Arabella remained parked. "You don't know how to change a tire, or you don't know how to drive?"

"Yes. Either. Both." Johnny slouched in his seat. "They're gonna fire me."

"Why didn't you tell Hale that you don't drive?"

Johnny shrugged. "They're already mad at me because I let the bull loose."

"Oh. That was kind of scary."

"Yeah. It came off the truck bucking. I was supposed to man the gate, but I wasn't fast enough when the cattle hauler pulled out of the corral. I didn't know a bull could move like that. Now they're gonna send me back to juvy."

"Juvenile detention?" Arabella blinked. She'd worked with troubled kids at Wengert Stables in Seattle. This boy didn't have the hard edge or defiance of the usual juvenile offender.

Johnny must have mistaken her surprise. He looked her in the eyes. "I'm not dangerous. I'm just stupid. I did some spray paint stuff with a couple of guys. I wanted 'em to think I'm cool, but we got caught. Since it was my first offense, the judge gave me work detention. Hale is my work sponsor, but I keep screwing up."

Arabella considered her new, young friend. "How old are you, Johnny?"

"I'll be sixteen in seven months."

Rather than scoffing at his attempt to claim an older age, she asked, "How do you reach the age of sixteen living in rural Montana and not learn to drive?"

The kid shrugged. "My mom died a few years ago, and my dad doesn't pay much attention to me."

"Okay. You're about to get a driving lesson. Trade seats with me." She unsnapped her seatbelt.

Johnny's eyes rounded. "I can't!"

"Sure you can," she said. "You're going to drive my pickup down to Leira's car, and I'm going to teach you how to change a tire."

Arabella talked Johnny into the driver's seat, then led him through adjusting its position, the mirrors, using the turn signals, brakes, and gas pedal; and how the transmission and ignition worked. Since he'd been watching people drive for years, he was a quick study. Johnny drove them straight down the road with no problem, but he balked when they got to Arabella's driveway. She asked him to turn in so she could change her clothes.

Johnny stomped on the brake, bringing the pickup to an abrupt halt. "Turn? I can't fit through there."

"It's plenty wide enough, just take it slow."

He drove through her gates without even coming close to the huge, empty planters on either side. Arabella directed him to park near her back deck and left him in the yard with Scheherazade while going inside to change.

She returned in a matter of minutes wearing a t-shirt, jeans, and tennis shoes. After she latched Scheherazade into the dog run, she cajoled Johnny back into the driver's seat.

Johnny stopped beside the truck. "No. Wait. Am I going to have to turn around?"

"Yes, but it's an easy three-point turn. How are you in math? Driving is all geometry and algebra."

They climbed into the rig, and Johnny stared at her from the driver's seat. "Okay, I get the geometry, but algebra? How?"

"An effective driver learns to estimate time, speed, and distance in a matter of seconds. Algebra is all about learning how to think in unknown numbers."

Johnny grinned at her. "Really? I'm pretty good at math."

"Then this should be easy. You're going to drive forward like you're turning into the garage, then stop at the door. Second, you'll reverse toward the tool shed and stop. Finally, you'll shift back to drive and crank the wheel to turn back down the driveway."

"I can do that."

"Good. Just take it slow."

Johnny made the turn without incident and grinned all the way to Leira's car.

Once there, Arabella talked him through changing the tire. He followed her precise directions and did all of the work himself.

Johnny continued to smile as he stowed the flat tire and closed the Subaru's hatchback. "I did it!"

Arabella gave him a high five. "Hop in and start her up. I'll follow you to my driveway, then watch you the rest of the way up. You should be fine."

Except the Subaru had a manual transmission rather than an automatic. Arabella couldn't very well give Johnny additional driving lessons in someone else's car.

Less than thirty minutes after leaving, Arabella returned to the ranch yard, this time driving Leira's car. She parked in the driveway beside the elegant, white, Victorian-style ranch house she'd been ogling through her kitchen window for the last ten months. What she wouldn't give to see the inside.

Johnny pulled up beside her. As they stepped out of the rigs, the house screen door slammed. They both glanced up to see Griff coming down the back steps. He crossed the yard in long, ground-eating strides, glancing from Arabella to Johnny to Arabella again. He stopped near Johnny but addressed Arabella. "Something wrong?"

Arabella shook her head. "No. Johnny doesn't know how to drive a manual transmission, so I helped him bring Leira's car home."

"Thank you." Griff nodded, then turned to Johnny. "Did Hale send you down to change that tire by yourself after that bull scared the tar out of you?"

Johnny shrugged. Griff put his hand on the kid's shoulder. "Tell you what; I'll talk to Hale. You take the rest of the day off."

"I didn't mean to let the bull loose," Johnny said. "I've never been that close to one before. I didn't know he was gonna be so big or move so fast."

"No harm done," Griff answered. "I expect you learned something today."

"Yes, sir." Johnny said. He thanked Arabella and walked away.

When he was out of earshot, Arabella turned toward Griff. "Johnny needs driving lessons. I only taught him enough to get from there to here." She pointed at the ground.

Griff blinked his amazing eyes at her. "You gave him a driving lesson?"

She crossed her arms. "Is there some reason I shouldn't have?"

"No, of course not. It's just—."

"Just—?" Arabella prompted.

Raising his hands in a shrug, he said, "You don't like me."

She grinned. "Yeah, but everybody else seems okay."

"Ouch." He spread his right hand over his heart, but his smile belied the gesture.

She laughed. "You look tough enough. I'm sure you'll survive the hit." She walked around the back of Leira's Subaru so she could get to her pickup without walking past him. As she settled into the driver's seat, she glanced up. He no longer smiled.

Jamming his hands in his hip pockets, he backed away. "I'm sorry."

Arabella squashed a tinge of guilt. Maybe he didn't precisely frighten her, but he set her on edge, and that was close enough, wasn't it?

Chapter Four

As Arabella pulled into Ty's place the next afternoon, he strode toward her rig with a big smile on his face. She stepped out of her pickup. "Hi, Ty. You got a ride for me this afternoon?"

He slid his hat from his head and combed his hand through his unruly brown hair. "Sure do. Jenny's Fortune is feeling antsy and could use a run."

"Oh, I love riding Jenny." Arabella grinned. That morning on her way into work, she thought she'd seen a Spitfire Ranch truck turn into Ty's driveway and wondered if Griff was up to something that might end her welcome here. Apparently, she needn't have worried.

Arabella walked beside Ty to the barn. She was five-feet, seven-inches tall, yet the top of her head barely reached his shoulder. She'd visited his ranch plenty of times over the past six months, and they'd often worked side-by-side while preparing to ride. She'd never felt threatened by him.

They worked as a team. Arabella secured Jenny's bit and bridle while Ty settled the saddle and tightened the cinch. They didn't chat or get in one another's way.

Griff said Ty was a murderer, but there was nothing in Ty's manner or the way he looked at her that engendered fear. Bryce Tyner was a giant of a man, but he was a gentle, kind giant. Whatever had happened in his past had nothing to do with here and now.

They walked out of the barn with the little Arabian filly named Jenny's Fortune prancing between them and stopped at the mounting block.

"I hear you have a new dog," Ty said.

"I hear you do, too." Arabella smiled.

"Yeah, she came up the driveway a couple of days ago, her belly swollen with babies and just about dragging in the dirt. Esmerelda—that's what Doc Turner said her name is—is in the house right now, but if you want, when you finish your ride, you can meet her."

"I'd like that."

Ty removed his straw hat and fidgeted with the brim. "Griffin Blake was here earlier. He said you might want to take Ezzie. I know it's only been a couple days and all, but I've kind of gotten attached." Ty held himself tense while awaiting her answer.

Arabella rubbed the filly's neck. "I have no idea why Griff said that. We certainly didn't talk about it."

Ty eased his hat back on and watched her from the corner of his eye. "I don't think he much liked it that you've been coming here."

Anger simmered in her voice. "Griffin Blake has no say in where I go, what I do, or who I'm friends with."

Ty swiveled to face her. "He's a good man, Arabella. He's just worried about you."

"You're defending him?" Arabella didn't even try to hide her outrage.

He shrugged his massive shoulders and raised his hands, palm up. "It's a guy thing. Let's just say I understand him."

"Well, I don't!" Arabella stepped onto the mounting block and swung into the saddle.

"I served time in prison. That makes folks nervous—and my size doesn't help."

Turning Jenny toward the corral, she glared down at Ty. "Griffin Blake's behavior concerns me a whole lot more than yours ever has!"

Ty's eyes darkened, and his brows lowered. He pinned her with his hard graphite gaze as, voice rumbling like thunder, he demanded, "Has he hurt you?"

Arabella's eyes widened. Okay, this ominous, glowering man Ty just morphed into must be the one who spent time in prison. She rushed to correct the impression she'd given. "No. Of course he hasn't hurt me. He just stomps around, glaring, yelling, and issuing orders."

And just like that, the Ty she knew returned. Laughter rolled out of him. He rocked back on his heels and said, "Ah, love at first sight."

"As if!" Arabella huffed. She settled her feet in the stirrups, pulled the slack from the reins, and nudged Jenny's Fortune toward the practice track.

After their workout, Arabella walked Jenny around the track a few times to cool down, then guided her toward the mounting block. Ty waited there, and Griffin Blake stood right beside him. She narrowed her eyes and glared at them both.

"I called him," Ty said as she came to a stop.

If she hadn't been astride an expensive horse she didn't own, she might have just ridden off. In fact, she was tempted to do so anyway. Apparently, Griff knew that, because he reached out and grabbed Jenny's bridle. Jenny snorted at him. Arabella understood completely. She glared at Griff.

"Ah, there's my city girl."

Arabella set her teeth and looked over his head toward the barn.

Ty cleared his throat and narrowed his eyes.

Griff shifted away from the bigger man, then returned his gaze to Arabella. "I'm sorry. I said some things I shouldn't have this morning. I was out of line. Now, could you dial back on your hostility just a little? You know," he jerked his head toward Ty. "Before he beats me?"

Arabella dipped her chin and studied Griff through narrowed eyes, then turned to Ty. "You selling tickets to that fight?"

"Private match." The giant man smiled.

"Alas." Arabella heaved a mock sigh. She did not acknowledge Griff's apology.

Swinging her leg over Jenny, she dismounted. At a hand-signal from Ty, a cowboy came forward and took Jenny's lead. Arabella turned to follow. Ty raised his arm to block her path but didn't touch her.

The man had a forearm big enough to balance a dinner table. Arabella looked from it to his face. "You know I always curry my own horse."

"Not today. Come on up to the house and meet Ezzie."

Arabella slanted a look at Griff. If he was going up to the house, too, she'd be just as happy to meet Esmerelda another day, but she couldn't very well say so. She fell into step between the two men.

The atmosphere hovering around the three of them was uneasy, but not hostile. Ty seemed even more enigmatic and laconic than usual. And why had he called Griff? For that matter, why had Griff come? Arabella swallowed a knot in her throat. It sunk to the pit of her stomach. She always seemed to lack inside information.

Ty lived in a little, two-bedroom bungalow probably built in the 1940s. He led them through the mudroom and into the kitchen, which, although clean, had worn linoleum flooring and minimal furnishings. The table, built to seat six, had only one chair. The white plastic dish rack beside the kitchen sink held only one plate. The room smelled like bacon and solitude.

Moments after the outside door closed behind them, a rotund, brown and white Shih Tzu waddled into the kitchen from an interior room. Her belly swished with each step. Freshly groomed, a dainty pink ribbon held her hair from her eyes.

"This is Ezzie," Ty said.

Ezzie shuffled to stand between Ty's enormous boots. She braced her feet and watched the newcomers with attentive eyes.

Arabella knelt in front of the dog. "Hello, little one. Come here." She extended her fingers. Esmerelda leaned forward, sniffing the air, but kept Ty between her and the visitors.

Griff knelt as well but kept a good three feet between himself and Arabella.

"Is she afraid of me?" Arabella whispered, forgetting to remain aloof.

"I got the same reaction this morning," Griff answered. He kept his voice low. "It's unusual for an animal not to come to me. She doesn't act skittish, but she isn't accepting, either."

"Is that why you told Ty you thought I'd take Esmerelda away from him?" Arabella tensed at the defensiveness in her tone.

Griff looked surprised. "I told Ty I thought you'd want Ezzie, which is altogether different."

Whatever his actual words were, she doubted his intent was positive. Instead of responding to his comment, she nodded toward Esmerelda, who sat just behind Ty's feet and peeked out at them from between his boots. "I think she's chosen her person."

"I made a bed for her in the mudroom," Ty said. "While I was outside feeding this morning, she tugged the blanket out and pulled it into my bedroom. It's under the bed. I think she's decided to have her pups there. She looks huge, but the doc says she's got a while to go."

"Are you up for puppies?" Griff asked.

Ty grinned, looking for all the world like a six-and-a-half-foot-tall toddler. "I'm kind of looking forward to it."

A few moments later, Esmerelda tired of holding court. She backed out from between Ty's boots and left the room via the door she'd entered. Griff and Arabella rose to their feet.

Ty looked at Arabella, "You sure you got no problems with me keeping her?"

Arabella thought they'd covered that ground. She cocked her head. "I'm sure." She turned to glare at Griff.

Griff shrugged. "This is between you two. I'm sorry I said anything."

They walked toward the rigs parked in the barnyard without talking. The silence wasn't comfortable. Arabella had no clue why. Obviously, she'd missed something. She wondered how quickly she could leave without appearing rude.

Ty strode straight to her pickup and opened the driver's door. "Thanks for exercising Jenny's Fortune." He said. "Same time Wednesday?"

Her step faltered. She was being dismissed. Politely, but dismissed just the same. Her breath hitched. She'd wanted to leave but being asked to leave was a whole different matter. Her gaze ping-ponged between Ty and Griff. She had no idea what she'd done to end her welcome. Seemed like that was always the way. Raising her chin, she nodded, avoiding Ty's gaze. "Sure. Whatever." She moved to brush past him. Again, his forearm barred her path. He didn't speak or try to touch her, just stood with his arm between her and her rig, waiting. She lifted her chin and glared past his head.

"I will see you on Wednesday." He enunciated each word, his voice warm and firm.

Arabella swallowed and jerked her gaze to his. Okay, it wasn't a complete dismissal. She was still welcome, just not right now. She could handle that. Arabella blinked and nodded. Ty shifted out of her path, and she climbed into her pickup, closed the door, and started the engine.

GRIFF ignored Ty completely and watched Arabella drive away. After her pickup turned a curve and rolled out of sight, he shifted his attention to Ty. "You want to tell me why you called and asked me to come back?"

Ty chuckled. "You want to tell me why you came?"

Griff didn't know if he could explain why he'd returned. He'd been over and talked with Ty that morning out of concern for Arabella's safety. He'd watched Ty interact with his ranch hands; show off Esmerelda, and calm an agitated mare. After talking to Sharee Lancaster, an old friend and one of Ty's horse trainers, Griff knew Arabella's safety wasn't in question. That still didn't mean he wanted her coming around. The feeling was almost like jealousy, but he wasn't willing to examine that thought too closely.

Ty motioned toward the practice track. "Let's talk." They walked to the fence and leaned against the rails while they watched the hands exercise the horses.

Looking at the practice ring brought Arabella's ride to mind and Griff said, "Arabella told me she could ride some—her exact words, 'I ride some.' I had no idea she could handle a horse like that."

"Started riding when she was five," Ty said. "Worked at Wengert Stables out of Seattle all through high school and college."

That image didn't fit with her flirty little suits, high heels, and manicured fingernails. "How did you find that out?" Griff stood with his feet apart, and his arms crossed.

Ty grinned. "It was pretty easy. I talked to her."

"I've talked to her." Griff wondered why he felt so defensive.

"Yeah?" Ty lounged against the fence, arms crossed on the top rail, right boot heel hooked on the bottom. "And how long do you talk to her before you start yelling?"

Griff felt his neck heating and hoped Ty kept his eyes on the horse rounding the track. "What makes you think I yell at her?"

"I suppose it might be that her description of you included' stomping,' 'glaring,' and 'yelling out orders.'"

That was a pretty accurate description of his behavior the previous morning. Griff wondered if she'd told Tyner why he'd been yelling. "It's not like I plan it."

"I'm sure that's true." Ty turned toward Griff. "But what you need to do is start planning for it to *not* happen."

Griff jammed his hands in his back pockets and wondered why he was even having this conversation with a man he'd just met that morning. Just the same, he blurted out, "And how would you suggest I do that? We've barely managed one civil conversation. I don't even know what sets her off half the time."

Ty motioned toward the spot Arabella's pickup had stood. "You just saw how easily her feelings get hurt."

"I did?" Griff had no idea what Ty was talking about.

"Just now, when I opened the door to her rig. You missed that whole thing?"

"I saw how fast her temper flared. If looks could kill, I'd be digging your grave right now."

Ty shook his head. "All her life, people have been pushing Arabella away. When I opened that pickup door, she thought I was telling her to leave, and I guess I was. But I didn't mean it the way she took it."

Griff crossed his arms. "And she went straight to battle stations."

"No. She went straight to defense stations." Ty drew a line in the air with his hand. "You know the old saying, 'Never let them see you cry?' You watch her and see. When she's hurt or scared, she straightens her spine and sticks out her chin. She won't meet your eyes, either. When she's acting like that, you stay calm, and there'll be a lot less fighting."

Griff stared at Ty, realizing he knew Arabella well. She wasn't just another riding stable customer. They were friends. *More than friends?* Arabella had said no, but Griff figured Ty felt differently. "I was straight with you when I came here this morning. I told you I was concerned about Arabella's safety. I asked your permission to talk to your people, and you granted it."

"I remember." Ty crossed his arms, too.

"Why didn't you tell me then that you're in love with her?"

Ty smiled. "Because I'm not."

That rocked Griff to the soles of his boots. Before he could examine the relief coursing through him, Ty continued. "Besides, it wouldn't matter if I were. She doesn't have eyes for me. I invited you here this afternoon so I could watch the two of you interact. I wanted to see if you have eyes for her."

"Eyes?" Griff managed to parrot, wondering where he lost track of the conversation.

"Eyes," Ty confirmed, pointing at his own hazel eyes. "That's where it starts. Just like a mare and a stallion. They get to looking at each other, all big-eyed. Prancing around. Sizing each other up. That's what you and Arabella are doing right now. But animals don't have a bunch of emotions muddying things up. Humans have hearts, and that complicates things."

Griff couldn't believe his ears. This was one of the weirdest conversations he'd ever had in his life. "You invited me over here to talk to me about the birds and the bees?"

Ty snorted. "No. You're here because Arabella has no family. That girl is all alone, so I've appointed myself her big brother. If all you've got for her is eyes, and you don't have heart, you need to back off and leave her be."

Griff uncrossed his arms and rested his hands on his hips. "Wait. You invited me over here to give me the 'don't mess with my sister speech'?"

Ty nodded. His eyes were serious, but he smiled. "But don't worry. I won't beat you up unless you give me cause."

Chapter Five

It rained all day Saturday, a relentless cold, gray, curtain of wet that just compounded the misery of an otherwise harrowing day. First, Griff told Red to grab the backhoe and clean the brush out of the flooding drainage ditch along the road. Red told Johnny to do it. And when Johnny said he didn't know how, Red told him to, "figure it out." While trying to figure it out, Johnny bashed the bucket through the corner of the big barn. The kid wasn't hurt, there were no stock injuries, a few boards and nails would set the barn to rights, but he also drove over the main water pipe and busted it below the shut-off valve. Between the rain, the ditch, and the water pipe, the stable had flooded by the time Griff got an ATV out to the well-house and shut the pump off.

He set wranglers to relocating horses and drying out the barn and spent most of the morning in the pouring rain trying to dig trenches in mud. Once he finally got the new pipe installed, the well pump refused to restart. Griff pulled the pump, drove into town for parts, returned to the ranch, rebuilt the pump, then reinstalled it in the well.

None of this would have happened if Tank, his foreman, hadn't gone to some family thing in El Paso, at the same time that Hale, Tank's second in command, took Leira away to celebrate their wedding anniversary. On top of that, Leira's absence meant Griff had just endured maybe his longest day since inheriting the ranch, and when he finally made it inside, he wouldn't even have a hot dinner.

He indulged in a hot shower instead and fell face down on his bed. His growling stomach forced him back up. Since he often cooked, the kitchen cupboards contained ingredients, not preprocessed food. He didn't feel like cooking, but the last thing he'd eaten was eggs and toast around 4 a.m. He could go out to the bunkhouse where there was always something on the stove. Red would be out there, and Griff knew he would either kill the wrangler or fire him. Right now, he didn't know which. Besides, Hale was the personnel manager. Hiring and firing was his job. Apparently, there were protocols for that sort of thing. Pity.

Griff grabbed his car keys. It was only eight p.m. He could head into town and snag a burger and a beer at the Big Pine Bar.

Less than three miles from home, he spotted hazard lights flashing on the far side of the highway. Tired, cranky, and hungry, he needed this day to be over. Even so, he lifted his foot from the gas pedal and applied the brakes. It just wasn't in him to leave someone out in weather like this without offering help.

THE truck drove past. Arabella's heart fell, then leaped for joy as she watched the brake lights glow. They reflected off the wet pavement. Second thoughts assailed her as the rig u-turned. What if her would-be rescuer was actually an ax murderer and she, his next hapless victim? And then she spotted the Spitfire Ranch logo on the truck. The rig rolled to a stop behind her pickup. Its headlights went out and the interior lights flashed on. Arabella got a good look at her rescuer as he emerged from the truck. Okay, he wasn't an ax murder, but she most certainly was a hapless victim.

Griff wore a green rain slicker and had what looked like a clear shower cap stretched over his Stetson. Beard stubble shaded his jaw. He looked like an ax murderer, although an ax murder would probably be carrying something scarier than an open yellow umbrella.

Long strides brought him to where she waited in her cab, running the heat to help her dry off and stay warm.

She opened the cab door and turned toward him.

He looked her over, probably deciding which part of her disheveled appearance to ridicule—the dripping hair, soaked skirt, shredded pantyhose, ruined heels, or filthy jacket? How about all of the above?

Instead, he asked, "Are you hurt?"

Arabella chanced a brief glance. She wasn't falling for his nice-guy persona. He looked grim and would likely revert to type any minute. "I'm fine. If I could use your phone, though, I would appreciate it."

"No problem," he sounded resigned and maybe just a little bit tired, but not unkind. "I left it in the truck. I'll have to go back and get it, but first, what's wrong with your rig?"

Arabella chanced meeting his gaze. There was nothing mocking or condescending in his expression. She considered him for a moment, then answered, "I have a flat. There's a nail in the front passenger-side tire."

"And you don't have your phone? How long have you been out here?" His tone conveyed concern, not censure.

She stuck her hand in her sodden jacket pocket and retrieved her phone, showing him the cracked, dark screen. "I slipped in the mud when I got out to check my tire. I dropped the phone and it bounced into a puddle. It's soaked, so it probably wouldn't have worked even if the screen hadn't broken."

"You were going to change your own tire?" His voice rang with disbelief.

Arabella jerked her head up, ready to do battle. He met her gaze openly. Surprise rather than contempt lit his dark eyes. She still didn't trust him not to turn on her but, since he was currently civil, she could be as well. She waved her hand toward the front passenger side of her pickup and explained, "I have the spare tire out, the hubcap off, and the jack in place, but I haven't jacked the front end up because I'm not strong enough to break the lug nuts."

He considered her in silence for a moment, then asked, "Are you sure you're not hurt?"

Arabella sighed. "I know I look a mess, but I'm fine."

"Then come hold the umbrella for me, and I'll change your tire."

He really was being nice, but she didn't want to owe him. Who knew when he'd turn on her again? She shook her head. "I can't ask you to do that."

He seemed prepared for that answer. "You didn't ask. I volunteered. You can't leave your rig out here. It'll be completely dark in an hour. Once the battery dies, your lights will go out, and somebody might crash into it."

"Let me use your phone to call road service." Arabella knew she was being stubborn, but it galled her to accept help from someone she knew disliked her. He'd get mad now, anyway, and be happy to leave her to the mercies of a tow truck.

Again, he surprised her. "Arabella, I'm already here. Please, don't fight with me. I've spent most of the day soaking wet. I'm cold. I'm tired. I'm hungry, and I'm on my way to town for food. It isn't going to take more than ten minutes to change that tire. Let's get this over with so I know you're safe."

Arabella realized that he'd just handed her some excellent reasons to turn down his help. But they were also solid reasons for him to have just passed on by in the first place. He was here acting considerate. Why not let him change the tire? And, if he could act like a civilized human being, she could at least save him the thirty-minute drive into town. "All right," she said. "You change my tire, and I'll feed you."

His mouth dropped open. He blinked those incredible eyes. A slow smile curved his lips. That dimple creased his stubbled cheek. "Deal." The rumble of his baritone voice made her toes tingle.

Arabella slid out of the pickup on rubbery knees. She pressed her hand to her stomach as she watched him walk to his truck for a flashlight. She reminded herself that she was safer with his anger than she was with his charm. It would be foolish to trust him.

Twenty-five minutes later, Arabella unlocked the door to her cottage. Griff followed her inside. Scheherazade shot between their legs and launched herself off of the porch into the darkness.

"I'll get her," Griff said, turning to go back out. Arabella grabbed his arm.

"Wait," she said. Less than a minute later, Scheherazade bounded back into the house. She shook herself violently. Arabella closed the door. "She hates being wet, but she's been in the house since I went to work this morning. She had to go."

"Hey," Griff looked around. "Where's Roy?" He put a damp paper bag he'd been carrying on the table, then hung his hat and rain slicker on pegs by the door.

Arabella headed for the laundry room, talking over her shoulder. "Fauntleroy is at Ty's. I took him over Wednesday so he could visit with Esmerelda. They were so happy together; I couldn't bear to separate them again."

Griff sat on a kitchen chair to pry off his boots. Scheherazade waited and watched from the edge of the puddle surrounding him.

Arabella returned to the room with two fluffy pink towels and a boot warmer. She put the towels on the table and plugged the boot warmer in by the back door. "Put your boots on this," she said.

Griff looked up at her in surprise. "Thanks." Then he grinned and hooked his thumb toward the dog, "Although it seems she's not as keen to sit on them when they're wet."

"She won't follow you into the shower, either." Arabella pushed the pink towels toward him. "You first. You know where the bathroom is. I'm sorry I don't have any dry clothes for you."

Griff indicted the paper sack on the table. "I always keep a spare set in my truck. You'd be surprised how often I need them. But why don't you shower first?"

Arabella shook her head. "I'll start dinner warming. Are you okay with leftover lasagna?"

Griff stopped in the act of peeling his soggy socks off. "Lasagna?" He savored the word, almost as though he could already taste the sauce. "Homemade?" he asked hopefully.

"Yes. I made it yesterday."

"With real noodles and meat sauce? It's not one of those vegetable things, is it?"

Arabella laughed. "Yes, with real noodles and meat sauce. No, it's not one of those vegetable things."

"Okay, then." Griff hopped up and grabbed the towels. "The sooner I shower, the sooner I can eat."

"Here," Arabella handed him a plastic bag. "Put your wet clothes in this."

GRIFF STRODE THROUGH the laundry room to the minuscule hall that served as a pivot point. Right to the bedroom and bathroom. Left to the living room. He flipped the light switch and stepped into Arabella's bedroom. The last time he saw it was the day he carted Tom to the hospital. The room had been dark and dismal. Then the east and north-facing windows had been covered in thick brown draperies, and the room held two sets of swayback bunk beds, a folding chair, and a dresser. Now the room was ... pink. Bright, girly, pink, like the towels in his hand. Well, the walls were white, but frilly pink curtains hung on the windows, a pink bedspread covered the bed with pink throw rugs alongside, atop the lighter pink wall-to-wall carpet. Pink. *Holy Hannah*.

By the time Griff stepped out of the bathroom, the house smelled like a feast of red sauce and garlic. He hoped she'd made plenty of lasagna. Opting to be nosy, he returned to the kitchen via the living room and dining room. It was hard to believe this had been Tom's house. The living room and dining room flowed together. The colors were white, and rose, and blue. Still pink, but not quite as jarring as her bedroom.

Arabella worked beside the sink chopping salad. She'd changed out of her wet clothes and stood zipped from neck to toes in a shapeless, purple fleece robe. She'd untangled her hair. It flowed wildly down her back. Griff stopped in the archway between the dining room and kitchen and leaned his shoulder on the doorpost. If he got any closer, he'd reach for those glorious golden curls.

"That didn't take long." Arabella didn't even glance up from the cutting board.

"Yeah," Griff said ruefully. "It was all that pink. I didn't want to stay in there too long for fear it would emasculate me."

She grinned and turned to look at him. Her eyes widened, and she gave him a slow once-over taking in his bare feet, blue jeans, and the pink towel draped around his neck. Her eyebrows slowly rose. It wasn't a come on. Griff fully expected to be tossed out of the house at any second. If she was afraid of him in broad daylight, when he was outside and fully clothed, she probably wasn't going to be thrilled with him half-naked, in her house, after dark, in the middle of a summer storm.

"Apparently, I didn't have a shirt in the bag." Did he sound defensive?

Her eyebrows lowered. She chewed her bottom lip and looked him up and down. Although her perusal wasn't as thorough this time, watching her mouth set his blood tingling and warmed him more quickly than the shower had. Unfortunately, Arabella didn't appear to be similarly moved. She shrugged and said, "All the important bits are covered."

Good thing, too, since she'd be getting an eyeful if they weren't. Griff needed to get his libido under control. He wouldn't even be thinking these thoughts if it weren't for the conversation he'd had with Tyner. Griff forced himself to exhale and tried to appear relaxed. "Thank you. I was terrified you'd throw me out. That lasagna smells fabulous."

She laughed. "Hungry, are you?" Her grin hit him right in the solar plexus and stopped his breath. If he hadn't been leaning on the wall, he'd have stumbled. She wasn't on the menu. He needed to remember that. Just because they'd managed a truce, didn't mean the war wouldn't resume. He answered her question, "Breakfast wore off about eleven hours ago."

She carried the salad bowl to the table. "The lasagna should be ready soon. I prefer it reheated in the oven. I've never much cared for microwaves. Why don't you toss your clothes in the washing machine with mine while I take a quick shower, then we can eat?" She crossed the floor and paused before leaving the room. "If you want coffee, you can make a pot. Otherwise the fridge dispenses cold water and ice. No beer, sorry."

"No worries. I rarely drink alcohol."

She smiled at him and left the room.

Chapter Six

Arabella closed her bedroom door and leaned against it, knees trembling. There was a half-naked man in her kitchen. A gorgeous, dimple-flashing, indigo-eyed, half-naked man. She'd heard him leave her bedroom, listened as he'd prowled around in the living room, and inspected the dining room. When he stepped into the kitchen, she'd known he was there but didn't realize he wasn't wearing a shirt until she'd looked up.

Had she drooled? The fuchsia towel draped around his neck only served to highlight his masculinity—and all his lovely muscles and bronzed flesh. She'd had to look. Then look again. At least she hadn't given in to the urge to touch him. And had anything she'd said even made sense?

How on earth was she supposed to sit across the table from him and eat? There'd be soup on the menu. Her. Puddled in her chair.

What was wrong with her? She didn't even like the man. Of course, not liking him seemed to make little difference to her hormones. Maybe it would serve her better to remember that he didn't like her.

It took her less than ten minutes to shower. Instead of dressing in a t-shirt and jeans, as she'd first intended, Arabella shrugged into her shapeless gray sweats, the least attractive clothing she owned. She didn't bother to try and straighten her riotous blond hair, just stuck a barrette in the back to keep the rampant curls out of her face. She considered it one of her least attractive looks and hoped the ugly factor would help curb her wayward thoughts.

It didn't work. By the time Arabella returned to the kitchen, Griff had tossed the towel in the washing machine with their clothes. He leaned, hips braced on the kitchen cupboard, in front of the coffee pot in all of his bronze-skinned glory, cradling a coffee cup in his right hand.

How could one shirtless man reduce her kitchen to less than half its normal size? What was it that took up so much room? The bulging muscles? The washboard abs? That lovely gold-limned dusting of curly, brown hair tapering from his chest to his jeans?

Staring and drooling was probably lousy protocol. Arabella grabbed hold of her self-control. She pulled out every lesson in poise Sister Pauline had taught her in boarding school, then she clamped them down over her fangirl hormones.

Of course, Sister Pauline would be appalled that any man would even consider coming to the table without first putting a shirt on. Arabella just wasn't that offended.

She grabbed two potholders and opened the oven door. Griff immediately came to her side, reaching for the pads. "Here, let me get that. It's hot."

Bent over as she was, her nose was about level with his belly button. She put on her haughtiest expression and eyed him from navel to nose and back again. "It is hot."

Griff cocked his head and arched his eyebrows.

Arabella felt herself blushing. "The lasagna." She stood up and looked him in the eyes. "The lasagna is hot. And since the lasagna is hot, *I* will carry it. You really don't want to expose all that skin to molten cheese, do you?" She waved her hand. "Grab the breadbasket. You could also get me a glass of ice water." *To pour over my head.*

They finally sat down at the table, him closest to the door and Arabella on his left. Scheherazade took up her coveted position on Griff's foot. When Griff asked for permission to say grace, Arabella couldn't hide her surprise. After the amen, she said, "Thank you. Do you attend church?"

"I used to." Griff grabbed the breadbasket and flipped the cloth back, sighing in pleasure at the stack of hot, buttered garlic bread. He grabbed two pieces and passed the basket to Arabella. "My mom loved church. We went every Sunday. Except for Christmas, I haven't been back since my parents died. Mostly I work on Sundays."

"I've been going to the United Methodist Church in Yellow Pine. The people are friendly, the music is lively, and the pastor preaches a good sermon."

"That's the one we went to," Griff said.

And remarkably, their conversation flowed smoothly.

Griff told Arabella about his horrible day and claimed her lasagna saved it from being a total disaster. She told him about taking Fauntleroy to see Esmerelda and her decision to leave him there. He described a more typical day on the ranch. She told him about her job as a design consultant for an architectural firm. "I work by appointment. When it's time to pick out paint, carpet, tiles, countertops, and other upgrades, the buyers talk with me. Sometimes they even want me to help them pick out decor."

"So, you're happy working there?"

"Happy?" She shrugged. "It isn't thrilling, but it keeps me up on the market."

"What would you rather do?"

"I'd rather do remodels and renovations. I miss the hands-on work. I want to be the one up to my neck in sandpaper, spackle, and paint. I have a website to advertise my services, but I don't have any local references. I have photos posted featuring the townhouse projects I did in Seattle. However, they don't really reflect western Montana values and culture."

Griff nodded. "Even if they did, there's not much call for a design consultant or hands-on decorator in Yellow Pine. Most people do their own remodeling and furnish their houses in contemporary American yard sale."

After the meal, they worked together to bus the table and wash the dishes. Arabella apologized for not having dessert. Griff said he was too full anyway. She went to put the clothes in the drier, and he grabbed two cups and poured them each an after-dinner coffee.

They sat back down at the table together.

Moments later, headlights swept into the yard. A truck rumbled to a stop behind Griff's and Arabella's rigs.

"You expecting company?" Griff asked.

"No," Arabella said. Griff walked across to the door and flipped the switch for the yard light.

They watched through the window beside the door as Ty stomped up the steps and across the deck. Griff opened the door.

A palpable tension flowed around Ty as he stopped over the threshold and took in the scene. He looked from Griff to Arabella and back again, staring pointedly at Griff's bare chest before pinning him with a hard-eyed stare.

GRIFF CONSIDERED THE tableau from Ty's perspective. Arabella's wild, blond curls were still damp, her face was obviously fresh-scrubbed, and she had on that ancient jogging suit she probably thought was modest, but that clung to her curves in all the right places. Then there was Griff himself, his hair still damp, wearing nothing but a pair of jeans.

"This isn't what it looks like," Griff said. He held his hands up in the universal pose for no aggression.

"What is it then?" Ty's voice was soft, but the look in his eyes was steel.

Griff knew what Ty wanted to hear. What Griff didn't know was how to tell Ty in front of Arabella. He couldn't very well tell Ty his intentions were honorable when Arabella didn't even know that he had intentions. Or could he? Griff met Ty's gaze, lifted his right fist, and tapped himself on the chest twice, right over his heart.

Ty studied him for another moment, then nodded, stepped back, and morphed from scary to mild-mannered in the blink of an eye.

Griff sighed.

Arabella rose from her chair and faced the two men. "What's going on?" She planted her hands on her hips and glanced from Griff to Ty.

Ty answered, "I called to see how you were weathering the storm. Your phone went straight to voicemail, so here I am."

Arabella studied him silently for a moment. Her bare toes tapped on the tile floor. "That's all?"

Ty nodded toward Griff. "Then I called Blake since he's closer to you. He didn't answer his phone, either."

"I think it's on the console of my truck," Griff said.

Arabella glared at Ty. "What else?"

"Nothing." Ty focused on Arabella.

"Then what was this all about?" Arabella made a motion with her hand between Ty and Griff.

Griff decided to answer. "That should be self-evident. Tyner arrived at your house late at night to check on your well-being and found you with a half-naked man he had no reason to believe you'd invite inside willingly."

"Seriously?" Arabella looked at Ty. The man was more than twice her size, and he still backed up from her glare. "I had a flat tire." Arabella enunciated each word clearly. "I was stranded on the highway in the pouring rain with a broken phone. Griff drove by, saw me, and stopped to change my tire. I invited him back here for dinner. That's all. Now, I don't know what this thing is between you two, but neither of you has any say over me so you can just stop!"

Ty reached for the doorknob. "Just making sure you're safe."

"Thank you," Arabella snapped, sounding not at all thankful. She started to turn away, then rounded on Ty again. "Sometimes he can be a jerk," she hooked her thumb toward Griff, "but even then, he's a gentleman."

Ty grinned at Griff. "I guess that settles that. Have a nice evening."
And he left.

Griff looked at Arabella. He couldn't decipher the look on her face,
and it made him a little uneasy. She hadn't gone all prickly. It was more
like she was waiting. Waiting for what? An apology? Which of his
thousand transgressions should he bring up? "I understand why you
think I'm a jerk," he said. "That seems to be my least offensive quality
whenever we're together. I have no idea why I get so riled up around
you—but in light of the other morning—" he waved his hand toward
the driveway, "—I was more than a little surprised to hear you call me a
gentleman."

She rolled her eyes. "What? I should have just let him beat you up
and trash my kitchen?"

Griff sighed. He walked to the table and lifted his coffee cup, surprised to find the coffee still hot. Not that it would have mattered to
him if it wasn't. "I'm glad we got that cleared up," he muttered into his
cup. Aloud he said, "At least it's over."

"About that," Arabella said, "there are still a couple little things...."

Griff froze. Arabella remained standing halfway between the table
and the door, where she'd been during most of her conversation with
Tyner. Feet planted, hands on her hips, she still looked braced for a
fight.

Griff sighed and put his coffee cup down. "Should I go put on my
wet clothes before we do this?"

"I suppose that depends on whether or not you're going to answer
my questions."

"I suppose that depends on what you ask."

Her lips compressed.

Griff pulled out a chair and sat. "Just ask. Let's see how it goes."

ARABELLA considered Griff. Dark smudges hollowed his eyes. Grilling him would be unkind. On the other hand, she wanted answers and if she asked now, he wouldn't be able to act like he didn't remember his actions.

She walked to the table and sat down. "So, tell me, what was that thing between you and Ty?"

"I thought we already covered that?"

"Not completely."

"I don't know what you want me to say. You saw what happened. Tyner came through the door already ticked. He was worried about you, and that had him on edge, and then I was here." Griff waved his hand at his bare chest. "It just made it worse."

Arabella shook her head. "Not that. I'm talking about the hand signal."

Griff stared into his coffee cup. "Hand signal?"

"Don't play dumb. You gave Ty some sort of hand signal. One second you two were squared off to fight, then you did that chest tap thing, and Ty stood down."

"It's a guy thing." Griff shrugged. "I just promised him that you were safe with me."

"Safe? What exactly does that mean?" Her voice rose. "And if he didn't think I was safe, why would some hand-signal convince him otherwise?"

GRIFF TOOK A DEEP BREATH and sighed. She was going to make him spell it out, and then they would fight. He snorted. Who was he kidding, they were going to argue whether he explained or not. "Monday after you left his ranch, Tyner gave me the *'stay away from my sister'* speech—"

Arabella's hand jerked, sloshing coffee across the table. She ignored it and focused on Griff. "First, why would he do that? He isn't even my brother. Second—" she waved two fingers—"what exactly is the *stay away from my sister speech*, and why did he think you needed it? And third—" three fingers. Her voice rose. "Did it occur to either of you that this is my life, and I have some say in it?"

Griff grabbed a sponge from the sink and blotted up the coffee spill. They didn't have to fight. He was not going to respond to her frustration with anger. He and Tyner had been talking about her behind her back and she deserved an explanation.

"Tyner wasn't trying to manage your life or make your decisions for you." Griff returned the sponge, rinsed and dried his hands, and sat back down. "He was trying to manage *me*. He has appointed himself as your older brother and protector."

"He ... what?" Arabella stared at Griff. He saw bewilderment in her eyes. And vulnerability. She jerked her gaze from his and stared down at her fingers clenched around her coffee cup. "Can he do that? Do people just ... adopt each other like that?"

"Yeah. Some people do. Family isn't just blood."

"But why would he want to?" Arabella whispered.

"I don't think Tyner has many friends. The other day you accused me of judging him unfairly. When he first moved into the valley, I heard the words' murderer' and 'ex-con' linked to his name and knew everything I wanted to know. I have a feeling most of the people around here have done the same thing. Then you came along and offered him trust, friendship ... loyalty. I completely understand why he set himself up as your protector."

Arabella still focused on her coffee cup. She took a shuddering breath. "I don't know how to do family." She glanced up at him through anxious eyes.

Something fierce roiled through Griff. He reached out and cradled her hands in his, coffee cup and all. Given her upbringing, it was a miracle that she had any tenderness and vulnerability left in her.

When he finally spoke, his voice was rough, "Every family is different. There really aren't rules, Bella. All you need is love and loyalty. The rest usually works itself out." He ached to gather her in his arms and ensure nothing could ever hurt her again. A staggering swirl of rage and tenderness roared through him. Griff completely understood why Tyner set himself as her protector. What he couldn't understand is why the man had chosen to be her brother and not her lover.

His breath hitched. *Is this what falling in love really feels like?* Tenderness and aggression warred inside him.

Griff sat back in his chair, trying to draw breath into his lungs. He looked at Arabella, considered their history. Remembered the first time he'd seen her, standing in Tom's kitchen, immaculate and classy, so out of place in that dingy little room. He'd ordered her outside and chewed her up. The next time he'd seen her was at Tom's funeral. She'd seemed cold and aloof in her elegant black suit. He'd paused, planning to say something cutting. Even though her eyes shimmered with tears, she'd faced him with her chin up. He'd given her an insolent once-over turned his back, and walked away. After that, their every encounter was a confrontation over her wayward dog or her insignificant scrap of land. Each moment replayed in his mind.

He couldn't fall in love with her. They had no chance of a future together. He'd given her nothing but reasons to hate him. Just the other day, he'd grabbed her arms and bellowed at her—what was wrong with him?

He lunged out of his chair and paced to the window, wanting out of his own skin. Unable to stay still, he spun back around, intending to get his wet clothes and leave. And Arabella was there, only inches away. He clasped her shoulders to keep from knocking her over. She gripped his arms, looking at him anxiously. "Are you okay?"

Griff closed his eyes and huffed out a bitter laugh. "Yeah, Bella, I'm fine." Her scent wafted around him, lilac shampoo, coffee, and a sweet something that was purely her. He savored the feel of her shoulders and searched for something to distract her from his odd behavior.

ARABELLA looked up at Griff. He wasn't fine. Something she'd said bled the light from his eyes and leached all of the color from his face. Then he'd jumped up and lurched across the room as though he'd been stabbed. She felt him tremble. She had no idea what she'd said to wound him so severely and clearly, he wasn't going to tell her. Picking a fight with him might get him to spit it out, but she wanted to comfort him, not do battle. Maybe she'd try for something lighter instead. She forced herself to step back and smile at him. "Okay, so you're fine. I'll pretend to believe that if you'll explain why you've changed my name."

Was that relief she saw in his eyes? His lip curved in a slow, one-sided grin. "Oh, that's easy," he said. "Arabella is the ice princess, suit-girl with trussed up hair, high heeled shoes, and icy glares." His voice lowered. "Bella is," he waved his right hand between them, "softer. Compassionate. Gentle." He lifted his finger and traced it down a curl near her forehead.

She inhaled the scent of soap and man and coffee. The heat from his body kindled an answering fire in her. Arabella wanted to touch his chest and slide her arms around him, but what she obviously needed was to work on her self-preservation skills. She took a chance on humor. "Is this your way of saying I'm schizophrenic?"

Griff chuckled and gently tugged the golden coil of hair he'd been teasing. "No. That's my way of saying you're a lot softer than you want people to know. Which brings us back to our original subject—Ty's *sister speech.* Brothers have been using it for years to warn off predators. "

"But if you two had this talk on Monday morning, what was with the hand signal today?"

"If you recall, that was the day I—" Griff stopped. His smile faded. He loosed her hair from his finger and stepped back against the sink.

"Monday...." He paused, staring at his hands. "Monday ...happened. So, when we talked, I didn't really answer Tyner. There was no point." Griff blew out a breath. "I'd just terrorized you—."

Arabella understood. It was her crack to Ty about Griff being a gentleman that triggered this reaction. She remembered the look on Griff's face just before he'd ridden away on Monday, then again in his yard when he'd gotten too close and she'd ordered him to stop and not come any closer. He'd been white and trembling then, as well. She needed to apologize. "Griff ..." she closed the space between them and flattened both her hands on his chest. The electricity that arched from their contact took her voice. She jerked back, but Griff's right hand was already at her waist, holding her in place. His big left hand came up to press her fingers against his chest.

He made a noise, low in his throat. Arabella didn't know if it was surprise or pain, but it helped her remember what she needed to say. "About Monday—I lied, Griff. I was furious. I accused you of manhandling me to end the fight. You didn't hurt me. I knew I was safe. And I wasn't frightened." She leaned more of her weight against him. "I'm sorry."

Chapter Seven

G riff couldn't breathe. It occurred to him that he'd forgive her of pretty much anything if she just stayed in his arms. The realization condensed in his throat. He was about to die of asphyxiation but, okay, it would be worth it. He tightened his arms around her and managed to whisper, "*Holy Hannah*, woman. You terrify me."

Arabella stilled. She licked her lips.

His gaze snapped to her mouth. He felt her breathing hitch. *Maybe Tyner is right. Maybe she is interested.*

He leaned toward her. "Bella, if you don't want me to kiss you, say so now."

Arabella trembled in his arms, lifted onto her tiptoes, and slid her hands to his shoulders. He cupped her head, angled it where he wanted it, and claimed her lips with his own.

"*Mine*," Griff thought. He splayed his hands on her back and pulled her closer. Arabella's arms locked around his neck. Nothing mattered but their kiss.

Griff raised his head and looked into Arabella's eyes, seeking permission to continue. She made a mewling sound and strained toward him. He lifted her into his arms. Their lips fused and clung. She went to his head like a shot of cognac, fiery, vibrant, and bold. All consuming.

He turned, backed her up to the counter, and pressed her close, rocking against her as they kissed. Every time they broke apart for air, she made whimpering noises and pulled him back, twining her fingers into his hair.

He found the hem of her sweatshirt and smoothed his calloused hand over her back, reveling in her softness. Feathering kisses down her throat, he caressed her shoulder, smoothed his hands down her back and over her ribs, drinking her sighs as he trailed kisses across her cheek. At last, he claimed her lips again, his hand slipping from her ribs to more intimate territory. The jolt that shot through her body jerked her mouth from his. She stiffened in his arms.

Griff lowered his hand and rested it lightly on Arabella's rib cage. He looked into her eyes. Her wide-eyed gaze clouded with trepidation. Griff knew he could continue. He could soothe her, and she would let him, but she was trembling like an innocent and that gave him pause.

He cupped her cheek and pressed his lips to her forehead. Her breath quivered against his jaw.

Resting his chin at her temple, he murmured, "Bella, do you have any condoms?"

She responded with a small, negative jerk of her head. Her answer didn't surprise him.

He kissed her eyelids, one, then the other.

"Are you on birth control at all?"

"No." Her breath puffed out. She trembled against him.

Griff loosened his hold in anticipation of her reaction to his next question. His voice emerged low and thick, "Bella, are you still a virgin?"

Her tension exploded, and she pushed him away. Griff stepped back, keeping her hands in his. He whispered, "Hey, it's nothing to be ashamed of."

Bella held herself rigid. Griff eased her into a loose embrace and rested his cheek on her head. He waited. Finally, she relaxed against him. "I ache."

"I know. I do, too. Just hang on, it will pass."

"Don't you have a condom?" she whispered.

Griff had no idea how someone as magnificent and passionate as Bella had made it to twenty-six years old still a virgin. His hard body raged at him to sink into her willingness and sort out all the repercussions later, but he followed his head and focused on what was best for her. Once her passion cooled, she was going to remember she didn't like him, and she didn't have the sophistication to deal with the dichotomy rationally.

He sighed. "No." He ran his fingers through her curls. "It wouldn't matter anyway. We can't do this."

Again, Bella tensed in his arms.

"Hey." He cupped her cheek and tried to turn her face to his. Eyes closed, jaw clenched, she resisted. "Oh, sweetheart, please don't get all prickly on me. I didn't say I didn't want to. I said we can't. I'm at the wrong end of a very long day—" he feathered kisses across her face as he spoke, "—and you've been the only bright spot in it. Right now, I'm running on adrenaline and coffee." He waved his hand between them. "This might be good for me, but it won't be good for you. Not like this. Your first time should be special. I don't want you waking up in the morning with regrets."

He rained small, slow kisses on her face, sipping away her frustration, defiance, and tears until she finally relaxed.

Griff lifted her and carried her into her bedroom, placing her gently on the bed. He was exhausted. He wanted to follow her down and sleep with her in his arms, but his own feelings were so raw and fierce and new, he didn't trust himself to wake beside her. He also didn't want to expose her to the gossip that would follow if any of his ranch hands saw him leaving her house in the morning. "I think the clothes drier stopped. I have to go, but I'll be back tomorrow."

Bella didn't answer. He had to content himself with a small nod of her head.

ARABELLA listened as Griff moved through her house. He rustled around a bit in the laundry room, ran water in the kitchen sink, and scooted the chairs up to the table. She heard him talking to Scheherazade, not his words, but the soft murmur of his voice, followed by the sound of his boots on the tile floor and more rustling as he donned his coat. He spoke to Scheherazade again. The little dog yipped excitedly. The door opened and closed, and then silence.

She tensed, waiting for his truck to start. Instead, the back door opened. She heard the sound of Scheherazade's toenails scrambling on the tile. Had he taken her out to the bathroom? The kitchen light snapped off. The door closed. Moments later, the engine of his truck roared to life.

Arabella grabbed a pillow and squeezed it to her stomach. What was wrong with her that she felt the need to set herself up for rejection? Griff had never made any secret of his contempt for her, yet the moment he'd shown a hint of kindness, she'd thrown herself at him. At least Griff was honorable enough not to take advantage of her. He'd stopped before her humiliation was complete. Arabella curled into a fetal position, trying to contain the jagged emptiness that swallowed her whole. *What is wrong with me? Will I never learn?*

THE sun shone bright and clear Sunday morning, which did not at all suit Arabella's mood. She woke to a pounding headache and figured she'd had maybe three hours of sleep. The bathroom mirror offered no mercy. Her fair complexion detailed the night's ravages, from the chaf-ing of Griff's beard to her puffy, pink eyelids resulting from her hours-long crying jag. She looked every bit as pathetic as she felt.

What happened to her common sense? Twenty-six years old and no one had ever tempted her beyond her self-control. Of all the men in the world to lose her head over, why would she pick Griffin Blake? Every cutting remark he'd ever made replayed in her head. He'd spent ten months underscoring just how contemptible he found her, then he was kind to her for a few minutes, and she turned wanton. She'd thrown herself into his arms and all but begged him to take her. The nuns were right, she was subject to her mother's sins.

Arabella gulped down three glasses of water at the bathroom sink, then stepped into the shower in an attempt to scrub her embarrassment away. After toweling off, she flat-ironed the tangles from her hair, then braided and twisted it into a tight coil on top of her head.

The pink t-shirt she pulled from her drawer contrasted horribly with her face. She tossed it back and grabbed a black one that better fit her mood and helped tone down the night's ravages. Even so, she wouldn't be showing her face in church today, for more reasons than one.

She took Scheherazade out for her morning jaunt, made coffee, ate a piece of toast so she could take two ibuprofens, then grabbed her stepstool and window cleaning supplies.

When Griff's truck rolled into the yard at ten-fifteen, she was on the stepstool washing the dining room window. She didn't get down and go to the door. If he hadn't spotted her when he pulled in, he'd see her through the window by the back door. She didn't care. She had no intention of subjecting herself to more humiliation. He'd get the message soon enough.

GRIFF was no fool. He knew he'd mortified Bella the night before, but that would have come about no matter how the night played out. She wasn't a twenty-six-year-old virgin accidentally. She was cautious about who she let close. Last night she'd reached out to test the chemistry between them, and he'd overwhelmed her with his own need, not recognizing her inexperience until almost too late. But if he'd continued, she'd have woken this morning remembering the history between them, then felt cheap and used. His rejection might have bruised her ego, but at least she wasn't in the shower trying to scrub the memory of him off of her body.

Even before he knocked, he knew she wasn't going to open the door. She had to have seen him drive by the window. He'd very clearly seen her. Since she wasn't already off the stool and headed toward him, she planned to ignore him.

He wasn't leaving. The longer they put off discussing last night, the harder it would be to talk about it. They needed to get it behind them if they had any chance of building a constructive relationship. He could sit and wait. Sooner or later, she'd have to let Scheherazade out.

Or—what were the chances? Griff reached up and ran his fingers across the top of the porch light fixture. Tom always kept a spare key ... and there it was. He hoped she hadn't changed the locks.

He turned the key in the knob, and the latch clicked inward. Arabella's back stiffened as he opened the door and stepped inside.

She didn't turn around. "Get out of my house." She bit off each word.

Griff kept his voice even. "We need to talk." He hung his Stetson on a peg by the door.

"I have nothing to say to you." The ice princess was in full freeze this morning.

"No problem. I'll talk, you listen." Griff bent down and gave Scheherazade a pat. At least she was happy to see him.

"Now, you've added breaking and entering to your repertoire?" She could goad him all she wanted. He wasn't here to fight.

Griff grabbed a chair, sat down, and toed out of his boots. He might regret it later, but he wasn't traipsing through her kitchen and dining room in his yard shoes. "If you hadn't wanted me to come in, you shouldn't have left a key outside."

"I didn't know it was there," she snapped, finally showing a glimpse of real emotion.

She still hadn't turned around. Perched on the second rung of the stepladder, she clutched the handrail.

"It's right here." Griff dropped the key on the kitchen table so she could hear it land. "Tom kept it on top of the light fixture. You can put it back or not after I leave."

She didn't respond.

"Bella—"

Her head dipped. She snarled, "Don't call me that!"

Another crack in her armor. Griff didn't know whether to push or back off. He stood in the dining room archway with the big cherry-wood table and an emotional minefield between them.

"Sweetheart—"

She took a deep breath to regain control. "Don't call me that, either."

He sighed. "Would you at least look at me?"

"No."

He moved until they were on the same side of the table but didn't crowd her. "Bella, look at us. You don't like me. You don't trust me. Think about how much more humiliating this moment would be for you if I hadn't stopped last night. Sweetheart, you wouldn't still be a virgin if you were comfortable with casual sex."

She wrapped her arms around her stomach.

Griff moved closer to her hunched back. Fine tremors shook her slender frame. Afraid she was going to fall, he wanted to lift her from the stepladder but didn't reach for her. She would break. All her pain would come gushing out, and he was going to bear it so she wouldn't have to.

"You offered me something precious and special, and I didn't take it because I don't deserve it." He spoke softly. "And because you deserve to be loved and cherished and honored. You offered me a kiss which I took, then demanded more. I pushed you too far, too fast. You can detest me, sweetheart. Hate me all you want, but Bella, don't hate yourself. You weren't the one out of line."

The silence between them stretched. Griff didn't know what else to say. He reached up and touched her shoulders.

A sob broke from her. She crumpled, and Griff caught her. He turned her in his arms, pressing her face to his chest, she smelled like Windex, lilac shampoo, and treasure.

"I hate you," she cried, but she clutched at his shirt rather than trying to push him away.

Griff drew a shuddering breath and tightened his arms around her. "I know," he whispered. "I'm sorry."

He carried her to the living room couch and held her as she sobbed, willing to absorb her anger and her bitterness. She'd already suffered enough rejection. Now he needed to give her the space to sort everything out in her own mind, and maybe, if he was lucky, she would realize he'd made the best choice he could, and not hate him for it.

Finally, her crying stopped. Griff looked down at the tight blond braid atop her head. "Are you okay?"

She nodded. Her hair brushed his chin. "I hate crying." Then she added, as if it had relevance, "Your shirt is wet."

He snorted. "It's had worse things on it. Trust me."

She made a sound somewhere between a sob and a laugh. He took it as a good sign.

"Listen, I'm going to go now, but I need to know you understand what I just said. I am the one who screwed up. If you want to talk, or call me names, or just tell me off, call me."

Shaking her head, she shifted from his lap. "I'm okay."

She kept her head down and turned her back. Griff considered her posture. She should be jutting her chin out, straightening her spine and ordering him gone. She wasn't doing so, which meant she was far from okay.

He raised his hand to her shoulder. "I'm going to need you to look at me before I leave."

She shook her head. "I can't."

Griff shrugged, even though she had her back turned. "No problem. I'll just sit here and wait until you can."

She sighed. "I'm fine. I'm just an ugly crier."

There was no anger or defiance in her tone. That was doubly unnatural. She wasn't refusing to face him because of some ugly crying, or she'd be snapping mad. She had to be lying. Why? A dread certainty coalesced in Griff's stomach. His hand tightened on her shoulder. "What is it you don't want me to see? Is something wrong with your face?"

Her shoulder flexed, something between a flinch and a shrug. Griff recognized the gesture as both confirmation and rejection.

He opened his hand and let her go. Looked down at his fingers. Had he hurt her? How? His throat clenched. He struggled to speak. "Bella, I need you to look at me."

She raised her head but didn't turn to face him. As though she'd read his mind, she said, "You didn't hurt me." There was heat in her voice, but that was no longer enough to satisfy him, especially when she added, "Besides, it was an accident."

"Please—." Using just two fingers, he gently pressed against her shoulder in the direction he wanted her to turn.

She resisted for a moment, then swiveled to face him.

Griff drew in a hiss. He raised his hands to cup her sad, ravaged face but stopped short of touching her. "Oh, sweetheart, I'm so sorry."

Now her chin came up. She glared at him defiantly. "It looks worse than it feels."

He snorted. "Sure it does." Cupping the back of her head, he turned her face toward the window. "Drat my beard. I didn't give a thought to my whiskers last night." Once she touched him, he hadn't thought of much anything until her innocence shocked him to his senses. "Have you put anything on this?"

She closed her eyes, probably so she wouldn't have to look at him. "Cool water feels good."

Even now, he wanted to kiss her. He stood to put distance between himself and temptation. "Water will chap. You need something to help you heal. I've got some salve in my truck." He went to the kitchen and stomped into his boots. Scheherazade followed him out the door.

SINCE Scheherazade always took her time during her second morning excursion, Arabella knew Griff would be gone for several minutes. She grabbed herself a cup of coffee and sat at the kitchen table. Reaching out, she put her index finger on the key he'd used to get into her house. She drew the small piece of metal toward her.

Arabella considered Griff's words. He'd said she deserved love. Did she? She didn't think anyone had ever loved her. Did some people deserve love and others not?

He'd said she would have woken this morning, remembered their history, and been doubly humiliated. That hadn't occurred to her last night, but this morning she recognized the truth in his words. She'd already used memories of his contempt and anger to flay herself.

But what now? The Griff who yelled at her and humiliated her, and the Griff who held her while she cried were the same man. How could she reconcile that? Which of them had changed? She moved the key back and forth on the table.

They both had. Through time and conversation, they'd come to know each other as people, not opponents.

He'd said she didn't trust him. She knew she'd had reason to distrust him, but last night, hadn't he proven himself trustworthy? Hadn't he put her feelings and needs before his own wants? And what about this morning? He didn't have to come here today. They could have just gone on their separate ways, wary neighbors whose paths crossed occasionally.

And didn't he try to shoulder all the blame for last night? He hadn't condemned her virginity. He hadn't castigated her for teasing him. Not that she'd meant to tease him. She'd just reacted. If Griff hadn't recognized her inexperience and stopped, their regrets today would be doubly bitter and much less salvageable.

Where did that leave them? She didn't know that she wanted him for a friend, but she did know he wouldn't deliberately do anything that might cause her physical harm. Somehow, she had always known that, even when he'd yelled at her.

When Griff and Scheherazade returned, Griff held a cube-shaped, green can. "Salve," he said. He stood on the rug by the door and didn't take his boots off. He wouldn't be staying, then. That was probably for the best.

Arabella crossed the room and took the salve. As she glanced down, her eyebrows and voice rose. "This has a picture of a cow on it!"

Griff grinned and shrugged. "It's Bag Balm. It was designed to use on cow's teats for chafing. I promise it will work on your face. It's pungent, and you're going to want to keep it out of your mouth and eyes, but it's almost as good as a miracle."

Arabella opened the can. She crinkled her nose at the medicinal aroma. "It looks like somebody mixed Vaseline with peanut butter."

Griff chuckled. "Yeah, it does. Will you at least try it?"

She looked at him. "Yes. Thank you."

His smile faded. "I guess I'll be going then." He reached up, collected his Stetson, and settled it over his dark hair, then looked down at Scheherazade perched on his boot. "Scoot," he said and jiggled his foot. Scheherazade backed away.

He turned on his heel and stepped through the door. "Griff," Arabella called.

He looked back over his shoulder. Arabella lifted her hand toward him, revealing the house key on her palm. "You want to put this back where you found it?"

Griff stared at the key for a moment, blinked twice, then nodded his head. His finger brushed her palm as he took the key and returned it to the light fixture. "Thank you," he said.

She watched him drive away, wondering what came next.

Chapter Eight

Two days later, Griff received a phone call from Tyner. "Arabella didn't show up Monday to ride and I haven't heard from her. My calls keep going to voicemail. Has she replaced her cell phone?"

"I don't know." Griff stepped out of the barn and into the sweet May sunshine and looked toward Arabella's cottage. From where he stood, he could see part of her garden, the garden shed, a blackberry hedge, the side of her free-standing garage, and the roof of her house. "From here, I can't tell if she's home or not. I haven't seen her since Sunday morning."

Ty was silent for several beats. "Wait," his voice was a growl. "You stayed all night Saturday, and you haven't seen her since?"

"No!" Griff snapped, startling a cowboy just heading into the barn. Griff crossed the gravel drive. "I don't appreciate what you're implying. I left at a respectable hour on Saturday night and stopped in briefly Sunday morning. I did not take advantage of her hospitality."

Tyner's sigh sounded through the connection. "I'm sorry. I have an over-developed protective streak."

Griff snorted. "I hadn't noticed."

"When you see Arabella, could you ask her to call me?"

"Yeah, I'm heading into town soon. I'll stop by her place on the way out."

They disconnected the call, and Griff went into the house to wash up. Not wanting to crowd Arabella, he'd planned for the next move to be hers, but stopping by to deliver a message didn't count as pursuit, right?

Turned out, his rationalization didn't matter. Arabella wasn't home anyway.

ON her way home from work, Arabella stopped at the hardware store in Yellow Pine to buy potting soil. She grabbed a fifty-quart bag and tugged it toward her cart. Two strong arms reached past her, hefted the sack, and settled it into her cart. She turned toward her helper with a smile on her face and found herself looking up at Griff. Her stomach climbed into her esophagus.

"Thank you," she felt her smile falter, but he apparently didn't notice.

He smiled. "How many?"

He sounded so normal, not that their relationship had ever had a normal. Arabella struggled to act naturally. "Two more." She held up two fingers.

"What are you planting?" He asked, just as though they were friendly neighbors.

"Lavender. I bought more than I needed for the hedge, and thought I'd put some in those two huge planters at the end of the driveway?" She really hadn't meant it as a question, but her voice rose.

Griff walked with her as she pushed her cart to the checkout stand. "Those planters have been empty for as long as I can remember. All Tom ever grew were weeds. You, however, are doing a great job of turning your acreage into a park."

Arabella shrugged. She glanced toward him but couldn't bring herself to meet his gaze. "I suppose you think I should plant alfalfa or hay?"

Griff reached out and stopped her cart. She stared at the paint department sign beyond his head.

"That was a compliment, Bella. Accept it." He chided. Her gaze flashed to his smiling face.

Arabella blinked. She never would have anticipated Griff looking at her like that. She caught her breath and stared.

He lifted his right hand and used his index finger to close her mouth, then trailed his knuckle along her jaw in a light caress. "The rash healed nicely. Did you use the salve?" His voice was low. Intimate.

Arabella tried to nod. His finger rested just below her left ear. The heat from that tiny caress twined down her spine and made her legs restless. She wrenched her gaze from his.

"Next!" The cashier called.

Griff removed his hand from Arabella's cheek and nudged her shopping cart toward the counter. Arabella fumbled for her wallet, wondering what had just happened.

While Arabella paid, Griff took the potting soil outside.

The cashier unabashedly watched Griff's long-legged, lean hipped stride as he walked away, "Oh honey," she said. "That is one handsome hunk of man you've got. He comes in here all the time. I didn't know he was taken. There go all my hopes and dreams."

Arabella had no wish to tell the cashier that Griff wasn't hers. She did, however, consider informing the odious woman that Griff was a person, not just some handsome hunk of man. Instead, she clamped her mouth shut, collected her receipt, and stalked away. Her own erratic emotions confused her. She had no business sorting out anyone else's.

Outside, Griff had already loaded the potting soil into the back of her pickup. She clicked her key fob to unlock the cab, and he opened her door.

"Thank you." Arabella climbed into her seat and motioned toward the front doors of the store. "Did you come here to buy something? You seem to be leaving empty-handed."

Griff jerked his thumb over his shoulder. "Already got it. I was loaded and ready to move out when I saw you pull in." Arabella looked in the direction he indicated. She saw a big, red, flatbed truck with a half dozen rolls of barbed wire cinched to its deck. Not Griff's usual rig, but it clearly bore the Spitfire Ranch logo on its side.

As she considered his truck, she considered his words. "You were ready to leave, but you followed me into the store instead?"

Griff shrugged.

Arabella was certain that kind of behavior should alarm her, but for some perverse reason, she was charmed. She tipped her head. "You've gone from breaking and entering to stalking?"

Griff flashed a white-toothed grin and held his hands up in an *'I'm innocent'* kind of gesture. "Would you believe I had a premonition you were going to need a big, strong man to help you carry something heavy?"

She rolled her eyes. "Seriously? This is Montana. There are literally big strong men everywhere to help carry things." One happened to be walking by and heard her comment. He winked at her and tipped his hat.

With a growl, Griff stepped between Arabella and the stranger.

She grinned. "Is there a problem?"

"That depends. Which one of us were you flirting with?"

Arabella gasped. "I don't even know how to flirt!"

"You just keep telling yourself that." Griff shook his head, then motioned for her to turn in her seat and put her feet in the rig. "You going home now?"

"Yes."

"Okay. You head out. I'll follow." He slammed the door. It took Arabella a couple of tries to fasten her seatbelt. She was too busy watching the backside of Griff's Wranglers to pay attention to her hands. She supposed the cashier had a point. He was a fine-looking man.

Arabella pulled onto the highway and glanced into her rearview mirror. Sure enough, Griff pulled onto the road behind her. Warmth curled through her stomach and a silly grin curved her lips. The realization gave her pause.

From their very first meeting, her interactions with Griffin Blake were nothing short of an emotional rollercoaster. Handing him her house key Sunday morning and letting him put it back on the light fixture was her way of admitting her own fault in their Saturday night debacle. She knew she could trust him not to wantonly hurt her, but it didn't necessarily follow that she had to like him or be his friend. After all that had passed between them, could they ever have a healthy relationship? Did she even want to try? The fact that she'd just enjoyed spending time in his company was incredible, but she doubted it would last.

Arabella pulled her pickup to a stop between the two large, cement urns that flanked the sides of her driveway. Moments later, Griff rolled in right behind her. He left his truck blocking one lane, but it didn't matter since the road only accessed her cottage and his ranch.

Standing in the back of her pickup with the tailgate down, Arabella tugged at a sack of planting soil.

Griff rounded the back of his truck. "You have got to be the most stubborn woman I've ever met."

Arabella turned, she had no clue why he sounded so irritated, but it fit their usual pattern. "What have I done now?"

He indicated the bag of soil at her feet. "I told you I'd follow you home, but you insist on wrestling that forty-pound bag for yourself rather than waiting for help."

She planted her hands on her hips. "First off, you said you'd follow me home. You didn't say you'd stop and help. Second off, I'm not only capable of lifting forty pounds, I'm also pretty used to taking care of myself."

"Point taken." He nodded his head. "I'll be more explicit next time."

Arabella studied him, pondering over his use of the term, *next time.* "Are we friends now?"

"I'm working on it." Griff grabbed the first bag of potting soil and lifted it to his shoulder. "Where am I taking this?"

She motioned toward the nearest urn. "I think one bag in each urn, then the other bag divided between them once I get the lavender plants in."

"Okay, you ready to do this now?"

Arabella looked down at her jeans and t-shirt. They were nothing special. She shrugged. "Sure." Then she looked at Griff. He was wearing his denim snap-front shirt rolled up at the elbows, blue jeans, and his cowboy boots. "Are you okay with getting dirty?"

Griff gave her a slow, half-smile. "Lady, if I do this right, I won't get dirty."

He walked to the nearest urn, reached into his pocket for his folding knife, and slit the bag open. The dirt poured neatly into the pot.

They had both urns planted and the lavender set and watered, in less than 20 minutes. And, other than their hands, both remained clean. Arabella smiled at Griff. "Thank you. I expected to spend most of the afternoon scooping dirt. May I offer you a glass of iced tea?"

GRIFF glanced at the barbed wire on his truck, then up the road toward his ranch before turning back to Arabella. She'd asked him to stay. Could he coax her a little further? "I'll make you a counteroffer," he said. "I have to get this truck up to the ranch while I still have men on hand to help me unload it. How about I come back here about seven and take you into town for a burger?"

Her spine stiffened, and she lifted her chin. Griff cajoled, "It's just Big Pine Bar. No big deal."

Arabella said, "I've never been there."

By the look on her face, Griff was pretty sure she meant to say 'no' and that her answer surprised her, too. He didn't want to lose her now. "Oh, where do you usually go? Would you prefer that?"

She shrugged. "I've actually never gone out to eat the whole time I've been here—well, except that chicken drive-thru down by the post office," she rambled. "So, I guess Big Pine Bar is fine."

Griff relaxed muscles that he hadn't even realized he'd tensed and smiled. "I'll pick you up at seven." He was three steps away when he remembered Tyner's call. "Oh, yeah." He turned to face her. "Did you get your phone replaced?"

Arabella stopped at her pickup door and nodded. "This morning."

"Tyner called me today. He said you didn't show up yesterday and weren't taking his calls?"

"Because of my face." Arabella touched her cheek. "I didn't leave the house Sunday or Monday. As to not answering Ty, when I got my new phone, I went ahead and got a 406 area code. I'll text him my new number."

Griff took a backward step toward his truck, telling himself to keep his mouth shut, but he had to ask, "Would you mind sharing your number with me, too?"

She smiled and reached for her phone.

Chapter Nine

Arabella was waiting when Griff's truck pulled into her yard. She'd showered, plaited a French braid into her hair, and let it hang to her waist, then dithered for thirty minutes over what to wear. Jeans and a t-shirt? Jeans and a dressy top? Maybe a blouse and a skirt? What did women wear to cowboy bars? She didn't own any western clothes, and she'd feel like an imposter wearing them if she did.

She wanted to look nice, but a casual nice. Not too dressy. Griff had asked her out for a burger as a friend. This wasn't a date sort of thing. They were just friends grabbing something to eat together. There was no reason to over-think her outfit.

Finally, she'd settled on a white camisole under a pink lace blouse, paired with a white denim skirt. On her feet, she wore white tennis shoes with pink shoelaces. Arabella hoped it was the perfect mix between casual and dressy. Plus, the camisole was modestly cut, and the skirt danced around her knees. She figured she'd look more like a kid sister than a dinner date.

Griff arrived at her door dressed in a western-cut red and blue plaid shirt with mother of pearl snaps down the front. His dark denim jeans looked new and fit him far too well. He also wore a fancy pair of caramel-brown cowboy boots she'd bet had never seen a horse stall or a pasture.

GRIFF followed Arabella across the back deck and down the stairs, watching that braid bounce at her waist. Why had he suggested taking her to a bar where all the cowboys in Ravalli County could see her? The competition would be lining up down the block. She'd have her pick of men who'd never given her reason to hate or distrust them, and he'd have no one to blame for that but himself.

Live music spilled out of the bar and into the parking lot. Since when did they have live music on Wednesday nights? They stepped inside and Griff frowned at the dance floor. It was packed.

"Hey, Griff, long time, no see," the barmaid materialized from the crowd. She had an empty drinks tray cocked between her wrist and her waist, wore a minuscule red tank top, short shorts, and a pair of red cowboy boots. She glanced at Arabella and turned back to Griff. "You want me to find you a table up by the dance floor in the thick of things?"

"Not this time, Katy-Bug. How about you take Arabella and me to a nice quiet table in the back?"

Katy looked surprised. "Sure thing. Follow me. Are you eating tonight?"

Griff nodded. Katie grabbed a menu from the hands of a cowboy they passed. "Hey," he yelled.

"Shut it, Gar," Katy answered. "You know this menu by heart."

Griff chided, "Hey, Bug, that's no way to treat your future husband."

Katy snorted and shook her head. "Gar and I are just friends and you know it."

Katy stopped beside a table for two near the back corner. "Will this do?"

Griff nodded. He put his hand on the small of Arabella's back and drew her to his side. "Katy, this is Arabella. Bella, this pest is Katherine Forrester. Her brother, Denny, is one of my best friends."

Arabella held out her hand and said, "Pleased meet you."

Katy ignored Arabella's hand and pulled her into a hug. "Oh no, girl. I'm pleased to meet you."

Arabella looked flustered. Griff pulled out her chair, and glared at Katy until she morphed back into a proper waitress and asked Arabella for her drink order.

Arabella looked at Griff. Katy said, "He's having a single malt IPA. Nasty stuff. Don't order it."

Arabella laughed. "I'll have a Corona with lime, please."

"Corona with lime?" Griff repeated after Katy had gone. "I thought all interior decorators drank white wine."

Arabella shook her head. The man was full of stereotypes, but she decided not to be annoyed. "Ah, but in high school and college, I worked as a stable hand, and stable hands don't generally go out for white wine after work. Not even stable hands in Seattle. If somebody brought wine, it was usually cheap and nasty. I prefer beer."

Griff shook his head. "I keep getting the real you mixed up with your city suits. I'm sorry."

They were ready to order by the time Katy returned with their beers. Some sort of commotion came from the bandstand, and then a girl's voice came over the speakers yelling, "Griffin Blake is in the house!" Then rhythmic clapping ensued, and everyone was chanting, "Grif-fin! Grif-fin!! Grif-fin!!"

Griff looked up at Katy. "There never used to be a live band here on Wednesday nights!" Then he turned to Arabella. "I'm sorry, I never would have brought you here tonight if I'd have known this was going to happen."

Arabella asked, "What's going on?"

The chant morphed into, "Dance! Dance! Dance!"

"You dance?"

Griff shrugged.

Katy answered Griff first. "Wednesday night music is something new the owner is trying out. So far it's been a big hit." Then she turned to Arabella. "Not only does Griff dance, he was the house line dancing champion until he quit showing up on Friday nights."

The small crowd continued clamoring for his attention.

"This is ridiculous." Griff stood and raised his hands to the crowd. "Not tonight, folks!"

That was followed by a round of booing and catcalls. A lean, dark-haired cowboy pushed to the front of the crowd. "What's the matter, Griff? Too old to take your title back?"

Griff said, "Not hardly, Joel, but unlike you, I've got a date."

Another round of cajoling and catcalls followed. Arabella wanted to see Griff dance. "Don't let me stop you."

Katy said, "Thing is, it could take a while. Everybody who wants in, gets a number. If someone wearing a number leaves the dance floor for any reason, they forfeit that number and are out of the contest. The winners are the last man and woman on the dance floor who are still holding their numbers."

"Sounds lively," Arabella said.

"It's exhausting," Griff muttered. Then he raised his voice, "I've got fence to string tomorrow!"

"Whoohoo!" The cowboy named Joel crowed. "Griff just admitted he can't cut it. Getting old, dude!"

Arabella leaned across the table. "Are you going to let him get away with that?"

"Bella, if I agree to this dance-off, you're going to be sitting here alone."

Arabella looked from Griff to Katy. "Why can't I—"

Katy snatched Griff's hat off his head and smacked him with it. "You are the dumbest man I ever met. What is your problem?"

"Ow!" Griff snatched his hat back. "What the heck did you do that for?"

Katy turned to Arabella. "Do you know how to line dance?"

"Some," Arabella answered. "I can do the Boot Scoot Boogie and a couple of the other easy ones."

"Well, if you want to learn the rest and this jerk—" she hooked her thumb toward Griff, "—doesn't want to teach you, I'm sure we can find a willing cowboy." Katy glanced toward the stage. "How about Joel?"

"Not Joel!" Griff reached over and took Arabella's hand. "I just did it again, didn't I, Bella? What say you forgive me one more time and come help me reclaim my title?"

"I won't know a lot of the dances and probably won't make it all the way to the end."

Griff smiled. "You don't have to dance well. You just have to dance."

Katy said, "Besides, you can dance whether you're in the contest or not."

They didn't order dinner. Griff jumped to his feet and called Joel out. The crowd went wild. Within minutes the dance floor was hopping. It didn't take long before people recognized Arabella as a novice, and she received an abundance of good-natured help—from the ladies. Griff somehow always managed to maneuver her away from any of the men who came to her aid. Luckily, Arabella didn't notice; she was too busy watching her feet.

Several dances later, after a tricky little number they called, *The Watermelon Crawl*, the lead singer called out, "Some of you are looking a little winded. We're going to help you stay on the dance floor by slowing things down a bit."

Griff caught Arabella's hand and tugged her toward him. She came up against his chest, still laughing from her attempts to master the fancy footwork from the last dance, and her hands flattened on the front of his shirt. He felt the same electrical jolt that shot through him Saturday night. His body recognized Arabella on a visceral level. Something primitive inside him claimed her as his. Their gazes locked. Arabella's breath hitched, and she froze. Griff watched amazement widen her eyes and fear crowd it out.

He immediately averted his gaze and stepped back, allowing her several inches of space, but kept her right hand clasped in his. He touched her waist with his fingertips, holding her lightly and hoping she wouldn't run. When the music started, he led her into a simple box step. She stumbled after him.

By the third turn, she flowed with him easily. Griff resisted the urge to pull her closer. She'd felt the connection between them as surely as he had, but she was fighting it. One wrong move on his part and she would bolt. He'd have no one to blame but himself.

He wasn't surprised when the dance ended, and she told him she wanted to sit the next one out. The only reason he complied when she asked him to keep dancing was so she wouldn't feel crowded.

THE next dance was, *Achy Breaky Heart*. Arabella huffed. She knew that one, but she wasn't getting back on the dance floor or going anywhere near Griff until after she'd stopped trembling, and maybe not even then. Her body had a mind of its own when it came to that man. He'd already given her a list of reasons why their relationship wouldn't work. The biggest one being that he knew she wasn't up for casual sex. Why didn't her body know that she wasn't up for casual sex?

Arabella realized that Griff knew she wanted him, and her reaction made him uncomfortable. She saw it in the way he jerked away after she'd touched him. Then he'd barely touched her as they danced. She'd almost left the dance floor then but didn't want to strand him without a partner and be the reason he lost the contest.

Not too long after Arabella returned to their table in the corner, Katy stepped up beside her and handed her a glass of ice water. "I saw you leave the floor and thought you might be thirsty." Then she pulled Arabella's dance number from her shirt sleeve. "Sorry I have to take this."

Arabella smiled her acceptance.

So far, only a few people had dropped out of the contest. The floor was crowded but orderly. Griff was easy to spot as he tapped and stomped. His long legs held her enthralled. Like his flashy cowboy boots, the jeans he had on were never destined for ranch work, they fit him much too snuggly for manual labor. As she watched his smile flash and his waist twist, Arabella realized she'd cool off faster if she danced beside Griff instead of watching him move.

On the last chorus, the band picked up speed. Griff made the dance look effortless. Arabella didn't want to turn away but also didn't want to get caught staring. She picked up her phone and activated the screen, pretending it had her attention while watching Griff from the corner of her eye.

After the song ended, Griff thanked his partner and stepped to the edge of the dance floor. He removed his black Stetson, wiped his forehead on his shirt sleeve, and smoothed his hat over his hair. The band leader called out a two-step. Griff looked toward Arabella. She willed herself not to respond. A curvy little brunette in skin-tight jeans grabbed Griff's hand and tugged him back to the middle of the dance floor. Griff let her change his course, but he didn't pull his gaze from Arabella until the music started.

Like line dancing, the two-step was a simple pattern dance, and as its name implied, it only had two steps, but every couple added their own variations. Griff and the brunette flowed with the music, a perfectly matched set. Arabella couldn't help but notice that the woman looked confident and experienced in Griff's arms, something Arabella herself would likely never be.

Arabella focused on Griff and didn't realize the "may I have this dance" question she'd heard was directed at her until a man's hand clasped her wrist and pulled her from her chair sideways. She stumbled but managed to gain her feet. A quick twist of her wrist freed her from the man's grasp. She backed away. "Thank you, but I really don't want to dance."

"Sure you do, sweetie. I saw the way you were staring at the dance floor." He was drunk. Arabella heard the telltale slur of his words.

"I am enjoying the music, but I'm tired. I've already danced quite a bit. Besides, Katy is bringing me a beer." That last bit was a lie, but the drunk didn't know that, and maybe it would encourage him to move along.

"I'm not taking 'no' for an answer." He reached for her again.

Arabella jumped away, moving closer to the dance floor. A large body brushed past her. Griff grabbed the drunk man's shoulder. "The lady said, 'no.'"

"Buzz off, Blake." The drunk pushed at Griff's wrist. "This ain't your ranch. I can dance with whoever I want."

"If the lady wants to dance with you." Griff agreed. "This lady doesn't."

The drunk snarled and took a swing at Griff, who must have been expecting it. He slapped the man's fist aside, grabbed him by the belt and the back of his shirt, and hefted him up. The man hung, his feet about three inches above the floor. He shouted an obscenity, and Griff shook him.

The bouncer arrived. "You again, Roger? We warned you last time. You're eighty-sixed."

"Ah, Tony. I just wanted to dance."

Tony looked at Griff. "You can put him down. I'll take him to the door and call a cab."

Griff set Roger on his feet and released him. Roger ignored Griff, turning toward Arabella. Tony's hand came down hard on Roger's shoulder. Roger nodded his head and said, "Begging your pardon, ma'am," then he allowed the bouncer to lead him away.

Griff stepped close and lifted Arabella's chin with his fingers. "You okay?"

Arabella tried to draw a breath. Why was it that every time her eyes met his, the bottom dropped out of her stomach, and the rest of the world disappeared? "You're a very scary man," she whispered.

She wasn't talking about the incident with Roger but Griff obviously didn't realize that. He cocked his head toward the door without shifting his gaze. "With him, maybe. With you, I'm a marshmallow."

It took Arabella a few seconds to process his meaning. She raised her eyebrows and snorted. "Since when?"

Griff's lips curled in that slow half-smile that rocked her heart. His voice lowered. "Oh, I'd say since about nine-thirty Saturday night."

Heat flooded her face. Arabella tried to turn away, but Griff still held her chin.

"Stop that," his voice was soft. He leaned in and kissed her on the forehead. "Now, what do you say we order some burgers? I'm starving."

Arabella's eyes widened in surprise. "Griff, you left the dance floor."

Griff stepped away from her and shrugged.

"You just walked off and left your partner." She turned and looked for the brunette, who was now dancing with Joel.

"No," Griff corrected. "My partner left me a couple of dances ago."

Katy materialized from the crowd again. This time she took the number taped just below the shoulder on Griff's shirt sleeve. "Sorry, sport."

Griff answered, "I'm happy with my choice. Can we get those burgers now, and a couple of fresh beers?"

Katy said, "I'll put your burger order in, but it'll be faster if you get your own beer."

Griff nodded. He held Arabella's chair and reseated her at the table. "Okay, Bella, I'm going to go get those drinks. You think you can stay out of trouble while I'm gone?"

Arabella glared at his chin. "I should be okay. I really don't think I can get two men to attack me in one night."

"Honey, I am not taking that bet."

After they ate, they decided to call it a night. Arabella had clients first thing in the morning, and Griff had fence to string. He helped

Arabella into his truck, then drove home with his arm stretched across the seat and his fingers resting on her left shoulder.

As the truck rolled to a stop in her driveway, Arabella reached for her door handle. "I'll get that," Griff said. In the dark cab, his deep voice spiraled down her spine and pooled in her stomach. She watched him walk around the front of the truck. He kept acting as if this were a real date, but it couldn't be. He belonged with someone like the sexy brunette, not an uptight, inexperienced, city girl.

What if he tried to kiss her good night? Should she let him? She really wanted to kiss him, but what she wanted seemed like a terrible idea.

Griff helped her from the cab, tucked her hand on his arm, and walked her across the back deck. When she dropped her keyring, he retrieved it, found the right key, and unlocked her back door. Scheherazade came tumbling out of the house in a froth of fur and danced around their feet.

Scooping the little dog up in one hand, Griff reached into the house and turned on the kitchen light. Then he moved his hand in the small of Arabella's back and nudged her into the house. She stopped just inside the door and turned to face him. He motioned with Scheherazade. "I'll be right back."

Griff carried the dog from the porch and put her down on the lawn. He waited patiently while she sniffed around and watered several of her favorite bushes. Finally, he picked Scheherazade up and returned to the door, placing her in Arabella's arms. "Thanks, it was ... fun," he said and left before Arabella found her voice.

She knew then that she definitely would have let him kiss her. She buried her face in Scheherazade's fur as she listened to Griff drive away.

Chapter Ten

Despite the fact that his house was slightly more than a quarter of a mile from her own, Arabella heard nothing from Griff on Thursday. Or Friday. Or Saturday.

She had plenty of time to examine her feelings and put them into perspective. Sure, she was attracted to Griff, what red-blooded female wouldn't be? That didn't mean she had to act like a dithering schoolgirl. The way Wednesday night ended—and his absence since—clarified that he wasn't interested in her in any romantic sense of the word.

That was okay. She knew how to be a decent neighbor. That wasn't even scary. And if he wanted to be friends, she knew how to do that, too.

Sunday arrived dressed in gray. By noon, bits of blue peeked through the clouds. Arabella and Scheherazade were in the dog run when Griff's truck turned off the highway and onto the dirt lane between their houses. He drove slowly, keeping the dust to a minimum. At the Y in the road, he curved north, into her driveway. Closing the gate to corral Scheherazade, Arabella went into the house, leaving the back door open.

Griff crossed the deck as she popped the lid closed on the coffeemaker. She pushed the brew button and turned toward him just as he stepped into the doorway.

He stopped on the threshold, pushed his hat back off his face with his index finger, and said, "I've come to proposition you," then he relaxed against the door frame.

Heat rushed to her face. Arabella firmly reminded herself that they were building a friendship, and played along, "Be still my heart." She fanned her hand slowly in front of her face. "I've always been a sucker for red flannel shirts, so you might be able to tempt me." She tried to sound skeptical. Her body temperature had risen dramatically, and she wasn't at all confident she'd pulled it off. That's why she added, "It'll probably cost you, though."

Griff chuckled. "I've been looking at your website and have absolutely no doubt of that."

"My website?" That surprised her, and her play-acting stumbled. "Really?" She motioned him inside. "Coffee's almost ready. You looked at my website?"

Griff toed off his boots and left them on the deck, then he hung his hat on the peg by the back door and pulled out his usual chair. He looked around. "Hey, where's my foot warmer?"

Arabella laughed. "She's out in the dog run."

The coffeepot sputtered to a stop. Arabella filled two cups and carried them to the table. She slid one toward Griff and pulled out the chair across from him, wanting to let him know she understood their boundaries.

"What, no cookies?" Griff looked longingly toward the red strawberry cookie jar.

Arabella clicked her tongue and turned back to the cupboard. She grabbed two small plates and lifted the cookie jar in the crook of her right arm. Behind her, she heard the furniture moving. She turned to look. Griff had used his long legs to pull in the chair across the table. He'd pushed out the chair to his left and angled it toward her. Arabella looked from the angled chair to Griff and back again. Smiling easily, he stood and took the cookie jar from her, placing it where it could be conveniently reached from either chair, then sat back down.

Still standing where he left her, Arabella clutched the plates in her hand and considered that angled chair. It would be rude to deliberately reclaim the chair across the table, and he did say he wanted to talk business. Still, her insides were liquifying just because he walked up to her door. This was not boding well for her resolve.

Griff nudged the chair a little closer to her. Arabella straightened her shoulders and sat. She pushed a plate toward Griff and asked, "Cookie?"

He shook his head. "No, thanks. I just had lunch."

Her startled gaze met his. She narrowed her eyes and tipped her head. What was he up to now? Had she misunderstood? "Are you flirting with me?"

He shrugged. "Can't help it. You're so dang cute when you blush."

She felt the heat climbing her neck. "Well, stop!" She needed a minute to regroup.

Griff leaned back in his chair. His grin faded, and the glow left his eyes. The sexual tension drained out of the room so quickly, Arabella clutched the table to keep from swaying.

"Right," Griff said. "No flirting."

Wait! Never mind! Arabella thought, but she couldn't really say that. Aloud she said, "So—." Her voice squeaked. She cleared her throat and tried again. "So, back to my website. What's on your mind?" There. That almost sounded casual.

WHAT was on his mind? Grabbing her out of her chair and kissing her perfect pink lips until neither of them could think straight. However, his immediate wants were irrelevant. He already had enough neanderthal moves to make up for. Plan A, now called the disastrous date, had made it obvious she didn't want to be in his arms. He'd better stick with plan B. He nodded toward her kitchen window. "I think you might be able to help me fix my house."

"Fix it? What's wrong with it?" She'd never been inside, but the sprawling Victorian ranch house with its grand turret was a pretty impressive sight. Painted white, the house sported green trim and sparkling leaded-glass windows. She longed to see the inside. "It's gorgeous."

"It's pretty old."

"How old?"

He shrugged. "1890-something old. It's been updated a few times. There's indoor plumbing and electric lights, but it's getting shabby."

Arabella walked to the kitchen window. She pushed the lace curtains aside and stared out at the upper story of his house, which was all she could see from there. "Dry rot?"

"No."

"Water damage?"

"No."

"Any sagging walls or ceilings?"

"The frame is sound."

"Fuse box or breakers?"

"Breakers."

"So, the electric wiring is up to date?"

"Maybe 30 years old. They re-did it when I was little, same time they put electricity in the barn."

Arabella turned around and looked at him. "What exactly is it you want done?"

Griff spread his hands, "Dress her up?" He shrugged. "I don't know. Maybe I could explain it better if you came to take a look?"

She stood with one hand on the counter and one hand on her hip. "This isn't a pity job, is it?"

"Bella, this is probably going to cost me a fortune. There's not enough pity in the world for that."

She bit her lip and stared at him, considering.

He met her gaze without flinching.

Finally, she said, "Okay, I'll look. When?"

He wanted to say, right now, but she might have something else planned. It was Sunday. Church was over. She was sock-footed and wearing blue jeans and a white t-shirt, so she probably wasn't going to work. Still, he shouldn't just assume she had nothing else to do. "Would you have time today?"

She shrugged. "I haven't made any other plans."

"All right. Then how about we finish our coffee, I eat a couple of these cookies, and we go on up to the house?"

Arabella scowled at him. "I thought we'd already established that you didn't want any of my cookies?"

His eyes widened. He most certainly *did* want her cookies. And anything else she'd give him. He knew better than to meet her gaze and glanced down at his coffee cup. She'd said no flirting. Maybe the double-entendre hadn't occurred to her? He gave her a quick glance from the corner of his eye. Her face glowed crimson. He shifted in his chair so she was facing his left shoulder. If he looked at her, he'd probably laugh, and she'd kill him. He grabbed his cup and poured hot coffee into his mouth.

She took a slow, deep breath and exhaled shakily. "Thank you," she said.

Griff nodded. He still didn't trust himself enough to turn around.

"I didn't mean—."

Griff raised his left hand to stop her. "I know,"

"Maybe I should just get my shoes, and we could leave?" Her voice squeaked a bit on the last word.

"That sounds good," he answered. Arabella turned and fled the room.

Griff put the cookie jar and plates on the counter, rinsed the coffee cups, and scooted their chairs to the table before going outside to wait.

ARABELLA paused just inside the back door. She looked at Griff. He stood at the top of the steps gazing out over the Bitterroot Valley with his feet braced apart and his hands jammed into his back pockets. He was pure sex appeal in cowboy boots. She really needed to tell him she wouldn't be doing anything with him or his house, but she wasn't going to because her brain obviously didn't function when he was around. Besides, she'd been staring at his house for almost a year now. She really wanted to see the inside.

She stepped out onto the deck. "I need to get Scheherazade and bring her inside." Thankfully her voice sounded normal.

Griff turned on his heel. "You could bring her along."

She arched her eyebrow. "I never thought you'd invite my nine-pound nuisance onto your property."

Griff laughed. He was already moving to the dog run, which was a little over an acre in size and pretty much served as her own personal doggy park. Scheherazade ran straight to him, and he picked her up.

"I cannot believe my own dog likes you better than she does me."

Griff held the little dog as she wiggled up his chest and tucked her head under his chin. "What can I say? She has good taste."

Arabella let out a huff and marched away. She stopped at the driveway and turned back toward Griff. "I should get her leash so I can walk her home."

"Or after we're finished, you could just get in my truck, and I could drive you both home."

"That's ridiculous. Your house can't be more than a quarter-mile away."

"Yeah, across the field. By road, it's a little more than a mile."

"Oh, a whole mile." She pressed her wrist to her forehead dramatically. "I'm just not sure I can walk that far."

Griff narrowed his eyes and stared at her. Just as Arabella wondered if they were about to have a contest of wills, he relented. She discovered why after he parked the truck in the barnyard. "We'll have to either leash or carry Sherry from here to the house. I don't want her anywhere near the cattle."

"Scheherazade," Arabella corrected while snapping the leash on the dog's pink halter. "I'll keep her away from your cattle."

Arabella unlatched the truck door. Griff reached across her and grabbed the door handle. His arm pressed her against the seat, and the spicy scent of his cologne filled her senses. She had the insane urge to run her lips along the ridge of his jaw. Thankfully, he moved away before she lost her self-control.

He didn't actually return to his own side of the bench seat. His hand rested on her shoulder, and their knees touched, points of incandescent heat.

"Listen," he said. "I've said a lot of things to you I shouldn't have. I'm sure I've implied several things no gentleman would have, but they weren't all arbitrary knee jerk reactions to the fact that you're a city girl. This one is to protect you."

He looked at her like he'd asked a question rather than made a statement, so she nodded her head to show she was listening.

"I am not worried about my stock. I have cattle dogs, and they're trained to run herd, but every so often one of them gets kicked or stomped. It isn't pretty, and Bella honey, even if I hated your guts, which I don't, it would kill me to have to bring your little girl home to you like that."

Leira had told her Griff wasn't worried about his cattle, that he'd actually been concerned about Scheherazade. She'd also claimed he was protecting Arabella from a broken heart. Arabella considered the way Griff cradled Scheherazade against his chest. Maybe he worried about breaking his own heart as well. "I understand," she said.

Scheherazade was leashed and in Griff's arms when they got out of the truck. Griff started toward the back door. Arabella stopped him. "Is it possible to go in the front door?"

He shrugged and altered his course.

Griff didn't ask for an explanation, but she offered one anyway. "It's a personality thing. Houses are like people. They have a public face and a private face. When I meet a new house, I like to meet the more social parts of it first, then make my way to the more private spaces. In a house like yours I think it is even more important. You have over a hundred years' worth of history here. I don't want to start by looking up her skirt."

Griff chuckled at her words, but he turned his gaze to the second floor of the turret. "You may have a point."

The lawn had been recently mowed, but wild grasses grew tall between the weathered slats of the picket fence surrounding it. Boards were missing, and here and there full sections of fencing were gone. Everywhere the paint peeled. Griff hadn't asked her about the fence, though, so she didn't mention it.

They could have walked around the front gate, closed and tangled with ivy, but Griff took the time to wrestle it open. "The front of the house isn't as social as you think. No one much comes this way anymore."

"That's so sad," Arabella murmured. "It is—exquisite."

The house faced west. The grand turret sat slightly north of center. Arabella studied the covered porch, which disappeared around the north and south corners. She asked, "Does the porch wrap all the way around?"

"No. I think it used to, but the kitchen was built on the back in the 40's. The porch ends at either side of the addition."

Arabella nodded. As they walked up the steps, she reached out and touched the railing. "The house has been painted recently?"

"Outside." Griff nodded. "Reroofed, too. Standard maintenance. We have a schedule."

That was wise, but it sounded so impersonal. This house should be loved, not merely maintained.

Griff opened the front door. Arabella looked up at him in surprise. "You don't use it, but it isn't locked?"

"We don't lock much of anything around here. It's not like the ranch is ever empty. There are people underfoot all the time."

"Well, at least you're not lonely."

"Sure I am," Griff said. "That's why you're here. It's time to fix the house up and catch me a wife."

Arabella knew her mouth hung open. She just couldn't seem to do anything about it.

"What," Griff said. "You find the thought of somebody marrying me that startling?"

She shook her head. "No," she said faintly. The truth is, her brain stopped functioning when he'd said, wife. Griff married? Everything inside her rebelled at the idea. He'd kissed her. Held her. "I guess it didn't occur to me that you were seeing anybody. I mean—." She couldn't, wouldn't complete her thought aloud.

"I'm not seeing anyone," Griff interjected quickly. "I'm just feeling my age and thinking maybe it's time to start looking. That led me to think about the condition of my house."

"Right." Arabella tried to shrug and nod at the same time. She could do this. She could go in, look at his house, and talk to him calmingly about fixing it up so he could share it with his future wife. Just because he'd kissed her senseless, didn't make this any different than any other house consult.

She took a deep breath and released it slowly, then squared her shoulders. She stepped over the threshold and—. "Ohhh!" the word escaped her on a sigh. Directly across from the door, a broad staircase flanked by spindle-railed banisters curved around on itself, leading the way upstairs. On her left, across a large, airy room, a massive fieldstone fireplace drew her attention. Its mantle was fashioned from the trunk of a tree, flattened on top. Arabella moved forward and touched the wood, running her fingers along the subtle growth patterns of the swirling golden grain.

Turning her head, she took in the classic leaded glass window covering most of the west wall, affording abundant natural light and a breathtaking view of the Bitterroot Mountains. Two wing back chairs and a reading table stood in front of the window, but the bulk of the worn, polished leather furniture in the room clustered around the fire-place.

Arabella slowly pivoted, taking everything in and not stopping until she faced Griff. He'd closed the front door and let Scheherazade off her leash. As usual, the little dog perched on his foot. Arabella lifted her hands, palms up, toward the ceiling. "This place is incredible."

The furniture had seen better days, and the paint could use touching up, but at most, this part of the house needed refreshing, not re-modeling. Arabella reached into her satchel and pulled out her iPad. She started taking photographs and jotting down notes.

Griff crossed the room with Scheherazade trotting across the hard-wood floor beside him. "You should have seen the place when my grandmother was alive. It glowed." He spoke of his home with apparent pride. "She was always cleaning and polishing. My mom was more about the ranch." He waved his arm, indicating the world outside. "Mom could be found wherever my dad was, working right beside him. She didn't put much into the house. In fact, after my grandmother couldn't care for it anymore, we had a series of housekeepers. No one has ever loved this house quite like my grandmother did."

Arabella wondered what kind of woman Griff wanted for a wife, a rancher like his mother, or a nurturer, like his grandmother? But that was none of her business. She came to do a job, best get to it. "The house looks clean and well cared for. Fixing it up—at least this part—shouldn't be that expensive."

"Come see the rest," Griff led her to the other side of the entryway into a semi-circular room with a one-hundred-eighty-degree window. Leaded glass windows rose from a built-in window seat and stopped just short of the ceiling, spanning the entire arc.

"Sunset," Arabella breathed. "It must be breathtaking."

"It is. When the sun hits the windows, the leaded glass creates hundreds of dancing rainbows." When he was a kid, he thought the effect magical. He couldn't remember the last time he'd stopped to appreciate the sight. "This is the formal living room. We never used it much." It was more for walking through than stopping in.

Arabella tapped a side table. "Antique," she said. Then she crossed the room and touched the heavy brocade drapes hanging at the junctions of the three massive glass sections, which comprised the arched window. "Sun damage." Some of the fabric flaked to dust on her fingers. "Are you attached to this look? The drapes don't close, and I think the windows would be much more impressive without them."

Griff shrugged. "They can be gone."

She took more photos and made notes.

The dining room extended north beside the formal living room. "Grams called this the banquet hall," Griff said. "My great grandfather built the table. It seats twelve comfortably, and the only time we ever ate here was Thanksgiving. Grams cooked a big meal and filled the house with friends. My parents changed the tradition to an all-hands potluck. I've continued the potluck, but the last few years, we've had it in the bunkhouse."

"This stays." Her hand caressed the expansive, oval tabletop. Griff noted she didn't ask his opinion. She turned to look at him. "This is a slab from a tree. The same kind as the mantle over the fireplace, and the banister?"

Griff nodded. "All the work of my great-grandfather. The wood is Ponderosa Pine, the Montana State tree."

"It's beautiful."

"He also made the double doors on the master bedroom suite. You'll see them when we get upstairs."

Both the northern and western walls of the dining room boasted sizable stained-glass windows. Arabella chose to focus on them instead of thinking about walking into Griff's bedroom. "All this glass had to cost a fortune," she said. "If for nothing else but transportation."

"It's all in the ranch journals." Griff motioned toward the other side of the house. "I have a bookcase full of handwritten histories from the time the first cornerstone was laid for Spitfire Ranch. There's some pretty amazing stuff in them. This whole place started from a one-room log cabin on a small tract of land in about 1866."

She looked down at her iPad and sighed. "It must be incredible to have that kind of history."

She sounded wistful. "Let's take a look at the kitchen," Griff said to distract her. "I'm pretty sure you're going be spending a lot of my money right here." He walked around the dining room table and pushed against a pair of batwing doors, propping them open.

Arabella grimaced. "Those doors ...." She shook her head.

"My mom had them installed. She wasn't much of a housekeeper, and she didn't like people being able to see into her kitchen. She had them specially made."

Arabella chewed her bottom lip. "Are they important to you?"

Griff shrugged. "Not particularly. I hated them when I was a kid. I was forever pinching my fingers in them."

She made another note on her iPad.

Griff watched Arabella's face as she stepped into the kitchen. Her mouth dropped open. She turned as she took a slow survey, noting the 1950s metal cabinets, yellow linoleum countertops, and matching, scuffed, sheet-linoleum flooring. The white kitchen range wasn't more than fifteen years old and didn't entirely fill the space provided for the previous model. The refrigerator was a two-door model about the same age as the range, and quite a bit bigger than the area allotted its original model. An unpainted scar marred the wall where the top cabinets had been removed to accommodate the new refrigerator's taller, wider girth. A high-tech, polished chrome expresso machine took up most of the kitchen counter.

Arabella touched the coffee machine and pointed toward the double-sided ceramic farm sink, deep on one side, shallower and longer on the other. "I like these," she said. "Everything else ..." She let her voice trail off and shrugged.

"I told you, this room needs some serious help."

"Two-thirds of it is wasted space. You could put an island counter right here." Arabella indicated the middle of the room. "It would double your counter space." She pointed at the northwest corner. "Build a coffee station right there to house your expresso machine, and there's still be plenty of room in the opposite corner—" she pointed, "—for a six-top breakfast nook. This could pretty much be my dream kitchen."

Griff nodded at her iPad. "Write it down. After I let you build it, I just might let you cook in it, too. Lasagna, maybe?"

Arabella's eyes widened and color flooded her face. Griff figured she was thinking about what happened *after* the lasagna. He pretended not to notice her embarrassment and offered a distraction. He pointed toward a closed door just beyond the refrigerator. "The next room is almost new."

"The pantry?" Arabella reached for the doorknob.

"It's a little more universal than that. We call it the utility room."

The room was nearly as large as the kitchen. One wall housed the washer and drier, complete with a hanging rod for freshly laundered shirts. There was also a stainless-steel deep sink and a glass-enclosed shower stall. Two of the remaining walls boasted built-in cupboards. A stainless-steel counter with a triple-tub industrial sink covered the fourth wall. Over the sink, a power wash hose hung suspended. "Until mom died, we kept a good-sized garden. This was where we cleaned the produce."

Next, Griff indicated the shower, "It's never been used. We had one installed in the barn about the same time, and I usually clean up there if I'm too dirty to make it upstairs." Griff opened a door beside the shower. It led to an ordinary half-bath. Arabella took more photos and made notes regarding the flocked, green wallpaper, and the sheet linoleum.

They passed through the bathroom, emerging just below the stairwell and to the right of the fieldstone fireplace. Griff indicated a set of double doors. "The study. It's the only room left on this floor. This room is special. It needs repainting and a couple of other finishing touches." He opened the door and stepped aside, motioning for Arabella to enter. "This time of year, the sun shines in here almost all day."

Arabella stepped into the room ahead of him and stumbled to a halt. She didn't even move when Griff bumped into her.

"Wow! Special doesn't even begin to describe this room." A massive mahogany desk dominated the floor space, but that isn't what riveted her attention. Two sparkling, stained glass windows came together at the southwest corner of the room. The afternoon sun slanted through the multifaceted panes, forming rainbows that danced on the otherwise unadorned walls. "I would never get any work done here," she murmured.

Griff chuckled. "It can be distracting," he said. But he wasn't looking at the room. He was looking at the woman who seemed unaware that her back pressed against his chest. He held her arms lightly, just above her elbows, and savored her weight against him as she basked in the rainbow glow.

The south and east walls of the room were a creamy white that intensified the dramatic effects of the fractured light arching across them. The north wall held a built-in mahogany wall unit. There were cupboards on the bottom and glass-enclosed shelving on the top that protected row after row of richly colored, leather-bound journals.

A high-backed, burgundy leather office chair sat behind the desk. It faced the window, which commanded a sweeping view of the Bitterroot Basin and the mountains beyond. Blue sky stretched endlessly overhead. The river glinted in the distance, and much closer, just off to the left, Arabella's cozy white cottage nestled like a precious gem in her tangled, flowering garden.

"I wouldn't change a thing," Arabella whispered.

Griff tightened his hold and turned her toward the east wall.

"I would like to change this," he said. "There's a good eight feet of empty floor space between my desk and the wall. I was thinking maybe one of those mini-couch things, and fussy tables with lamps on either end, so if she wanted to, my wife could curl up there and read at night while I worked on the ranch accounts. Then over here," Griff turned to the south wall, "maybe an easy chair, in case we have a baby to rock."

Arabella stepped from his side and turned to face him. Laughter danced in her eyes. "A mini-couch and fussy tables?" she queried.

Griff shrugged. His neck grew hot. He was thirty-two years old and would not blush. Why in the world did he even want a woman who could tie him up in knots this way?

She laughed, and the heat from his neck pooled low in his stomach. That probably wasn't good right now, either, but thankfully she'd turned away from him again and studied the blank wall.

"Not a love seat," she said. "And certainly not fussy tables."

He really didn't want to let go of that dream. "And why not?" He bristled. "You don't think my family would want to spend time with me?"

Arabella turned toward him, a look of surprise on her face. "That's not it." She covered his wrist with her slender fingers. Her soft pink hand looked delicate beside his weathered skin. "What I was thinking," she said, "is that if I were your wife, I would want a couch big enough for both of us and any babies we might have." He was so surprised she'd taken his hand, that his defenses weren't up. Her words hit him right in the solar plexus. He must have made a sound because her head turned, and their gazes locked. Griff couldn't get his lungs or his brain to function, but it didn't seem important. He hung suspended in her green eyes.

Her fingers tightened on his arm. He watched her eyes widen and stepped toward her, reaching out with his free hand to touch her face. She jerked backward, pulling her hand away from his. The current sizzling between them snapped.

Arabella practically teleported to the door. "I think we should go look at the rest of the house now, don't you?" Her voice was too high and too bright. She turned and fled, pausing a moment at the staircase then hurrying toward the kitchen.

Griff took a moment to compose himself before following.

He had his breathing under control by the time he made it to the dining room. His knees weren't shaking, and his heart rate had almost steadied.

He stopped in the kitchen doorway between the open batwing doors. Arabella stood near the sink with a coffee cup clenched in her hands. She didn't look at him. "I hope you don't mind?" She waved her cup at the high-tech coffeemaker looking out of place on the ancient, battered counter.

"Coffee sounds good," Griff said. He took another step into the room. She shot away from the coffee machine as though it was a bomb three seconds from detonation. Griff froze, then slowly lifted his hands where she could see them. "I'm sorry," he said.

He watched her struggle to swallow. She slowly nodded her head. "I ... uhm ... me, too." She shuffled a little closer to the back door.

"My fault," Griff said. "I should have warned you." He stood immobile, arms bent at the elbow, hands splayed wide in a universal gesture of safety and peace. He didn't want to fight with her, but he'd rather have her fury than her fear. "It's no big deal. The room does that." He forced himself to shrug.

"What?" Arabella went still and narrowed her eyes. "What do you mean, the room does that?" Her voice rose.

"Well, supposedly, that room has some kind of love charm on it."

"You can't be serious?" Her chin came up. She'd gone all frost-maiden on him.

He smiled. She was stubborn and spunky and beautiful. And he had it bad. "I am serious. You've really got to be careful who you go in there with."

She looked away from him then. "You've experienced this before?"

Damn his stupid hide, she probably thought he was mocking her. "Not me," he said quickly. "Most of those books you saw in there are journals written by my ancestors. That room has seen a lot of romance. That's why I suggested the couch. I was kind of hoping to carry on the tradition."

"Don't you think you should wait for your wife?" she snapped.

This probably wouldn't be a good time to tell her he'd thought he had.

Chapter Eleven

They stood in the kitchen and drank coffee. Her professional voice firmly in place, Arabella talked about color schemes. Griff didn't like it, but at least she hadn't walked out.

This whole thing was such a bad idea. He should thank her for her time and send her back down to her own end of the driveway—where he could watch her from afar like some lovesick fool.

No, that already wasn't working for him, but he hadn't really thought this through step-by-step. If he wasn't careful, he was going to say the wrong thing and frighten Arabella even more.

She tapped her iPad to wake the screen. "Since you don't know who you plan to marry, I suggest a neutral color scheme. It would suit the character of the house, then your wife could add her own touches with throw pillows, wall art, and conversation pieces."

Griff studied Arabella. Plan B wasn't working out very well, either. Arabella had no qualms about linking him romantically to another woman. He'd come up with the idea of having her in his house and decorating it so they could spend time together and she could get to know him—hopefully, even forget about the raving lunatic who'd spent the last ten months yelling at her—now she just thought of him as a raving lunatic with a future wife. Her reaction in the study made it clear she wasn't interested in that wife being her.

Unfortunately, he didn't have a Plan C, and Plan A wasn't even worth reconsidering. After Wednesday, there was no way she'd go out on another date with him. She'd been afraid to slow dance with him; he'd let a drunk accost her, and when he brought her home, he'd opened the door to help her out of the truck and saw pure terror in her eyes. If he told her he was falling in love with her, she would run.

Griff shook his head. "I don't think I thought this through very well." Understatement of the year.

Arabella closed the cover on her tablet. "No problem. It's not like you've committed to anything."

Not true. He was committed to her, and he wasn't giving up. "Look," he said. "There is no girlfriend. There's just the idea of a wife. And maybe a kid or two. Someday. But look at this place. If I were dating you and I brought you out here, what would you think when you walked in?"

"Are you serious?" Arabella exclaimed. "This house is gorgeous. It has it all. An incredible turret, leaded glass windows, a river stone fireplace, tongue and groove hardwood floors ... what's not to like?"

"Bella, the couch is covered in duct tape."

Arabella huffed. "Cosmetics. Totally fixable. They don't make houses like this anymore." She rinsed her coffee cup and put it in the sink, then turned to look at him. "Besides, when you do pick a wife, do yourself a favor and pick one who cares at least a little bit more for you than she does the house."

"I'll try." He wasn't holding out much hope, though.

Griff rinsed his own coffee cup and then continued their tour. "There are four bedrooms and three bathrooms upstairs," he said as they climbed the staircase. "There's the master suite, a mini-suite, and two bedrooms that share a connecting bath. The bathrooms were redone in the seventies, so they won't shock you quite as badly as the kitchen did."

Arabella raised her eyebrows. "The seventies?" They'd reached the top of the staircase. "Am I about to encounter green or orange shag carpeting?"

"All hardwood floors except the linoleum in the bathrooms," Griff promised.

The staircase ended in an anteroom. Arabella and Griff stopped facing a set of intricately carved, golden grained, double doors that led to the turret rotunda. She moved toward them for a closer look. Griff motioned her away. "Let's save that one for last." He directed her instead toward the south wall, which housed an antique rolltop writing desk. It was flanked on either side by a closed door. Griff opened the nearest door. "Guest room," he said and directed her inside.

The room was long and narrow. The door opened to the sleeping area. On the left a generic queen-sized bed shared space with two mis-matched end tables. A mirrored dresser in bird's eye maple stood on the right. Beyond that, a sitting area opened up. A love seat buttressed by end tables served as a room divider. It faced the room's single win-dow. Another leaded glass expanse; it looked out over the ranch build-ings.

"I'm surprised your guests ever leave," Arabella said. "The night sky from here must be incredible."

"Big Sky Country," Griff said. "Day and night. This house has the views."

Arabella turned away from the window and indicated the walls, "I thought you said there wouldn't be any green shag."

Griff grinned at her description of the flocked wallpaper. "I take it that has to go?"

She nodded.

Next, they looked at the walk-in closet. "All this space for one hang-ing bar?" Arabella shook her head. "This closet needs built-ins." She made a note.

"The room next door is identical to this one." Griff pointed toward an open doorway. "The bathroom connects them."

The bathroom fixtures were right out of the seventies, a mint green pedestal sink with matching commode reflected in the mirrored sliding doors of the tub-shower combo. Black starburst flocking decorated the silver wallpaper.

"Oh, my," Arabella said.

Griff sighed. "I suppose it all has to go?"

"No," Arabella said. "The wallpaper, yes." She waved her iPad and shook her head. "And mirrored doors in front of the toilet? Why?"

Griff snorted.

"I'll recommend removing the linoleum countertops and flooring in favor of cultured marble and tile. All your porcelain is in excellent condition, so it can stay. Colored fixtures are back in these days."

They walked out through the second bedroom, which, as Griff had said, was identical to the first. They returned to the anteroom. Arabella said. "I'll mock-up drawings and a per room estimate. That way, you can approve or decline any line item. But as you noted, the only considerable ticket expense I've seen is the kitchen. I mean, I still have to look at the other two bathrooms, but so far, I won't be recommending you change any of the porcelain."

"That sounds promising," Griff said, leading the way past the staircase to the door on the north side of the anteroom. He stopped with his hand on the doorknob and turned to Arabella. "I'm going to let you go in here alone. Take as long as you want. Take photos, whatever, but I'm staying out here."

"Okay," Arabella studied him. "Any particular reason?"

"Yes," Griff said, backing away from the door. "This is my room, and if I go in there with you, I'm sure you'll be uncomfortable."

HER GAZE SNAPPED TO his boots. Yeah, he was right. She was already uncomfortable. "If it's too personal—."

Griff shook his head, opened the door, and backed away.

Arabella stepped into the room hesitantly. She didn't know what she expected, but her surprise told her it hadn't been this. A familiar piney, citrus tang welcomed her. She breathed it in and studied his room. The upper part of the northern wall was primarily window. It struck Arabella that the only window dressings she'd seen in the house were the curtains in the kitchen windows, which were not stained glass, and the faux drapes in the formal living room. How did one live in a house without curtains? She made a mental note to ask, then turned her attention to the rest of his bedroom.

He slept in a queen-sized bed. It boasted four pillows, each with a plain white pillowcase. A star-patterned blue and tan quilt served as his bedspread. The headboard of his bed, matching end tables, and six drawer chest were unremarkable, functional rather than ornate, and made from lacquered pine. A colorful collection of rodeo ribbons framed the mirror above the dresser. One corner of the room held a curio cabinet filled with trophies. Another corner held a straight-backed chair sporting a stack of novels—paperback crime dramas from the local library. She conjured up a mental picture of Griff reading, barechested, propped up in bed on all those white pillows. Oh my.

Resolutely turning her back on the bed, she opened his closet door. Again, she found a large, walk-in closet with one simple hanging bar. It held a couple of suits, an assortment of colorful western shirts, and a half-dozen or so blue denim, pearl snap-front work shirts. Four western hat boxes rested on the top shelf and a tidy line of cowboy boots and a few pairs of shoes toed the baseboard.

His bathroom was just as neat as everything else. Of course, Arabella told herself, he'd planned on her coming, so he might not always be this organized. The porcelain fixtures were pale blue with the linoleum countertop and floor being several shades darker. The sliding glass shower door wasn't mirrored.

So far, everything she'd seen, in his bedroom and throughout the rest of his home, spoke of quality care. The wallpaper was old—and ugly—but not ripped, or torn, or peeling. The kitchen was the only real eyesore. She wasn't entirely certain why Griff thought his house needed fixed. For the most part, a little refreshing would do nicely.

When she emerged from his room, Arabella found Griff sitting on the floor, leaning against the balustrade post. One of his long legs stretched out before him, and the other bent at the knee. Scheherazade reclined on his lap. Griff rose to his feet, still holding the dog, and said, "Well?"

Arabella wasn't entirely sure what he was asking. She said, "I didn't look in your dresser drawers or under your bed or in your medicine cabinet, but I did open your closet. All that organization is a little disconcerting.

Griff shrugged. "I like things neat." He sounded defensive.

Arabella smiled. "You know it's not exactly a fault." She guessed from his tone that he hadn't been entirely comfortable with her presence in his private space. She hugged her tablet and waited for his next directive.

HE tipped his head toward the double doors across from them. "Last but not least."

"The master suite?" Arabella walked toward the doors. "I kind of expected this to be your room."

"Not until I'm married." Griff reached out and put his hand on her shoulder. "Wait."

Arabella turned and looked at him questioningly. He put Scheherazade down and smoothed his hands down the thighs of his jeans, almost as though he were nervous.

Her deduction must have shown on her face. Griff shrugged and motioned toward the doors again. "I could never sleep here alone. This room has an ... aura. It's kind of like the study downstairs."

Arabella's eyes widened in surprise.

Griff said, "I just wanted you to know before you went in, so you'd be prepared. It starts right here. He indicated the outside of the doors. "Even when I was a kid and couldn't read, I knew these doors were special."

Arabella studied their carvings. Each image flowed into another. Birds and butterflies, flowers, bees, and vines, all twisted together to create an intricate pattern. She saw sunshine and flowing water. Stars. A dancing lamb, a sleeping lion, a flock of sheep. She turned to look at Griff, "Somehow, this reminds me of Bible stories?"

He nodded his head. Raising his arm, he flipped the light switch at the top of the stairs. A chandelier glittered overhead. The light changed the flowing patterns on the door, and now Arabella could clearly see words. She drew in an awed breath.

Griff stepped up behind her and read from the first door. "*I thank my God upon every remembrance of you. Philippians 1:3.*" Then he motioned to the second door and continued, "*What therefore God hath joined together, let not man put asunder. Mark: 10:9.*"

"That's—" Arabella searched for words that would express her wonder "—sacred. This room is consecrated. Like a marriage sanctuary."

A sigh escaped Griff. "Yes, that's exactly how I've always felt. Even before I understood the meaning behind the words." He stepped up to the doors. "My great-great-grandfather gifted my great-great-grandmother with these doors on their twentieth wedding anniversary. Only love has passed over this threshold. I want my marriage to be the same."

He pushed both doors open. Like the formal living room, the western wall was all stained-glass window. Curving one hundred eighty degrees, it rose from a built-in window seat and looked out across the Bitterroot Valley. Arabella crossed the hardwood floor to the wall of glass. "Incredible," she said.

She sat on the window seat. Griff leaned in the doorway with his hands in his pockets and Scheherazade on his boot. Arabella smiled. "If somebody had told me two weeks ago that you were both tenderhearted and a romantic, I wouldn't have believed them."

Griff flashed his dimple at her. "That's because I'm also bad-tempered and ill-mannered."

"Well, just for the record," Arabella twirled her finger in the air, "I like this side of you better."

"Duly noted." Griff's voice lowered. The look in his eyes went to her head like mulled wine.

Arabella shifted her gaze to her iPad. "Why do none of the bedrooms have curtains? I agree that covering them seems a sin, but—" she shook her head "—privacy?"

"The house is built on a rise. No matter where you stand outside, even at night when the interior lights are on, all you can see is the ceiling." Griff pointed at her. "With the exception of standing directly in front of the windows themselves. Right now, you could be seen."

That made sense to Arabella. She made a note on her tablet and asked her next question. "Why isn't there any furniture in here?"

Several moments passed. Arabella glanced up. Shoulders hunched; Griff stared at Scheherazade. Arabella realized that his parents were likely the last couple to use this room. "I'm sorry," she said. "Was that insensitive of me? I didn't think."

Griff waved his hand. "No. It's okay. It's just ...." His voice trailed off.

"You don't have to explain."

He responded anyway. "My parents went river rafting on their thirtieth wedding anniversary and never came home. New furniture for this room was supposed to be delivered while they were gone." Griff waved his hand. "They were always so wrapped up in each other they'd forget to share things, or maybe they thought I knew." He shrugged. "But I was still living in the apartment above the bunkhouse and I didn't even know the room was empty. Not until I was making arrangements to have their bodies shipped home from Tennessee and the furniture truck showed up." He gave a rueful laugh and finally looked up at her. "I'm afraid I didn't react very well. When you're pricing furniture for me, you might want to skip the Dream Bedroom store in Missoula. They probably won't deliver here."

Arabella started across the room toward him. Griff held up his hands to stop her. "I'm all right. Or at least I will be as long as you don't offer me any sympathy."

She knew that feeling. Arabella nodded and activated her tablet. Back to business then. The double doors to the master suite actually opened into an alcove created by two rooms on either side of the portal. She pointed to the room on Griff's left. "What's in there?"

Griff answered, "I think when the house was originally built, it was the nursery, but it has no windows. Now it's a closet and dressing room."

Arabella noted that then pointed to the room on his right and said, "Then this would be the master bathroom?"

"Yes, and you're going to have to see it to believe it." Griff reached down, scooped Scheherazade into his arms, and motioned for Arabella to proceed him.

She looked over her shoulder and asked, "Are you two following me into the bathroom?"

"Oh yeah," his grin was back. "I get to watch your face when you see this."

"Okay, suit yourself," Arabella turned away to hide her grin. She hoped he enjoyed watching her surprise as much as she planned to enjoy the surprise Scheherazade had in store for him. She paused outside the bathroom door, not knowing what to brace for. From Griff's behavior, she anticipated a decorating disaster similar to the kitchen. She reached in and flipped the light switch.

First she gasped, and then she sighed. "Oh, Griff. If you want a wife, just pick any woman in the world and promise her this bathroom."

Griff looked pleased with her reaction, but protested in mock outrage, "Didn't you say that my wife should love me more than she loved my house?"

Arabella waved her arms expressively. "I'm sorry. That's not going to be possible once she sees this."

The focal point of the room was a replicated clawfoot bathtub obviously built for two. Embellished with gold fixtures and feet, it sat square in the middle of the room, wide enough for two lovers, side by side, yet both ends curved, so if those lovers chose, they could sit face to face with their legs entangled. Arabella caressed the edge of the tub. "I have never seen anything so elegant and classic, yet so sexy at the same time."

The room also included dual sinks, a huge walk-in shower with multidirectional showerheads, and a private alcove for the commode. It was a dream in white marble, polished gold, and glass.

"The floor is heated," Griff said. He stepped into the bathroom. Scheherazade exploded in his arms, nine pounds of panic and fur struggling for freedom. "*Holy Hannah*!" Griff juggled her frantic body, trying to lower her to the floor safely. The little dog's legs churned desperately even before her feet hit the tile. She caught traction and bolted.

Arabella leaned against the counter, laughing. Griff looked up at her. "What was that?"

Green eyes sparkling, Arabella prompted, "Do you remember noticing that Scheherazade had no interest in sitting on your wet boots?"

Griff looked down at his feet, then back to her. He clearly wasn't following her train of thought. "So?"

"She has a similar aversion to bathrooms."

It took a couple moments, then Griff's eyes widened. "She thought I was going to give her a bath?"

"Apparently so, and if she behaves true to form, you are in the doghouse for the next several hours."

"You couldn't have warned me?" Griff bristled.

Arabella continued to grin. "Nope. That was way too much fun to miss."

Griff arched his eyebrow. "It seems to me that a dunking is in order." His grin sent a shock of adrenalin through her. "Maybe you shouldn't have come into the bathroom, either." He stepped toward her.

She skipped sideways, keeping the tub between them until she was parallel to the door, then she bolted, too.

Griff followed. Their dash ended in the kitchen.

"Ha! I won," Arabella sang. She knew if he'd really tried to catch her, she wouldn't have made it out of the bedroom, but she wasn't telling him that.

"Indeed," Griff said. Something in his purposeful stride had her backing away cautiously. He walked to the kitchen sink and retrieved his coffee cup. She relaxed. He flipped on the water, grabbed the sprayer, and doused her from head to toe.

She shrieked and jerked her tablet above her head.

Griff released the sprayer. "Oh, crap! I'm sorry." He stared at Arabella. The look on his face told her he thought he'd gone too far.

She arched her eyebrow, planning to take advantage of his guilty conscience, but his eyes widened even further, and she couldn't contain her laughter. She put her iPad on the counter and dashed the water from her cheeks with her fingers. "Competitive much?" Her clothing dripped.

Griff opened a drawer and handed her a tea towel, tossing several more onto the floor. "Uhm, Bella—." He motioned toward his own chest with his hand.

Arabella looked down. Her green cotton t-shirt clung lovingly to her skin and outlined her bra faithfully, right down to the little bow between her breasts. She could even see the indentation of her belly button, but her shirt wasn't transparent, so she was still basically decent. She grabbed the shirt and peeled it away from her body. "I am going to remember this," she said as she rung the hem out onto the towels on the floor. "And when you least expect it, I will get even. But first, I think I'll go home and dry off."

SCHEHERAZADE refused to come out of hiding. After shooting out of the bathroom, she'd found herself a secure refuge and wasn't budging.

Arabella asked, "Could she have gotten out of the house?"

"I don't see how," Griff had searched while Arabella dripped on the kitchen floor. "The doors and windows are all closed."

"She can pout for hours," Arabella said, chewing her lip.

Griff sighed. "I'm sorry." He was not doing an outstanding job of impressing Arabella. In the last hour and a half alone, he'd grabbed at her, told her a sob story, soaked her, and lost her dog.

"It's not your fault," Arabella shook her head. "I should have known this would happen." She shivered despite the towel wrapped around her shoulders.

"You're cold. I shouldn't have gotten you wet."

She shrugged. "It was fun, but I am cold. I need to change."

Griff nodded. He'd planned a different ending for their day, but any clothing he could offer her would be way oversized. "Come on, I'll drive you home."

"Scheherazade?"

"She'll be fine here by herself for the few minutes it takes to run you home. And when she finally comes out of hiding, I'll bring her down to you."

Several hours later, Griff leaned back against the pillows on his bed with a novel open in his lap, but he wasn't reading. Arabella told him she would draft a proposal for his house. She'd seemed excited. Even so, he wasn't confident she'd accept the job. They'd had a few good moments today, but they'd had a couple of bad ones, too.

He should have let her go into the study alone. Maybe, if she hadn't touched him, if she hadn't mentioned being his wife and cuddling on the couch, he could have kept it together, but his mind conjured up her in his arms, holding their child. The image seemed so real that his reaction was as automatic as breathing. He'd needed to touch her.

At least he'd had sense enough not to follow her into his bedroom—and he'd managed to keep his hands to himself the remainder of the evening. She'd taken getting doused with the spray nozzle well, but he still wished he hadn't done it. She'd wanted to go home, ending his chance of talking her into the grilled steak dinner he'd planned.

He finally heard the click and clatter of Scheherazade's toenails on the hardwood floor. She climbed the staircase and stepped into his room.

Griff tossed the novel aside. "I should have been asleep two hours ago, you little brat."

Scheherazade, undaunted by the tone of his voice, jumped onto the bed and wiggled into his lap.

"None of that," he said, setting the dog aside and peeling back the covers. He stepped into the jeans on the floor by his bed, then retrieved his shirt from the doorknob. He shrugged it over his shoulders without bothering to tuck it in or snap it closed.

"Let's get you home." Grabbing a pair of socks from his dresser, he headed out the door. Scheherazade didn't follow.

Griff stepped back into the bedroom. The little dog sat on the bed and just looked at him. "Stubborn." Griff sighed. "I totally see why you're her dog." It was a grumble, but he was smiling.

Scheherazade went into his arms willingly. She tucked her head under his chin and cuddled up to his chest. "Nice," Griff said. "Suppose you could teach her that?"

Scheherazade swished her tail.

ARABELLA heard Griff's truck moments before his headlights flashed across the living room windows. She climbed out of bed and tugged into her robe as she hurried through the house, flipping light switches.

By the time she got the yard light on, Griff had already climbed the deck stairs. He'd left his truck running. The headlights were on, and the driver's door stood open.

She opened her back door. "Hey." Looking up at Griff, her smile faltered. He was hatless, practically shirtless, and beard stubble shaded his jaw. His hair stuck out in unruly curls. He looked tired and impossibly endearing. Like Scheherazade, she wanted to crawl into his arms and curl up. "I...uhm...." Yeah, last time she'd tried that, it hadn't worked out so well for her. She stammered, "T-thank you."

Griff stopped about two feet from the door. The smile faded from his face. "She turned up in my bedroom about eleven o'clock," He said. "I have no idea where she'd been hiding."

Arabella wiped her palms on her robe and reached for Scheherazade, surprised her hands didn't shake. Her stomach quivered. "I'm sorry she woke you."

He hadn't moved. Scheherazade still sheltered in his arms. Arabella stepped forward. Her bare toes curled on the cold metal threshold. She glanced at Griff. Their eyes locked. Heat swirled through her, spiraling out from just below her belly button. She jerked her arms back and crossed them, trying to resist the pull of his indigo eyes.

"You're cold," Griff said. "I should let you get back inside." He shifted and leaned forward, offering Scheherazade. The scent of pine and leather, with a sweet tang of citrus, overwhelmed her senses. She accepted the wiggling dog into her arms and whispered, "Thank you." She didn't have the air for anything more. She hastily backed away from temptation.

Griff stared at her for a minute. He reached up like he intended to adjust his hat. His hand encountered air and he let it fall to his side. He nodded and walked away without a word.

Chapter Twelve

Monday Ty called with a birth announcement. Esmerelda was the proud mother of four. He asked Arabella to plan to stay a little while after her Wednesday ride to meet the new family. Arabella spent most of Monday and all of Tuesday working on the specs for Griff's house. She strove to keep the prices as low as she could in hopes he'd approve it. She'd promised to complete the specs by Wednesday, and was ready to deliver, but the day seemed to conspire against her.

She'd met with three sets of clients in the architect's office and didn't make it to Ty's until almost three-thirty in the afternoon. It was close to five by the time she'd finished her ride and curried her horse. At this rate, Griff would be headed in for supper and bed before she made it back to Spitfire. Arabella wondered how quickly she could hurry through meeting Esmerelda's new puppies without hurting Ty's feelings.

Thinking only of reaching Griff as soon as possible, she emerged from the barn to discover him leaning on her truck. "Hey." A smile brightened her face. "Are you here to meet the puppies, too?"

"Yeah. Tyner called me." Griff nodded toward the practice ring. "I caught the last of your ride. You know, you have access to horses much closer to home."

Surprise halted her feet. Arabella stared at Griff with her mouth open. "You'd let me ride your horses?"

Ty came around the back of her truck. "Hey, don't go trying to poach my free labor."

Griff reached out with his finger and tapped Arabella's chin. "It's really not safe to leave your mouth hanging open in the barnyard."

Arabella swatted at his hand and replied, "It's probably not safe to put your fingers that close to my teeth, either."

Griff grinned and winked.

Her smile didn't fade, but Arabella shook her head. "You're racking them up, I still owe you for the water."

"This sounds interesting," Ty said. "What about the water?" He turned and swept his hand toward his house to get them moving in that direction.

Arabella fell into step between the two men and nodded her head toward Griff. "Mr. Competitive lost a foot race, so he turned the kitchen sprayer on me."

"I'm not so competitive," Griff countered. "After all, I could have pushed you down the stairs and jumped over you."

"Wait." Ty held up his hand and stopped walking. They turned to face him. "You were running in the house?"

"Bella started it!" Griff hooked his thumb toward her as they resumed their walk.

Ty shook his head. "You two need adult supervision."

ESMERELDA wasn't any more impressed with Griff and Arabella this visit than she was the last. Still, she was proud of her babies and allowed them to be praised. She had four plump, brown and white fluff balls lined up at her side. She allowed finger petting, but when Arabella reached with both hands to lift a puppy, Esmerelda leaned forward and growled.

Arabella jerked her hands back to her knees. Griff, kneeling beside her, reached out and rested his hand on the small of her back. She shifted away, prompting Griff to say, "Sorry, that scared me."

She nodded, moving just a bit further still.

Ty glanced at Arabella and questioned Griff with a look. Griff shrugged.

When it came time to go, Griff offered Arabella a hand up. That she allowed.

On the back step, Arabella stopped. "Wait. Where's Fauntleroy?"

"Roy," Ty answered, emphasizing the shortened name, "is out of favor with Ezzie. He's probably sleeping on the front porch. He spends most of his time in the front yard and only comes inside for the night when I do. Did you want to see him?"

Arabella looked up at Ty. "Do you mind?"

"No, go right ahead. Griff and I will wait here."

Arabella disappeared around the corner of the house. The men crossed to stand in the shade of a gnarled apple tree several yards away.

They watched quietly until Arabella rounded the corner.

"What's up with you two?"

Griff waved his hand. "Every time I get close, she runs. I keep reminding myself that I can't expect to undo ten months of damage in a couple of weeks."

"It's not just ten months," Ty answered. "It's her entire life. She isn't used to being touched, and she's learned that people don't stay. Her defenses are automatic and ingrained."

There was more to it than that. Griff knew he'd pushed Arabella too far, too fast. First, with anger, and then with intimacy. She held a tight rein on her emotions, and he'd broken those barriers without offering her a safety net. It was a miracle she even tried to trust him. He needed to be patient.

Ty echoed his thoughts. "Building a relationship with her will take patience and restraint. It will be frustrating."

Griff shook his head. "Yeah. I sabotage myself. I always act first and think later. It's just that touching is so natural to me. It's not something I think about. It's just something I do."

"I don't suppose it occurred to you to tell her that? She doesn't know how to react to touch. You're going to have to teach her."

Griff blinked. Could it be that easy?

A few minutes later, Arabella came back around the house and paused when she didn't see the men where she'd left them. Ty waved.

"Do you want me to take Fa...uh, Roy home with me since Ezzie doesn't want him near the pups?"

"No. We're doing just fine," Ty assured her. His cell phone buzzed, and he glanced at the screen. "Give Ezzie a couple more days to relax, and everything will go back to normal." Ty raised his hand to indicate his cell phone. "Sharee says there's a potential buyer in the barn who's interested in Cosmic. I need to go."

"GO AHEAD, WE'LL SEE ourselves out." Arabella moved to Griff's side.

Ty left them at their rigs, and Arabella opened the passenger door on her pickup. She retrieved a manilla envelope from the seat and handed it to Griff. "The specs for your house."

"That was fast."

Arabella shrugged. "I told you I'd have it for you today. You don't need all that much done. Mostly wallpaper removal, painting, some flooring, bathroom countertops, and that kitchen. Any furniture you need can come later. You don't have to do it all at once."

Griff tapped the envelope against his hand. "Should we go back to your place and talk about it?"

"It would be better for you to look at it alone first." She gave him the same advice she gave every client. "You'll find an itemized, room-by-room list of price options and choices in the prospectus. I don't want to influence your decisions any more than I already have." Arabella closed the passenger door and walked around the front of her rig.

Griff followed. "What if I want you to influence my choices? You're the expert. Just do what you think best."

She faced him, shaking her head. "That would be foolish. It's your house. You have to live in it." She remembered his reaction to her bathroom towels and sent him an impish grin. "Give me free rein, and I'm painting it all pink."

He looked horrified, then laughed. "You would, too, wouldn't you?"

Probably not, but he didn't need to know that. Arabella nodded toward the prospectus. "Look it over. Take notes. Jot down your questions. Then you can call me, and we'll talk."

They said their good-byes. Arabella glanced in her rearview mirror as Griff pulled onto the highway behind her. She knew she had no reason to be so ridiculously happy, but she was. Griff hadn't even looked at the specs yet. She really needed to quell her enthusiasm. He might want extensive revisions, or he might nix the project all together once he saw the bottom line. He hadn't given her a budget, but he'd be hard-pressed to get the work done any cheaper without doing it himself. She hoped he knew that.

She pulled over at her mailbox and hopped out of her pickup. Griff honked and waved as he drove past. She grinned and waved back with a handful of weekly sales papers, then climbed into her rig. She was just far enough behind him that she'd barely reached the turn to her driveway when he pulled up at his barn and stopped. He stepped out of his truck. The door on the little yellow station wagon sitting nearby popped open and a woman emerged. She ran straight into Griff's open arms.

Arabella jerked her steering wheel to the right, narrowly missing the planter on the left side of her drive. Griff said he didn't have a girlfriend. If that was true, what had she just witnessed? She parked her rig, gathered her possessions, and headed for the house.

Scheherazade shot outside doing her potty dance and ran straight to the dog run. Arabella followed the little dog into the enclosure and latched the gate. It was a pleasant afternoon for sitting on a bench in the shade and trying to breathe. It wasn't as if what she'd seen at Griff's really mattered. What mattered was the shock she'd felt. Why hadn't she learned by now to stop pinning her hopes on other people? She needed to remember that just because Griff was kind and caring, it didn't mean he'd suddenly developed a romantic attachment to her. And that was okay. If the last twenty-six years had taught her anything, it was that she was awkward and odd. And not the kind of person others loved.

Her phone rang. She'd left her purse by the back door and really didn't feel like retrieving it. She wasn't expecting a phone call anyway. A few minutes later, a ping announced a text. It was probably somebody contacting her mistakenly. After all, it was a new number. Only three people even knew she had it; her boss, Ty, and Griff. She decided she'd better check on the off chance it was her boss.

As Arabella reached into her purse, her phone rang again. Caller ID flashed: *Griffin Blake*. What could he possibly want with her when he had company? She didn't answer the phone, but she did look at the text, also from Griff. *Call me, please.* The phone went silent in her hand. She bit her lip, staring at the screen. Another text came in. *I need help*.

Arabella pushed the call back button.

He greeted her with the words, "Could you come up here? Katy's here. She's crying, and I can't get anything coherent out of her."

"Katy?" Arabella remembered the cute little waitress that Griff had introduced as his best friend's little sister. "From Big Pine Bar?"

"Yes. Please, Bella. She's locked herself in the bathroom. I don't know what to do." Griff sounded stressed.

Arabella didn't know what to do, either, but Katy had been kind to her. "I'm on my way." She disconnected the call as Griff said thank you.

When she arrived, Griff opened the back door and jerked Arabella into his arms for a hug. "Thank you!"

Already defensive and out of her element, Arabella put her hands in the middle of his chest and pushed. "I'm not here to comfort you. Where's Katy?"

Griff stepped back. He heaved a sigh and rubbed his forehead. "Ah. *Arabella*. Right." He motioned toward the utility room. "She ran through there and locked herself in the bathroom."

Arabella narrowed her eyes at his name crack. Obviously, he thought she was behaving like an ice princess again. Maybe she was, but what did he expect? She'd never had close girlfriends and didn't have the faintest idea how to proceed. "Hasn't Katy got any family you can call? You said her brother is your best friend?"

"Denny shows up when Denny shows up. He comes home maybe once a year. There's a number where I can leave a message, but Katy needs help now." He took off his hat and pointed it toward the bathroom. "I suggested calling Gar and she flipped. Now I don't know what to do."

Arabella said, "And you think I do?"

"You're female."

Her mouth fell open. She snapped it closed and spun on her heel. "That attitude—" she jabbed her finger in the air, "—is why you get *Arabella*. Not all women are the same!"

Arabella stalked through the house to the bathroom door that opened beside the staircase. She paused for a minute to compose herself, then knocked. "Katy, it's Arabella. May I come in?"

A click sounded, and the doorknob turned. The door eased open just far enough to reveal one red-rimmed, brown eye. "Where's Griff?" Katy asked. "I'm not coming out if Griff is with you."

Arabella, knowing Griff was right behind her, said, "Why, did he say something insulting to you, too?"

Katy wailed, "He's going to call Gar!"

Arabella turned her head and glared at Griff. He shook his head, waved his hands in a "*no*" gesture, and backed away.

"Griff won't call Gar." A moment later, Arabella heard the front door close. "And we're alone in the house. Come on out and tell me what's happened."

They ended up in the kitchen drinking coffee. Katy washed her face with a paper towel. "I suppose you think I'm crazy," she said.

"I think you're upset," Arabella corrected. "Can you tell me why?"

Katy tore off little pieces of another paper towel and piled the confetti on the table. Arabella waited. Finally, Katy whispered, "I had a horrible fight with Gar."

Arabella wasn't certain how to proceed. She knew absolutely nothing about Katy and Gar's relationship beyond Griff's quip about them getting married and Katy's denial. "So, do you want to talk about it?"

Katy shrugged. "I thought I did. I came to talk to Griff, but when he saw I was upset his first thought was to call Gar." She shook her head. "Except Gar is the problem. Besides, Griff is too decisive. There's no way he's going to understand why I'm having trouble with this. He'll just say, *'Do this,'* and tell me whatever he'd do to solve my problem."

Arabella snorted, then slapped her hand over her mouth.

Katy looked at her wide-eyed.

Fighting a grin, Arabella said, "I'm sorry. I'm not laughing at you. It's just your description of Griff is so spot on."

Katy nodded. "I don't think he's ever had trouble making a decision in his life. I second-, third-, and fourth-guess every decision I make."

"Me, too."

"Then maybe you'll understand. See, Gar and I—" Katy stopped and shook her head. "He asked—" She stopped again. "I don't even know where to start so you can understand."

"The beginning is usually best."

Katy inhaled deeply, blew out her breath and nodded. "Gar and I met when we were eleven years old. He and his dad moved in next door, and pretty soon he hung out at our house all the time." She smiled and shook her head. "Probably at first because my mom always fed him. Gar's dad wasn't very good at keeping food in the house."

Arabella made a sympathetic sound, encouraging Katy to continue.

"And we've been friends ever since." Katy stopped and stared into her empty coffee cup. "But maybe not anymore."

"The two of you have been friends for what? At least ten years?"

"Seventeen." Katy grabbed another paper towel and swiped at her eyes. "We've been friends for seventeen years." And then she whispered, "Then I ruined it."

"Seventeen years carry a lot of history. Surely there's a way to work things out?"

"I don't see how." Katy swiped at her eyes impatiently. "The jerk asked me to marry him!"

Arabella blinked and sat back in her chair. Relationships were so confusing. Was she supposed to have seen that coming? "Wait. I don't understand. He asked you to marry him? But I thought you were just friends? Plus, you said you ruined it, and—Wait! Did you turn him down?"

"Of course I did! I can't marry him. He doesn't love me. He only proposed because—" Katy paused, then took a deep breath and blurted. "—he doesn't want the bank to repo the farm. He said—." Her voice broke. "He said it would be no big deal. Just marry him for a few weeks to meet some weird condition in the Garfield Family trust, then we could file for a divorce and pretend the whole thing never happened."

"Now there's a dream proposal." Arabella rolled her eyes. "Did you let him live?"

Katy snorted. "I just grabbed my car keys and left. I drove around for a while, then tried to go back home, but Gar's car was still parked at my apartment."

"Then you came here?"

"Yeah," Katy shrugged. 'I couldn't think what else to do. Usually when I'm confused, I talk to Gar, but now I can't." She stared at the table. One slow tear rolled down her face. She didn't even try to brush it away. "I'm in love with him. I've loved him forever. In high school, I watched him date other girls and always hoped he'd notice me that way.

He never has. I've tried dating other guys, but no one measures up to Gar. Now he's asked me to marry him, but it's not for real."

"Have you ever told Gar how you feel about him?"

"No! That would just be too humiliating. He'd end up feeling sorry for me, maybe even feeling responsible for me." Katy jumped up and paced to the high-tech expresso machine. "I don't think I could take that."

Arabella understood the cold comfort of being someone's unwanted responsibility. She still thought Katy and Gar needed to talk but understood why Katy didn't want to face it. "Okay, Katy. You came here for help. What do you need?"

"I thought I could talk to Griff but then I realized he's just going to get all bullheaded and take a side. That won't help solve the problem." Katy squared her shoulders. "I just need a little time to get my head together. Time to process. Garfield Farm was founded in the early 1900s by Gar's great-great-grandparents. As his friend, don't I have a responsibility to help him save it?"

"Marriage really isn't a *hey do me a little favor* kind of thing."

"Maybe, if I could do it without breaking my own heart? I just wish Gar would back off and let me think." She pulled her phone out of her back pocket and showed Arabella the screen.

Owen Garfield 11 missed calls.

Arabella bit the side of her lip and contemplated the phone screen. She lifted her gaze to Katy. "How much time do you think you'll need?"

Katy shrugged her shoulders.

"Well," Arabella said. "You can come home with me tonight. Gar's probably never heard of me and wouldn't even think to look for you there. But, just in case he's worried about you, why don't you text him and tell him that you're safe, and you'll talk to him later?"

Arabella left Katy to text Gar and went out to the front veranda to talk to Griff. "She and Gar had a misunderstanding, and she's not ready to talk with him."

Griff spread his hands. "They've been friends for over fifteen years. Did she say what they fought about?"

Arabella crossed her arms over her stomach. "Yes, but she asked me to keep her confidence. All I can tell you is that she wants some space so she can think without being told what she should or shouldn't do."

Griff nodded. "No problem." He pulled his truck keys from his front pocket. "I'll just go talk to Gar—."

"No, you won't." Arabella stepped in front of Griff and blocked his path. "Gar and Katy need to sort this out themselves."

"I don't get it. If Katy doesn't want my help, then why did she come here?" Griff demanded.

"Wasn't it you who explained to me about adopted family? Katy came here looking for security, then she realized that if she talked to you, you'd want to solve her problem for her. She needs the time and space to make up her own mind."

Griff heaved a sigh and rubbed his forehead. "What does she need me to do?"

"I'm letting her stay at my place tonight. If Gar calls, you can tell him you've seen her and she's safe, but please don't tell him where she is."

Chapter Thirteen

The next morning, Griff arrived at Arabella's door just as she was filling the coffeemaker. Since the door wasn't locked, she motioned for him to enter. Katy entered through the dining room just as Griff stepped into the house. The citrusy, pine scent of his cologne came with him, mixing with the rich aroma of freshly brewing coffee. Griff dropped his hat on a peg. He wore his everyday work jeans, a denim shirt, and his blunt-toed, battered yard boots, which he kicked off at the door.

Arabella figured that meant he'd be staying for a while. She motioned toward the table and asked him, "Have you had breakfast yet?"

He shook his head in answer to Arabella. "No. When I opened the bathroom window this morning, I heard Sherry barking and figured you'd be up. I got dressed and came right down." He crossed the room and gave Katy a quick hug.

Katy ventured further into the kitchen. Arabella motioned her toward the table. "Scheherazade loves chasing the magpies out of her yard. They can happily torment each other for hours." Arabella crossed to the refrigerator, where she collected bacon and eggs. Griff and Katy stood beside the table.

"Well, sit down," Arabella ordered. Her kitchen was compact, and Griff seemed to take up more than his fair share of the room anyway. Katy sat. Griff crossed to the utensil drawer and collected three sets of silverware. He carried them and the napkin dispenser to the table and laid out three place settings.

Katy watched him, looking from Griff to Arabella and back again. Griff opened the cupboard and grabbed three plates. Arabella, at the stove, said, "I'll need those here for the eggs." She nodded at the counter then looked up at Griff as he placed them beside her. "Oh." She tapped the egg carton. "How many?"

He gave her a half-smile. "Three. Over easy?"

She jerked her gaze away from his impossibly blue eyes and nodded. "Katy?" Her voice sounded a little thick.

"Two," Katy answered. She stared at Griff, but questioned Arabella, "I thought you said you two weren't an item?"

Griff almost fumbled the chunky red coffee mug in his hand.

"We're not." Arabella turned to look at Katy.

Griff lifted two more mugs from the cupboard and poured coffee into all three.

Katy waved her hand, encompassing Griff and the table in her gesture. "He sure seems mighty familiar with your house."

Griff hooked his thumb toward the window and said, "We're neighbors?" He slid one of the coffee cups toward Arabella and carried the other two to the table.

"Come to think of it," Katy said. "You seemed pretty familiar with Griff's house yesterday, too."

"I've only been inside once," Arabella said, "But it would be pretty hard to miss that coffeemaker."

Katy snickered. "Yeah, it's the only decent thing in the kitchen."

"I'm going to let Arabella fix that," Griff said. "I'm hiring her to redo the place."

Arabella turned to him. Surprise lit her green eyes. "You've looked over my prospectus already?"

Griff shook his head, "No. I'm sorry. It's still on the front seat of my truck." He nodded toward Katy. "I got distracted."

Arabella stood with a spatula in her hand. She stared at him. "Then how do you know you're hiring me?"

"The idea occurred to me the first time I saw this place. If you could make this—" Griff raised his hands, indicating the house, "—out of the mess Tom left you, I figured you'd be able to turn my place into the Ritz. I just didn't mention it right away because we had ...issues."

Arabella huffed. "We still have issues."

His lips curved into a slow smile. The look in his indigo eyes tangled up with her breathing, and his baritone voice rumbled smooth and low, "Yeah, but we're working on it."

Arabella's mouth dropped open. She jerked her attention back to the frying bacon, but she still saw Katy look at Griff with a question in her eyes. Griff hid behind his coffee cup.

Before the silence grew awkward, Arabella said, "I'm about to start the eggs. We're going to need butter and toast."

"I'll get the butter." Katy went to the refrigerator.

Griff didn't say anything, but he crossed the room to the breadbox and the toaster.

Arabella cracked eggs into the skillet then turned to Griff. "The Ritz, huh? I did not charge you enough."

Katy giggled.

When it came time for Katy to leave, Arabella said good-bye at the back door. Griff walked Katy to her car with his arm around her shoul-ders and Arabella busied herself with laundry so she wouldn't be tempt-ed to stay and watch them through the windows. She returned to the kitchen when she heard Katy's car drive away.

Griff stood in the driveway staring at the ground. He had his hands jammed in his back pockets. Arabella wondered what he was thinking. On cue, he glanced up at his truck, toward her house, and back to his rig. That was pretty clear. He was thinking about leaving without coming back inside.

The dejection in his stance compelled Arabella to open the back door She stood on the threshold. "You okay?"

She hadn't meant to speak so softly, but apparently, he'd heard her anyway. He shrugged and answered, "Yeah, I guess." Then he shrugged again, looked up, and said, "I don't know." He pointed down the driveway. "There's something she's not telling me, and I feel like it's important."

"She's a grown up. You have to let her make her own decisions."

"Yeah? I don't even know what her decision is, but I feel like it's wrong. I shouldn't have promised to stay out of it."

"I don't think she's made her decision yet." Arabella motioned toward the house. "Come back inside and have another cup of coffee."

Griff looked toward his truck. "I'm not good company right now. Besides, I've imposed on you enough."

Arabella smiled. "You're better company than you used to be." She crossed the deck toward him.

He lifted his hand and rubbed his forehead. Arabella walked down the steps and touched his arm. Griff hauled her into his arms, hugging her convulsively. Arabella didn't struggle. She knew Griff was hurting and simply needed comfort.

She felt his tension and remembered something one of the college counselors had tried to tell her about healing hugs. Arabella splayed one hand over Griff's heart and slipped her other arm around his back. With her cheek on his sternum, she counted his heartbeats; at ninety-two, he started to relax. At one hundred thirty-seven, his breathing evened out. At two hundred forty, his arms slackened. She eased back and put some space between them, keeping her hands on his forearms.

"Better?" she asked.

His eyes were sad, but his dimple peeked out when he tried to smile. "Yeah. Thank you."

She nodded. "Are you ready for that coffee?"

When his smile came this time, it was much more real. A light kindled in his indigo eyes. "I am," he said. Gripping her shoulders, he turned her toward the house. "Give me a second, I'll be right there."

Griff came through the kitchen door before she had their coffee mugs refilled. He held the manilla envelope with her specs in it in one hand and Scheherazade in the other. Arabella carried the coffee to the table. She tipped her head in question and nodded toward Griff's hands.

He put Scheherazade down, removed his hat, and shucked his boots off. "Sherry was standing at the gate, giving me sad puppy eyes. I couldn't leave her out there."

"Hmm," Arabella took her usual seat. "I'm beginning to think you like my dog."

Griff grinned.

She tapped the manilla envelope in his hand. "I thought we agreed you'd look at this without me?"

He shook his head. "That was your idea. I don't remember agreeing to it." He opened the envelope and drew the specs out. "I'm the client. Humor me."

Arabella heaved an audible sigh.

Griff extended his left arm and draped his hand over her right wrist. She noted the difference between his sun-bronzed fingers and her fair skin. They were a study in contrasts and incompatibilities. Even so, she quelled her impulse to shift away.

The prospectus lay on the table in front of him. He lifted the top page and studied it silently before placing it face down above the stack and raising the next page. He used only his right hand. His left thumb methodically caressed her wrist. Arabella wasn't even sure he realized he was doing so.

She had to force herself to sit still. Griff sipped his coffee as he went through the pages one-by-one. He did not shuffle backward to double-check, nor did he ask for a pen to take notes. Not even his expression helped her gage his thinking.

As he studied the second to the last page, his thumb hesitated for a moment on her wrist and then resumed its rhythmic stroke. He barely glanced at the final page—the one that was most crucial to her—before he used both hands to gather the papers and turn the stack over. Once the pages sat neatly, face up in front of him again, he lifted his head and pinned her with his indigo gaze.

She noted his clenched jaw and tensed. He spoke in a measured tone, "I see where you've marked that you'll need two, possibly three people to help with manual labor, and their wages." It wasn't a question, but she nodded. "And then I see that you've included your own labor and wages." Again, she nodded. "Why is it," his eyes narrowed, "that your wages are lower than those of your employees?"

Arabella relaxed. That was an easy explanation. "Because part of my remuneration comes from that last page. I am requesting formal permission to use before and after photos in my advertising. That will include your name and reputation and is no small thing. It's not unheard of for a first client in a new market. You'll get a break for helping me earn future contracts."

Griff braced his elbows on the table and leaned toward her. "Photo permission and my honest testimonial are a given." He tapped his finger on the prospectus. "Underpaying you isn't."

"But—"

"Do you want the job?"

Arabella nodded.

"Fine." He lifted the specs and slipped them back into their envelope. "I'm inclined to go with column three. Get me paint chips, tile samples, and for countertop samples, I'm leaning toward quartz, but might consider granite." His voice lowered. "And revise your salary to market value."

"Column three all the way across?" Arabella said faintly. "That's—."

He shrugged. "I told you I was going for the Ritz." He rose, tipped what was left of his cold coffee into the sink, and refilled his cup.

She grinned. "You don't have enough bedrooms for the Ritz. You'll have to settle for being a really, really expensive bed and breakfast destination."

He topped off Arabella's coffee cup. "I'll keep that in mind if the rodeos go out of business and people stop eating beef."

"Seriously, no one ever goes for column three full stop. The most expensive item isn't always the best choice."

Griff sat back down. "You want to save me money? Great. I'm all for that, but it's not going to be on lesser quality materials or workmanship. You need muscles to tote and carry and move furniture? Fine, use mine, or I'll send a couple of my men over. I'm already paying them anyway. That wouldn't even need to go through you."

"We can do that." She whispered, finally believing he'd actually authorized the dream column without reservation. She pressed her hands to her face and looked at him. "Oh my gosh. This is unbelievable."

Chapter Fourteen

The three rooms in his house that Griff said he used most often were the kitchen, his bedroom, and the study. The kitchen would take the most time to rebuild. He asked Arabella to start in his study while he had his men strip the kitchen down to its walls.

From her cottage, Arabella could see only the upper story of Griff's house. When she arrived on the first day of renovation, she found the lawn freshly mowed with a brand-new white picket fence standing guard around it. She smiled at Griff. "It's beautiful."

"It's also practical," he answered. "You can bring Sherry to work with you."

Her green eyes lit with joy. "That's so sweet." She skipped beside him as he led the way up the front walk.

Griff smiled. "You seem pleased about thoroughly disrupting my life for the next couple of months."

Arabella's smile faded. She paused and looked up at him. "Are you having second thoughts?"

He snorted. "I'd better not be." He opened the front door and lightly touched Arabella's shoulder to usher her in.

A vast expanse of hardwood floor greeted her. The furniture, the throw rugs, the wall art—all of it—gone. As she looked around in shock, Griff explained, "Only my bedroom is furnished. The old table and chairs are still in the kitchen. They'll go after the remodel is done, so you don't have to be careful with them. The coffeemaker is out there, too. I'll move it into the utility room later. The fridge won't fit, so we'll put it on the veranda."

"Wow." Arabella didn't have the brainpower required for speech. She turned full circle. Even the wooden double doors to the study were gone. "Wow." She spread her arms. "When you commit to something, you commit."

He smiled his slow, sexy smile. "You might want to remember that."

She nodded, not really registering his words. She had other concerns. "Are you going to be okay living like this? Most people do one or two rooms at a time."

"When you finish my study, we'll put the doors and that furniture back. I'm in there almost more than any other room in the house. For now, the TV is in my bedroom, and I can take meals in the bunkhouse. I'll be fine."

"I hope so." Arabella smiled. "This ought to shave a few days off my completion time since I won't be waiting around while furniture gets shifted."

They unloaded Arabella's pickup, carrying in paintbrushes and trays, drop cloths, a case of painter's tape, ladders, buckets of paint, and a paint sprayer. "You know how to use this thing?" Griff asked.

Arabella raised her eyebrows. "Of course. If I used a roller, I'd be painting all year."

Griff stepped back and looked her over. He tilted his head, first this way, then that.

Arabella considered what Griff saw as he looked at her paint-splattered blue jeans, t-shirt, and tennis shoes. The baseball cap protecting her braided and coiled blond hair fared no better. However, an occasional blot of paint here and there didn't make her incompetent at her job. If he had questions about her abilities, he was free to repack her truck and she'd leave. Her chin came up, her hip jutted out, and she planted her arms akimbo. "What?" She glared.

Griff laughed. "That's perfect. You want an advertising poster? Stand just like that and dress exactly the way you did when I first saw you. With those sparkly princess things in your hair, that boob-hugging jacket and minuscule skirt, and those strappy pink high heels —post a picture of you like that with a paint gun in your hands and every man in the valley will want his house redone."

"That is the most sexist—" She floundered for words, outraged. "Why don't I just wear a bikini?"

He growled low in his throat.

Arabella squared her shoulders and snapped erect. She pointed at the door and ordered, "Out!"

Griff left, laughing.

Arabella ripped open the case of blue painter's tape and slid two rolls onto her wrist. She jerked a paint tarp into the study and started viciously taping it to the hardwood floor. That man was a serious trial. One-minute charming, the next sweet and caring, but he could morph into a conceited, pompous, arrogant, egotistical jerk in a blink. Not to mention chauvinistic. How dare he—she stopped taping and sat back on her heels—*think she was sexy in her business suits?*

She pondered the thought. It must be true. Why else would he remember the details of her outfit better than she did?

She resumed taping, but her thoughts were more analytical than judgmental. When she'd first moved into the cottage, almost every confrontation she'd had with Griff had been as she was either coming from or going to work. Of course, she'd been wearing a suit. As best she could recall, the day he'd brought her Fauntleroy was the first time Griff had ever seen her in blue jeans. That was the day they'd finally started to communicate—not that they'd gotten very good at it, but they were better. Some days she even liked him.

Once again, she reminded herself that she didn't need to worry about how she felt about Griff. He might find her sexy in her business suits, but he'd made it clear that he didn't care for city girls. That prob-ably hadn't changed, even if he were trying to make friends with her.

The fact that she was here right now getting ready to paint his study underscored his preference. If he'd held any romantic interest in her, he'd have asked her out again, not put her to work.

She thought of their evening at the bar, and Griff's unwillingness to touch her as they danced. At least he was no longer unkind to her. She knew she should be content with that. It wasn't as though she could ever count on a long-term relationship anyway. Her own family hadn't wanted her. Why would anyone else?

She'd worked steadily all morning. As soon as she finished taping the huge, multi-pane window, the room would be ready to paint. Cowboy boots thumped across the hardwood floor and Arabella turned toward the sound. Griff came to an abrupt halt in the doorway. He faltered when he saw her atop the scaffolding with the expanse of leaded glass behind her. His gaze riveted on hers. He shoved the two coffee cups in his hands onto a five-gallon paint bucket and stepped in front of her. He held up his arms. "Bella, come down."

It was an order. Griff kept his voice soft, but he wasn't asking her to join him for coffee. He wanted her off the scaffolding. Arabella sighed. "Griff, I'm a competent professional. You have to let me do my job."

"It isn't your competence that concerns me. It's your equipment. Please come down." His voice was too measured. Arabella noted the tension in his jaw and the fine white line around his lips. This was not an angry man to argue with. His rigid stance and the strain evident in his gaze communicated fear. She wouldn't be able to reason with him until her feet were on the floor. He simply wouldn't listen.

Arabella nodded her head. She dropped the tape rolls, walked to the end of the platform, and descended the ladder.

Griff closed his eyes and let his arms drop to his sides. His fists clenched, but his voice remained controlled. "Thank you. I didn't think you were going to be reasonable."

She considered the tension still running through his body and answered drily, "Shouldn't that be my line?" Moving forward, she stopped in front of him. From where she stood, she could see the pulse point beating in his jaw.

His eyes snapped open, then narrowed. "I thought you were going to fall!" He reached for her.

Arabella braced herself.

Griff faltered, then waved one arm toward the scaffolding. "All I could see was your body going through the flipping window!"

Okay, he wasn't reasonable yet, but he was trying to be. She kept her voice soft. "Both your window and I are safe."

He told her what she could do to the window in very explicit terms.

Arabella smiled. "That really would be unsafe." He snorted. More of the rigidity eased from his shoulders. Stepping closer, she reached up and rested her hand on his jaw, "Stop grinding your pretty white teeth before you break something."

Griff closed his eyes and covered her hand with his own. She felt his jaw relax and he said, "*Holy Hannah*, woman, you scared me."

"Yes, I realize that. I'm sorry." Gripping his wrist, she tugged him toward the scaffold. "Come and look at this. It's perfectly safe."

"No," he said. "It isn't. It's a flipping board between two ladders."

Arabella showed him the platform anchor and demonstrated that it wouldn't slip. She also pointed out the extra-wide foot base on both of the ladders and the heavy rubber stops on all eight feet. "I could tap dance up there and it wouldn't fall over."

Griff hadn't finished arguing, but he wasn't yelling. "There are no safety rails to protect you."

Releasing his hand, Arabella pointed at the coffee cups. "Did you bring one of those for me?"

He looked over at the coffee. "Yes. It's lunchtime. I came to ask if you wanted fried chicken from the bunkhouse." He turned his gaze back to her, "But you're not changing the subject."

Raising her hands in exasperation, Arabella said, "This is my equipment. What do you expect me to do?"

He planted one hand on his hip and jerked the other, pointing toward the barnyard. "We have OSHA approved scaffolding out in the equipment shed. I am going to call my foreman and ask him to send a couple of men in with it—" Griff's voice rose again, "—and I expect you to use it!"

Arabella selected a coffee cup and took a sip. She looked up at him and smiled. "Okay."

"Okay?" Griff couldn't believe what he's just heard. He raised his hands in frustration. "That's it? Okay?"

Arabella cocked her head. "You want me to fight with you?"

"No," he growled. First, she scared him half to death. Now she mocked him. He'd gone from overwhelming relief that she was safe to wanting to kill her himself. "It's not like you to be reasonable. I just—" He tensed as soon as he heard the words leave his mouth. He swallowed and tried for a more conciliatory tone. "That might have come out wrong."

Arabella raised her eyebrows. "It *might* have come out wrong that it's not like me to be reasonable? You really do want me to fight with you, don't you." Her tone was even and she still had that amused grin on her face. How was he supposed to react? Griff closed his eyes and rubbed his forehead. Whatever he said, it probably wasn't going to come out well. Did it matter? As long as she used the safer scaffolding, he'd live with her anger. "Just tell me you'll use the safer scaffolding."

"Hey," she said. She held both cups of coffee and extended one toward him. He eyed the cup, wondering if it was poisoned or a peace offering.

She laughed. "Take this. Your tone of voice wasn't prudent, but your offer is. I'm not fighting with you because using the safest equipment I can makes good sense."

Griff accepted the coffee cup. Studying her face, he considered her words. Her eyes were guileless and clear. He sighed. "I'm sorry I yelled."

She nodded. "Next time, try talking to me."

The last of the tension eased from him and he smiled. "Next time, try not scaring me half to death."

"I'll note that in my fight planner," Arabella said. "Did you offer me fried chicken?"

Motioning toward the door, Griff nodded. "Come wait in the kitchen. I'll go get us a couple of plates."

Arabella followed him, wondering why they couldn't just go eat in the bunkhouse together. Ferrying food back and forth seemed like a lot of bother. "Can't I just come with you?"

Griff crossed the dining room and opened the batwing doors. "I suppose you could," he said as she passed through to the kitchen. "But I would rather you didn't. Except for special occasions, like the holiday party when all the families come, I don't allow the men to have women in the bunkhouse. I'd rather not break my own rule." He crossed to the back door and opened it, waiting for her answer.

Arabella moved to the kitchen table and pulled out a chair. "That makes sense. I'll wait right here."

Griff stepped through the door, then swiveled back and winked at her, "Bella, try not to be too reasonable. That's scary, too."

She laughed.

GRIFF returned carrying a mounded, foil-covered cookie sheet. He slid the tray across the table toward her as he asked, "Have you got open paint anywhere?"

Fingers working the edges of the foil, Arabella answered, "Not yet. Why?"

"Can I bring Sherry in?" He hooked his thumb toward the back door.

She grinned. "You want to let her in your house again? You remember what happened last time?"

"Don't worry. I won't be taking her into any of the bathrooms." He opened the door and whistled. Scheherazade bounded excitedly through the door and danced around his boots.

Arabella frowned. "Wait a minute. I left Scheherazade at home this morning. How did she get here?"

Griff shrugged, staring down at the dancing Shih Tzu. "I might have gone and gotten her."

"Why would you do that?" Arabella tipped her head in question. "I'm beginning to think you really do like her."

He laughed and pointed toward the floor. "Being adored kind of grows on a man." Of course, Scheherazade had already settled onto his boot.

Arabella smiled and shook her head as she lifted the foil from the cookie sheet. The aroma wafting out made her mouth water. The amount of food made her gasp. "This is lunch? Who is going to eat all this?" The cookie tray held two plates piled high with fried chicken, mashed potatoes and rivers of gravy, steamed peas and onions, and fluffy biscuits oozing butter. There were also two smaller plates, each holding a huge slab of chocolate cake.

"We work hard around here," Griff said. "That's fuel. I suspect I'll eat most of it, but you can have some."

Tilting her head, she gave him a slow once-over starting at his boots and working her way up. The look on her face was curious, not provocative, even so, Griff felt his body quicken beneath her scrutiny. He turned and sloshed his cold coffee into the sink, then jammed his cup onto the tray of the coffeemaker and pressed several buttons. "You ready for a refill?" Rather than looking at her, he watched his cup fill.

"You don't have an ounce of fat on you," she said. And then, "I didn't make you enough breakfast the other day, did I?"

Carrying his brimming coffee cup, Griff sat across from her at the table. They were going to have a pleasant, *neutral* conversation and eat lunch together. "Generally, I cook my own breakfast. I have four pieces of toast and three eggs. I ate that at your house and four pieces of bacon." He indicated all the food in front of them. "This is our dinner and my supper. I try to stay out of the bunkhouse as much as possible. Only a handful of my men live here full time, but our work often requires weird hours, so they all have bunks out there. It's their personal space. They don't need their boss in it."

"Leira said she lives on the ranch?" Arabella lifted the two pieces of cake from the tray and set them aside. She handed Griff a set of silverware.

Griff nodded. "There's another house just over the rise." He pointed north with his fork. "When I was a kid, our foreman lived there with his family. Now Hale and Leira have it. Tank, my foreman, is single and lives in the apartment above the bunkhouse. He's also the one who cooked this fabulous food." He indicated the tray. "Let's eat."

"This smells incredible," Arabella said. She didn't reach for a plate but looked up at Griff instead; her green eyes hesitant. "Did you empty everything out of the cupboards?"

"Yes. What do you need?"

"A plate. I don't want to eat off of one of these and leave you my sloppy leftovers."

"Ah, manners." Griff smiled at her. "I've lived alone too long." He rose and disappeared into the utility room, returning with two paper plates, a roll of plastic wrap, and a couple of serving spoons. "I did keep some kitchen stuff nearby."

They served themselves. Griff took Arabella's hand and offered grace. Afterward, she picked up the thread of their conversation. "So, until your kitchen is fixed, you're going to be eating the same thing twice a day?"

"Not all the time," Griff explained. "Leira is my housekeeper. She comes in a couple of times a week and tidies up after me, and usually leaves a covered plate or two in the fridge, so I don't have to cook every night. I imagine she'll still do that." He indicated the utility room with a nod of his head. "I'll move the coffee machine in there. I have a microwave, a toaster, and a hot plate. It's all good."

"I'll start the kitchen as soon as possible. When are your men pulling the cabinets?"

"They can start tomorrow if that suits you."

THE rest of their meal passed with ease. Arabella told Griff she'd have the study ceiling painted that afternoon. After that, she said she'd like to start taping the downstairs bathroom, but needed the toilet, sink, and countertop pulled. "I probably should hire my own help. I can't keep taking your men."

"About that—," Griff said, "—I'd like to give you Johnny. He'll work with you all the time, and if you need extra muscle, I'll come in."

"Johnny?" Arabella smiled. "How's he doing?"

"Not well," Griff said. "As you know, he's wrecked the barn and broke the water pipe. Since then, he's also managed to tip the tractor over and back the combine through the corral. I want him away from heavy machinery."

"And you want me to give him a crowbar and a hammer?" Arabella cut one of the slabs of chocolate cake in two pieces, lifting half onto her plate. Griff took the other half. She wondered if Johnny was in danger of being fired. She worked on forming the question politely when Griff answered it.

"Johnny is a good kid. His mom died about six years ago, and his dad—whom you've met—has taken to drinking."

"I've met ...?" She frowned, trying to remember when she'd encountered a drunk, then her eyes widened. "Roger from the bar?"

Griff nodded.

"So, you're giving me Johnny because you'd rather have him destroy your house than your barn?"

Griff laughed and shook his head. "I don't think it will come to that. Johnny is only fifteen. He got caught spray-painting graffiti on the high school doors. The boys with him all had priors, but it was Johnny's first offense. The judge put him in the work program and Hale signed on as his mentor, but Hale gets busy and we all keep forgetting to keep an eye on the kid. He has a good work ethic. He wants to help but nobody's taught him much of anything."

Arabella considered his words. When she worked at Wengert Stables in Seattle during her college days, she taught a riding class with a particularly inept and angry young man in it. With that kid in mind, she said, "He's going to take offense at being separated from the other men. He might even consider it a punishment. You have any plans to address that?"

All of a sudden, Griff was very interested in his fork. He stared at it as he pushed it back and forth on the table with his index finger. "I did have one thought," he said.

After several long moments of waiting, Arabella lifted her right foot under the table and popped him lightly on the knee. "Spit it out!"

Griff lifted his indigo gaze to her and gave her that slow half-smile that always seemed to tickle her belly button from the inside out. "You have a history with the kid. I thought, maybe, if you asked him ...."

Arabella dipped her chin and challenged him. "Excuse me?"

He shrugged. "You're a beautiful woman. If you ask him—."

"I'll have a lovesick teenager following me around!" She scooted her chair away from the table. "I will not agree to that."

Griff's eyes widened. He raised his hands in surrender. "Good point. I hadn't thought of that."

She stood. "What do you mean you hadn't thought of that, you just said—."

Griff talked over her. "I was only thinking about how to get him to agree, not all the possible consequences." Arabella stopped and stared at him. He waved his hands again. "I'm sorry. I only thought it halfway through."

She nodded, sat down on her chair, and reached for the plastic wrap.

Griff gathered the paper plates and dirty utensils.

She wrapped the remaining lunch plate.

He refilled their coffee cups.

Pulling the second slab of chocolate cake toward herself, Arabella sliced it in half horizontally.

Turning back to the table with their coffee, Griff froze, watching her. She lifted the top section of the cake up and flipped it over, so the frosting nestled in the middle, then sealed it, plate and all, in plastic wrap. Griff grunted in surprise. "Why'd you do that?"

Arabella slid the plate toward him. "When you unwrap it later, you won't lose your frosting to the plastic wrap."

He puffed out a small laugh. "That's brilliant."

"There's frequently another way to do something," Arabella said. "I have an idea about how to approach Johnny. Would you like to hear it?"

Griff slid her coffee across the table and sat. "Tell me."

She explained as they washed the dishes. Just as they finished, the big, red Spitfire Farms flatbed backed up to the fence. Johnny hopped out of the cab and opened the gates. The truck rolled over the green lawn, stopping at the kitchen door.

Griff scooped Scheherazade off his foot and handed her to Arabella. "Looks like your scaffolding is here." He wiped his hands on a dishtowel and tossed that at her, too. "I can't have the guys seeing me do dishes. They won't respect me." He winked.

The towel hit him in the back of the head as he opened the door. He swiveled back to face Arabella, his arm cocked to throw the towel. She looked down at the dog in her arms and said, "I do not know why you like that horrible man."

Griff swiveled just a little bit further and tossed the towel on the counter. He went out the door and down the steps without a word.

Arabella looked from the towel to his retreating back, then down at Scheherazade. "He knew I was joking, right?"

Griff and three of his men, Hale, Johnny, and Art, unloaded a rolling scaffold. It had a waist-high safety bar around its platform. Griff briskly demonstrated how to lock and unlock the wheels, change the platform height, and maneuver the scaffolding through doorways. Several times as he talked, he reached toward Arabella, but always stopped short of actually touching her. Finally, he dismissed Hale and Art. "Johnny, if you'd shut the gate behind the truck and wait for me, I'd appreciate it. I'd like to talk to you."

Johnny's shoulders straightened. "Yes, sir." He nodded and moved backward, staring at Griff through rounded, gray eyes.

As the door closed behind the boy, Arabella murmured, "Oh dear. That frightened him." She looked at Griff. "Do you yell at him, too?"

Griff froze momentarily, then took a step back. Arabella had seen that look on his face enough times now to realize she'd shocked and maybe even hurt him.

She bit her lip and shrugged. "I'm sorry. I just—. He seems so nervous. I thought maybe you intimidate him, too."

Griff raised his left hand and motioned for her to stop. "I have never yelled at him." Without meeting her gaze, Griff crossed to the door and opened it. "I don't know why Johnny's afraid of me, but it's not for the same reason you are." He latched the door behind himself and took the steps in two bounds.

Arabella stared at the closed door. Griff still thought she was afraid of him? She distinctly remembered telling him she wasn't afraid of him the night she threw herself in his arms and kissed him. How had he missed that?

Chapter Fifteen

Twice inside of an hour, Griff had walked out of his own back door feeling like he'd been kicked in the gut. How would he ever get Arabella to trust him if he couldn't control his mouth and hands? He'd wanted to hug her when she came down from the scaffolding. He'd reached for her, but she'd tensed, flinching away. Then, her first thought when Johnny seemed nervous, was to automatically accuse him of yelling at the kid. And why wouldn't she think that? He'd spent the past ten months granting his temper free rein. This was nothing more than he deserved.

Griff glanced toward Johnny. The kid did look apprehensive. He stood with his shoulders hunched and his hands stuffed in the front pockets of his jeans.

Stopping a couple feet from the boy, Griff said, "Thanks for waiting. I need to ask you a favor."

Johnny gasped audibly. "Huh?" The kid pulled his hands out of his pockets. He blurted, "I thought you were going to fire me!" Then blushed horribly. "I'm sorry I keep screwing up," he mumbled, and jammed his hands back in his pockets.

Griff waved dismissively. "We all screw up. I know Hale was upset at you for not telling him you couldn't drive, but we've failed you." Griff put his hand on Johnny's shoulder. "And I think you've done pretty well considering how little teaching or supervision you've been given. Somebody tells you to do something, and you do your best to get it done. I know grown men who don't have half your guts and determination."

"I ... gee, thanks." Flustered, Johnny pulled his hands from his pockets again and motioned toward the barn. "You have all been awesome. You all talk to me like I'm somebody."

"You are somebody, Johnny. And right now, you're the only man on this ranch who can do a job I need doing."

Johnny stood up straighter when Griff called him a man. "Yes, sir, what do you need?"

Griff motioned toward the house. "Bella—oh, you're probably going to need to call her Miss Arabella—needs a helper. Have you noticed that she's a pretty girl?"

The boy blushed again and nodded.

"I've hired her to remodel my house. She's a skilled professional, good at her job, but a lot of tasks require two people."

"You want me to work in your house?" Johnny interjected. "Gosh, what if I break it?"

Griff laughed, mostly because of what Arabella had said, but he answered, "You're not going to break it. I explained to Bella that you'd need to be taught what to do, and she's willing to teach you."

"But why not just send her one of the others?" Johnny hunched his shoulders again. "They wouldn't need to be taught."

"Actually, that's exactly why I can't send one of the others," Griff answered. "Bella is the professional. She knows how things should be done, but the other men won't listen to her—mostly because she is a pretty girl—and they'll want to tell her how they think she should do her job."

"Oh, so you want me because I don't know anything?" The boy seemed to shrink even smaller.

Griff tightened his hand on Johnny's shoulder and held him in place. Finally, Johnny looked up.

When their gazes met, Griff said, "No, John, I want you because I know I can trust you to pay attention, learn, and to correctly do whatever job Bella gives you."

Johnny's silver eyes widened. He blinked and swallowed. "I will, boss. I won't disappoint you."

Griff said, "Come on, then, let's go in the house and tell her."

They walked back to the house. Griff knew that everything he'd said to Johnny was absolutely true. He also knew he wouldn't have thought to say it if Bella hadn't told him that Johnny's self-esteem would be better served if the boy knew he was valued and respected by another man.

"Think about it," she'd said. "His dad pays him no attention. He ran with the wrong group of boys and got into trouble looking for valida- tion. If you want to make a better man out of him, treat him like a bet- ter man."

ARABELLA watched as Griff talked to Johnny. As their conversation ended, she could tell from Johnny's posture that he'd accepted the job. Now they walked toward the house together. Griff glanced up and saw her standing at the window. His gaze slid past her. He turned to Johnny and said something that made the kid nod. They exchanged a high five, then Griff walked off toward the barn, and Johnny continued into the house.

It seemed to Arabella that she spent an inordinate amount of time watching Griff walk away when she still had things to say to him. She turned from the window as Johnny came through the door. She wasn't about to chase Griff down over a minor misunderstanding.

Four days later, she still hadn't talked to Griff. He never came any- where near the house during her working hours. After the paint in his study dried, he'd had Johnny and Art return the furniture to the room. The day after that, Art and the cowboy they called Red rehung the doors.

Art, Red, Johnny, and Arabella stripped the kitchen to the floors and walls. They'd also pulled the toilets, sinks, and counters from the downstairs and guest room bathrooms.

Johnny made an excellent assistant, but Arabella missed Griff. She'd texted, asking him to make a final decision on the additional furniture he'd requested for the study. Griff replied with a thumbs-up emoji. No choices and no further communication.

Johnny looked over her shoulder at her phone screen. "What's up with you and the boss, anyway?"

"I don't know what you mean." Arabella shoved her phone in her back pocket.

"Right," the kid answered. "Every morning you ask about Griff. Every evening Griff asks about you. Why don't you just talk to each other?"

Griff asked Johnny about her? She wanted details but decided against asking in light of Johnny's present complaint. "We seem to have a communication problem. Sometimes it's better if we don't talk."

Johnny stared at her like he wanted to say something. Then, he shook his head and turned back to masking off the stair rail. Arabella climbed onto the scaffold to swaddle the fieldstone fireplace in plastic wrap and protect it from overspray. She slipped the masking tape roll onto her wrist like a bracelet and looked at Johnny. "Go ahead, speak your mind."

"You'll just tell me it's none of my business and that I'm only a kid." Johnny kept his head down.

"I might tell you it's none of your business," Arabella faced him with her hands resting on the scaffold guard rail. "But I probably won't insult you by telling you you're just a kid while you're working for me and doing a man's job."

He looked up at her then. Arabella waited. Johnny stood and shoved his hands in his back pockets, standing just like Griff. "It's easy to see you don't like the boss. I don't understand. I mean, he's pretty cool. I'm a regular screw-up, and he keeps giving me chances."

"I don't dislike Griff," Arabella exclaimed. "Why would you think that? We started out with some misconceptions we're having trouble getting past, but that doesn't mean I dislike him."

"So why do you tense up and back away every time he comes near you?"

Arabella shook her head. "I don't."

"You do," Johnny said. He motioned with his right hand. "When the boss showed you how the scaffolding worked the other day, every time he reached toward you, you froze. I don't think he knows how to talk to anybody without holding their shoulder or slapping them on the back. He probably just wanted you closer to be sure you understood what he was showing you, but you kept moving away. And the more you backed away from him, the more tense he got. By the time he finished talking to you, he was pretty upset."

"I—." Arabella shook her head. "No. If I was tense, it's because Griff was making me nervous."

She knew exactly what Johnny was talking about. Griff did grow tenser and grimmer as he spoke, and it did make her more and more anxious, but he started it. Didn't he?

"I don't know who started it—" Johnny said as if reading her mind, "—but one of you has to make it stop."

"Griff and I have been fighting since I moved in next door. It's complicated."

"When my mom was alive, she'd just tell me to kiss and make up." Johnny bent down and grabbed a fresh roll of painter's tape.

Arabella huffed out a little laugh. "Yeah, well that didn't work out so swell for us, either."

Johnny's mouth fell open. He stared at her through wide silver eyes.

Arabella shrugged. "Go back to work. I'll think about what you said." A few minutes later, she added, "Oh, and Johnny? You are not a regular screw-up. I'm glad Griff picked you to be my assistant."

About ten minutes after that, Johnny asked, "Do you think I'm enough of 'not a screw-up' that the boss would let me keep working after my probation is up?"

"I can't answer that," Arabella said. "You'll have to ask Griff. But won't school start by then?" She climbed off of the scaffold and moved it to the other side of the fireplace.

Johnny shifted up a step to mask the next spindle. "I'm thinking about maybe not going back to school."

"Going to college isn't a requirement," Arabella said. "You can get plenty of good-paying jobs by going to trade school, but you will need your high school diploma. If nothing else, it tells your prospective employers that you can see something through to the end."

Another few minutes of silence passed. Johnny said softly, "I can't go back and live with my dad. You don't know what it's like. He's always drunk. There's never any food in the house. If he's home, he's screaming at me, or worse, crying or puking. I can't have any friends over." His voice choked to a stop. Johnny spun and snatched his white straw cowboy hat off the staircase behind him. Slapping it over his blond hair, he pulled the brim low to shade his face and swung his hand toward the front door. "I just need some air," he said. "I'll be back."

When the door closed behind him, Arabella pulled her cell phone out of her back pocket and texted Griff.

Arabella: We need to find time to talk.

Griff: Text me whatever you need.

Arabella: This isn't something we can do over text.

Griff: Sorry, that's all I've got time for.

Arabella stared at her phone, finally coming to realize Griff had no intention of seeing her. Obviously, their last miscommunication wasn't just a minor misunderstanding. Now Arabella regretted not following Griff to apologize. But what difference would it have made? They'd have come to this sooner or later anyway.

Arabella started to put her phone away. She really didn't need more rejection, but this wasn't about her. She sent one more text.

ARABELLA: Johnny wants to quit school.

Griff stared at his phone. He felt like a jerk. His mood over the last few days had his ranch hands acting surly, and they'd probably be just as happy if he left them to finish moving the irrigation pipes on their own.

He didn't have time to talk to Arabella because he didn't want to have time.

First, she'd texted him about the furniture for his study. He saw no point in picking anything out when he'd blown all of his plans over that stupid scaffold. She'd been so reasonable and sweet one minute, then terrified and calling him a horrible man the next. He'd no idea what had gone wrong. How was he supposed to combat that fear in her eyes? He loathed himself every time she looked at him.

Now it's, '*We have to talk*.' Well, she could talk to him via text and have done with it. Neither of them needed the pain they inflicted on each other when they were together.

He reread her text. "*Johnny wants to quit school*."

Fine. He could talk to Johnny about that. There was no reason to talk to Arabella. He turned his phone off and jammed it into this pocket.

ANOTHER three days passed. The contractors worked to install the new cupboards, backsplash, and countertops in the bathrooms and kitchen. Arabella and Johnny finally finished masking the wood and stonework. They were ready to start painting the downstairs, but first, they decided to take a break. Johnny went to the bunkhouse for lunch. Arabella returned to her own home and flipped through her mail while eating a sandwich.

Her cell phone lit up with a text.

Griff: Where are you?

She dropped her sandwich remains onto the paper towel she'd used as a plate and tossed everything into the trash. According to her con-tract, she had one hour for lunch every day. Not even half her allotted time had passed. He'd ignored her for a week. He could darn-well wait thirty more minutes for her answer. She grabbed a trowel and donned her garden gloves. She had plenty of time to weed a row or two in the garden before returning to work. Leaving her cell phone beside the kitchen sink, she headed outside.

Righteous indignation powered her steps. Arabella marched around the front of her garage. She skirted the blackberry bush, skidding to a halt mere feet from Muerte Manchado, who stood munching on the tender greens in her spinach patch. He lifted his massive head and eyed her.

Arabella didn't move or breathe. *Don't look him in the eye.* Hadn't she read that somewhere? Was she supposed to try and look big and threatening, or small and inconsequential?

The bull snorted and stepped toward her. *Oh crap. I am small and inconsequential.*

Her knees began to quake, but she held her ground. *Don't panic. Don't panic. Don't panic.*

Muerte Manchado stared at her for a few more moments, before lowering his massive head. He continued munching on the spinach greens, keeping one black, beady eye trained on Arabella. If he stayed on his current path, he'd chew his way right past her.

As if keeping an eye on the bull without looking at him wasn't enough to contend with, she heard another large animal approaching. The garage and towering blackberry bush blocked it from view. Was it yet another bull? Where was Griff? Did he know his bull was loose? And why hadn't she answered his text?

She didn't have to wonder how Muerte Manchado had gotten into her garden. A section of white fencing lay shattered on the ground, evidently no match for the weight of a hungry bull.

The slow thumping of hooves sounded from behind the blackberry bush, and the speckled nose of the Appaloosa came into view. The bull sidled around, swinging his backside away from the approaching horse and turning to face it. Now Arabella stood at his rear. She shifted her right foot backward. Muerte Manchado turned his head toward her and snorted.

"Don't move." The whispered command came from whoever rode the Appaloosa. Arabella didn't recognize the voice but obeyed it just the same.

The sotto-voce continued, apparently talking into a phone or walkie talkie. "Boss? I found him. He's in Miss Arabella's garden." Silence, and then, "No. She's here, too. Standing about 8 feet from him." Another wait. "Yes, she's on the ground."

Arabella listened as the cowboy talked, straining to hear Griff's answers. She never caught the sound of his voice.

The cowboy spoke again. "No, he won't go down fast enough. Besides, that would be darned expensive hamburger."

Hamburger? Had Griff just ordered his prize bull shot?

"He's pretty calm, Boss. Just come in slow. We'll herd him back through the fence and into the pasture."

A few moments later, Griff walked a broad-barreled chestnut roan up the driveway and into the garden, moving slowly but steadily until he stood between the bull and Arabella.

Another horse and rider followed Griff, stopping beside him. Muerte Manchado snorted and backed away, toward the break in the fence. "Crowd him slowly," Griff kept his voice low. "Don't spook him while Bella is still on the ground."

Both cowboys nudged their horses another step closer. Griff kicked his left boot out of its stirrup and leaned low, extending his arm toward Arabella. "Bella, honey, I need you to grab my arm. I'm going to pull you up behind me. Can you do that?"

She didn't have to. Muerte Manchado snorted and turned tail. Trotting back through the break in the fence and into the field beyond.

The two cowboys moved forward and blocked the gap with their horses.

Griff ordered, "Get this bull out to section seven. Find out who put him in this pasture. And get somebody down here to fix that fence asap." He swung from his horse and turned toward Arabella. Probably to yell at her for not answering his text. Like she hadn't already realized her mistake.

Arabella wanted to run toward him. She wanted to back away. Indecision and a full week of silence gripped her throat and locked her feet to the ground. Griff wore the red and blue plaid shirt that brightened his indigo eyes to tourmaline. Solid and safe, she needed to touch him and hated herself for the weakness. It would be stupid to trust him again. Why did she always yearn for what she couldn't have?

He strode toward her. She focused on the pearl snap below his Adam's apple and opened her mouth to tell him she was fine. "Gr-iff," his name emerged on a sob. She covered her face with her hands as he pulled her into his arms.

"I'm here, Bella. You're safe."

She shook her head. Her next sob took out her knees. Griff caught her, swinging her up into his arms. He carried her into her kitchen and lowered her feet to the floor. She clung to his neck, refusing to let go. Wrenching sobs shook her slender body.

GRIFF didn't remember ever being more frightened in his life than the terror that gripped him when Vince said Arabella was on the ground and at the mercy of Muerte. The bull wasn't particularly ferocious without a rider on his back, but he was a bull. Power and aggression were fundamental to his nature.

Now that she was safely in his arms, Griff had no wish to let go of Arabella, either. He carried her to the living room and settled them both into the recliner. He still wore his yard boots and had probably made a mess of the floor. At the moment, he didn't care. When she recovered, she could yell at him for her floor, the destruction of her garden, and whatever else she wanted. She was safe. Nothing else mattered.

It was a long while before her shuddering sobs slowed. First, they transitioned to tremors, then quivering sighs, and finally, she dropped into an exhausted slumber. The last time he'd held her like this, her tears had stemmed from humiliation and pride. She'd held herself stiffly and struggled for control. This time, she'd clung to him like he was the only anchor in her maelstrom. Griff eased the recliner back. His hat slid forward over his eyes. Grabbing the black Stetson, he flipped it toward the couch, not bothering to watch it land. Arabella stirred. He tightened his hold and soothed her with comforting whispers. Eventually, his breathing synchronized with hers and he slept, too.

Griff woke as Bella attempted to climb from his lap. He forestalled her only long enough to right the chair, then lifted her to her feet. She motioned toward the bathroom. "I have to ... go." She didn't look at him. He chose not to force it, afraid of what he might see in her eyes.

He removed his boots, fished his hat out from under the coffee table, and carried everything to the kitchen. After locating a broom and dustpan, he collected the bits of dirt and straw he'd strung through her house, relieved he hadn't tracked in something worse. Arabella entered the kitchen as he put fresh coffee on to brew.

She paused in the laundry room doorway. Griff glanced at her, then busied himself with not looking at her. She'd changed out of her paint clothes and into white shorts and a light blue t-shirt that complimented her ash-blond hair. Her braid hung free, her red-rimmed eyes glistened like emeralds, and she'd looked positively frightened—again. Or was it still? He expected her to order him out of her house. He took a deep breath and tensed his shoulders for the hit.

"Do you know—," her voice came softly from behind him, "—you are the closest I've ever come to having a real friend? I know I keep screwing things up, but please, talk to me."

His lungs froze. *Holy Hannah*, she was good with those sucker punches. He braced his hands on the counter and tried to exhale.

Her bare feet pitter-pattered across the floor. "Griff?"

He could not turn around and look at her, but he did manage to grate out, "I'm the one who screwed things up. I quit talking to you so I wouldn't hurt you anymore."

"Yeah, um, that didn't work." Her voice sounded teary again.

"Listen—." He finally managed to catch a decent draught of oxygen. "—every time we're in the same place, one or both of us ends up hurting."

"I'm sorry I hurt you. Until the other day, I didn't even consider that a possibility."

Bitterness seared his gut, spurring Griff to face her. He leaned against the counter and crossed his arms. "Why, because I'm such an ass?"

"Ugh!" She stomped over to him. "Yes! You are the most pigheaded, obstinate, obnoxious—-." She gave an inarticulate shriek. "What is your problem?"

A pulse beat in the side of his jaw. "Bella, you're terrified of me, if I so much as move my little finger, you'll teleport across this damn room."

"Seriously? Didn't we just spend the last three hours in the same chair?" She planted her hands on her hips. "Yes, you startle me sometimes. You are twice my size! I grew up in an all-girls school. I am not used to large men or shouting." She shouted.

He remained logical and calm. "You don't flinch when Tyner walks up to you. He's four inches taller and at least fifty pounds heavier than I am."

Arabella waved her hands in exasperation. "Ty's not you! He's soft-spoken. Mellow. He doesn't make fast moves and has never picked me up or yelled at me." She clasped her hands together, took a deep breath, and continued. "Look, I know I'm socially awkward. I don't always react the way a normal person would, but that doesn't mean I'm afraid of you."

Griff stepped forward and raised his hands toward her shoulders. She braced herself but didn't back away. He stopped short of touching her and sighed. "You just flinched. Why?"

"Anticipation of my feet coming up off the floor?" She shook her head. "I never know what you're going to do."

"And you don't trust me not to hurt you." He crossed his arms again.

She crossed her arms, as well. "I do trust you."

He snorted.

"Look, I don't have the words to explain something even I don't understand." Tears flooded her eyes. "See this?" She pointed at her face. "Until you came along, the last time I full-on cried in front of another person, I was ten years old."

"See, that right there—."

Arabella made a slicing motion with her hand to silence him and snapped, "I don't trust you at all, and I trust you completely. Dammit, having a friend scares me near to death, and it hurts!"

The hurt he understood thoroughly. He hurt. And he had to touch her. This time he used common sense and acted instead of reacting. Opening his arms slowly, he held out his hands. "Bella?"

She took a small step toward him. He stepped forward as well. Her hands came up, reaching for his waist. He slowly clasped her shoulders and drew her into his embrace.

His throat tightened. He closed his eyes. Arabella's willingness to try again both humbled and terrified him. She'd given him her trust, could he coax it into love, or would he let her down and destroy them both?

He held her lightly and spoke into her hair. "Listen, I'm a toucher. It's what I do. I don't think about it. It just happens." He gave her shoulders a brief squeeze. "I'll try to be mindful, but it'll be an adjustment—likely for both of us. I'll overlook it when you flinch if you can forgive me when I reach."

She nodded and whispered, "I'd like to try."

"Me, too."

"But ..." She tensed. "Could you ...." She tried to pull out of his embrace.

Griff tightened his hold. "What, Bella?" Then he realized what he'd done and released her.

She stayed here she was, with her forehead on his collarbone. Drawing in a shaky breath, she whispered, her voice more insubstantial with each word. "Could we promise to always talk to each other, even when we're upset?"

He remembered what Ty had said about people always pushing her away. When he'd chosen not to speak to her, he'd thought it would end the pain. Instead, he'd made it worse for both of them. He sighed. "Yes. I'm sorry I hurt you. No wonder you called me a horrible man."

Her hands tightened on his waist. "I was teasing when I said that. You know, because you'd thrown the towel at me. I didn't even really understand why you weren't speaking to me until Johnny told me off."

Startled, Griff gripped her shoulders and braced her away from him so he could see her face. "Johnny told you off?"

Her chin came up. "Don't be angry. He was polite about it, and I needed to hear it. I'm not used to people caring about me, so I've never wondered if they care how I feel about them."

Griff closed his eyes. His voice was thick when he answered, "You're important to me. I care what you think. Let's both keep that in mind from here on out."

Arabella nodded. "Okay." She dropped her gaze to his shirt front.

Griff sighed. *Lord, please help me not screw this up.* After dropping a light kiss on her forehead, he stepped away. "Hey, have you got any cookies to go with this coffee?"

Chapter Sixteen

Arabella carried plates and the strawberry cookie jar to the table. "Pecan-chocolate chip," she said, but didn't move to put the jar down.

Her first few years at Seaview Girl's School, she'd worked at making new friends. At the end of each school year those friends returned home, and Arabella stayed behind. Sometimes the girls never returned to the school. Those that did return had changed. They had new interests and experiences that Arabella couldn't relate to. She hadn't seen the latest movies, knew nothing of fashion beyond her school uniform, and was woefully ignorant about popular music or celebrity crushes.

Arabella studied Griff as he collected mugs and poured the coffee. She noted the size of his hands, his bulging biceps, the corded muscles in arms, and the width of his shoulders. She'd grown up in a female world. Even Wengert Stables and the university she'd attended in Seattle were Christian-based businesses with fraternization between the sexes governed by strict codes of conduct that she'd never even considered violating.

After college, she'd moved on with her professional life. She had colleagues, not friends, and preferred that her personal space stay personal. So why was she trying to forge a friendship with Griff, who'd already proven unreliable? Did she never learn?

Griff moved to the table, put two full, chunky red coffee cups down, and turned to Arabella. She stood motionless, staring at the tabletop. He raised his right hand to her chin and tilted her face toward his. "What's wrong?"

She shuddered. His baritone voice scraped the raw places inside of her, but she couldn't turn away without struggling. She remained motionless.

"Hmmm," Griff released her chin. He lifted the cookie jar from her arms and placed it on the table beside the coffee. Opening the top, he pulled out a cookie. "I think a little sugar and a little caffeine is in order." He held the cookie to her lips. "Take a bite."

She jerked away from the cookie and glared at Griff.

"Ah, there you are." Griff smiled. "Hello, Bella. You had me scared there for a minute. I thought I'd lost you." He took a bite out of the cookie and pulled out her chair. A tiny tourmaline light flickered in his indigo eyes and calmed her fears. What was it about this man that both unnerved and calmed her?

She settled into her chair and raised her coffee cup. "I'm sorry," she said. "I think it was just an aftershock."

"Shock," Griff agreed. "Drink your coffee and talk to me."

"Talk about ...?" Her gaze focused on Griff, and she sat up straighter. "How did your bull get into my garden?"

"Much better." Griff nodded as he settled into his own chair. "You look alert now. And, I'd say the bull got into your garden because your fence posts are rotten. I probably should have had Hale check that out when he repaired the fences in your dog run, and somebody had better be taking care of that right now. As to Muerte, he got close enough to your fence to knock it over, I don't know. For as long as I can remember, that strip of land between our outbuildings and your place has been a buffer zone. We usually plant it with feed. I didn't order anybody to put the bull there, and I'm sure Tank didn't, either. No one else has the authority." He reached into his pocket for his phone. It wasn't there. He bolted out of his chair. "My horse!" Griff went out the door in his stocking feet.

Arabella followed him to the threshold. His horse wasn't where he'd left it. A leather satchel sat on the deck. Griff fished his phone from inside. He activated the screen and flipped through his messages. "Vince took took my horse back to the corral."

Tension returned to her stomach as she watched him scroll through his phone. He'd stopped work because of her. Again. She spent a lot of time interfering in this man's life. It's no wonder he got irritated with her. In fact, shouldn't she be working right now? And where was Johnny? Was he off the clock because of her as well?

She moved to the kitchen counter and palmed her own phone, finding a series of texts, all from Griff.

Griff: Where are you?

Griff: Pick up your phone.

Griff: The bull is missing.

Griff: Are you safe?

Griff: Bella, please answer me!

She had indulged in a temper tantrum and put everyone in danger.

"You're white as a sheet." Griff stepped behind her and tilted the screen of her phone so he could read the messages.

"I'm sorry." She back against him. "I received your first text, but I was angry and figured you could wait until I was ready to answer you. I never saw the others."

Griff slipped his arm around her waist. "I suppose I deserved that. I promise, Bella, if I ever go silent again, it isn't because I'm deliberately ignoring you."

She shook her head. "If I hadn't been pouting, you and your men wouldn't have been in danger."

"My men and I knew what we were doing. We were safe. You were the one in danger. I'm going to kill whoever put the bull in that field." He motioned toward the table and tried to guide her toward it with his hand on her back.

She didn't move. "I should get back to work."

"No, you shouldn't," Griff said. "Neither one of us is going back to work. We've both shot enough adrenalin through our systems for one day. Besides, it's almost five o'clock. I just texted Johnny to come and get us. You and I are going up to my house, I'm grilling some steaks, and we're going to sit on the porch and relax. Nice and quiet and peaceful."

She turned to face him. "Was that an order from my boss, or a request from my friend?"

"Yes." Griff put his hands on his hips. "A little of both. Your boss says you're off the clock today. Your friend says he's still really freaked about seeing you facing down a two-ton bull and isn't quite ready to let you out of his sight."

Her eyes rounded. "Two tons?"

Griff shrugged. "About one-point-seven-thousand, but close enough."

Arabella let Griff lead her back to her chair. She sat down and then stood right back up. "Where's Scheherazade?"

Griff caught her shoulders and pressed her into her seat. "Safe and sound in my yard where you left her. You'll see her in just a little bit." He grabbed another cookie.

"You're going to spoil your dinner."

He shook his head. "We still have to bake the potatoes. Dinner is going to be a while yet."

She took a cookie, too.

GRIFF discarded the seven of hearts. Arabella picked it up and slotted it into her rummy hand. She studied her cards for a moment, spread them out on the table, then discarded the two of spades. "Gin." She grinned.

Griff's dimple flashed. "That's three in a row. I vote we put the cards away and eat while I still have some pride left."

"Beginner's luck," Arabella shuffled the deck and set it aside. "That's what you get for teaching me to play. How can I help with dinner?"

Griff had a kitchen of sorts set up on his veranda, comprised of the barbecue grill, refrigerator, kitchen table, and four ladder back chairs. He tested the foil-wrapped potatoes. "These are ready. You want to bring me the steak and corn?" He spread the glowing red charcoal briquets evenly across the bottom of the grill. "How do you want your steak cooked?"

"On the rare side of medium," Arabella said.

"Good choice. If you'd have said, 'well done,' I'd have just tossed my boot on your plate."

Arabella laughed. "I was in college before I ever had a grilled steak. Somebody in the dorm had a barbecue birthday party and my roommate talked me into going with her. The food was fabulous, but I wasn't as fond of the rap music and beer pong. I left when people started getting drunk." She shrugged. "I never seem to fit in."

"I rarely drink alcohol at home." He pointed at the two glasses of ice water she'd just set out on the table. "You fit in just fine here, Bella."

As she collected plates and cutlery from the utility room, she wondered how long she'd fit in. Probably only until Griff found a wife, then she'd definitely be in the way.

They cleaned up after dinner, carrying the dishes to the utility room to wash them. Afterward, they brewed coffee and settled on the porch swing. Arabella sat with her legs crossed and her feet tucked under. Griff sat sideways, facing her with his right foot on his left knee. His left foot propelled the swing. When his phone rang, he fished it out of his pocket and glanced at it. "It's Tank. My foreman." He swiped to take the call and hit the speaker out of habit. "Yeah, Tank? What's up?"

"Tonight, at the dinner table, Mason started bragging about setting the bull loose in the buffer field. He said that after the fright Miss Arabella had today, you'd probably have your five acres back in no time."

Arabella dropped her coffee cup. It shattered on the white veranda floor.

Griff snarled, "Fire him!" He leaned forward, grabbing Arabella's hand as she struggled off of the moving swing.

"Hale already did," Tank answered.

Griff dropped his phone and stood, stocking footed, in the warm coffee. "I did not authorize that!"

Arabella jerked her gaze to him in surprise. She lifted her free hand to his chest. "I didn't think you had."

He captured the hand on his chest as well, and said, "Then where were you going?"

Nodding toward the floor, she answered, "To get something to clean up the mess, but you seem to have taken care of that."

He glanced down at the coffee soaking into his wool socks, and then back up at Arabella. "I know you're upset. You dropped your cup."

"I was startled that anyone would do something like that on purpose, but I didn't for one second think it was your idea." She stiffened as Griff jerked her into his arms and hugged her. After a moment, she relaxed and slipped her arms around his waist.

"He must have remembered the things I said when you first came here, but even then—."

She patted his back. "It's okay. I know."

Griff's hold tightened. "Given the things I've said to you, I don't see how you could possibly believe me."

Pushing against his hard abs, she forced him to give her enough room to look up at his face. "Griff, you ordered that cowboy to shoot your bull."

"In a heartbeat, sweetheart."

The murmur of voices reached them from the barnyard. Turning toward the sound, they spotted three cowboys approaching a beat-up red pickup parked near the main barn. Griff named them. "Tank, Hale, and ... Mason." He growled the final name, setting Arabella away from him and turning toward the steps.

"No!" She pushed in front of him. "You're too angry to go out there."

"He could have gotten you killed." Griff gripped her shoulders. Arabella braced herself, fully expecting to be picked up and set aside, but Griff's hands gentled. Over her head, he watched the three cowboys at the pickup.

Arabella pressed her hands to Griff's chest and whispered fiercely, "He's lost his job. That's enough."

"It's not nearly enough." Griff captured her wrists.

Maybe he wouldn't pick her up, but he was still planning to go after Mason. She needed his attention. "Really? Because I think we should thank him."

"Thank him?" Griff focused on her. "Are you nuts?"

"Probably. After all, we were both much happier not speaking to each other. Mason ruined all our lovely angst, and now here we are, reduced to having dinner together."

Griff blinked at her. A shiver coursed through his body. He let go of her wrists and skimmed his hands up her arms, drawing her into a hug. "Yeah, and I'm really enjoying my socks soaked in coffee."

Chapter Seventeen

Griff and Hale had gone to the cattle auction in Bozeman. They'd been gone for three days and were due home that afternoon. While they were gone, Arabella and Johnny focused on completing the kitchen. Arabella planned to surprise Griff by having dinner waiting when he arrived.

She couldn't decide what to cook. For almost a month, they'd eaten together two or three times a week. Griff had cooked most of those meals on his barbecue grill. They'd play cards, eat, then wash dishes together, finally ending their evening side-by-side sipping coffee on the porch swing.

Tonight, she wanted to do something for him. She decided to prepare a meal he wouldn't likely prepare for himself. Usually, lasagna was her go-to special occasion dish, but she doubted she'd ever be able to make that for him again without reliving the humiliation of his gentle rejection. Even though he wasn't interested in her in a romantic way, he made an excellent friend, and every day his friendship grew even more precious.

Around noon Griff called. Arabella answered, "Hey, how'd it go?"

"Still going," Griff said. "We got a good price on our beef, but the paperwork is taking longer than expected. I know I told you I'd be home around four, but it's looking like it's going to be closer to six. You'll have packed up and gone by then. I was really looking forward to seeing you."

"And you have no idea where I live?"

Griff laughed. "I was hoping to talk you into letting me take you out to dinner."

"I don't think so," Arabella answered. "You've been feeding me barbecue here for over three weeks. Why don't you let me cook dinner for you?"

"But ... I like doing stuff for you."

"Okay, you want to do something for me? Come home and eat the food I cook."

His voice lowered, resonating through the phone. "I can do that."

"See you tonight."

IT was almost six-thirty by the time Griff turned onto the ranch access road. He was anxious to see Arabella but wanted to shower and change first. Did he have time? As he rolled past her cottage, he was surprised to see the windows dark. His gut tightened and didn't relax until he pulled into the barnyard and spotted her truck parked near the garage.

"Looks like Arabella's still working," Hale said.

"Yeah, it does." Griff didn't know whether to be happy or disappointed. He wanted time to shower and shave, but he was hungry, and with Bella still painting, it would probably be a while before dinner.

Scheherazade greeted him at the back gate. He scooped the little dog into his arms and looked toward the veranda. No cooking happening there. Oh well, seeing Arabella was more important than food. He climbed the back steps, opened the kitchen door, and stopped in his tracks.

"Surprise!" Arabella stood in front of him. She wore a pretty, blue-checked sundress, and her hair flowed free.

Griff pushed the door closed and lowered Scheherazade to the floor. "Beautiful," he said. He held his hands out and beckoned her closer with his fingers. "Come here. I get a hug before I take my boots off." Arabella stepped into his arms and tucked her head under his chin. As his arms closed around her, he said, "You've been busy."

"Johnny and I," she agreed. "We wanted to surprise you."

"You've succeeded. The kitchen looks fabulous. The aroma is fabulous, too." He took a deep breath. "Red sauce, garlic, and fresh bread fabulous."

"Chicken cacciatore," she said, easing out of his arms.

Griff let her go reluctantly. He wanted a kiss but was afraid to chance it, especially since she wouldn't meet his gaze. "Do I have time to shower?"

She nodded. "Yes. All I have to cook is the pasta. How long do you need?"

"Fifteen minutes?"

She nodded.

Griff returned to the kitchen in twelve and a half minutes. Arabella stirred angel hair pasta into a vat of boiling water.

She glanced toward him and smiled, focusing on the little piece of toilet paper stuck to his chin. "You shaved?"

"It seemed appropriate. You've gone to a lot of trouble here." He'd also put on a dressy pair of jeans and a tailored western shirt in a summery blue, almost the color of her dress.

She smiled. "You look nice. Thank you."

Again, he felt the urge to kiss her, and it must have shown on his face because her eyes went big and she tensed. Griff swallowed his disappointment and turned his attention to the room. "You were right, the chestnut-colored quartz countertops are perfect with the ponderosa pine cupboards."

Arabella indicated the matching kitchen table and chairs in the breakfast alcove. "That really surprised me. I didn't know you'd ordered it." She poured the pasta into a strainer.

"I asked the cabinet guy if he could make a table and chairs that matched the cupboards and countertops. He said he could so ... "Griff shrugged, his voice trailing off. Where had their normal easy companionship gone?

She transferred the pasta to a serving bowl. "If you want to sit, I'll bring the food to the table."

"No." He wasn't sitting down without her. "I want to help."

"Oh. Okay." She studied him for a moment and then pointed at the fridge. "Caesar salad, ice water, serving tongs."

They put dinner on the table together, and Griff said grace. "Lord, thank you for this food and the hands that prepared it. Thank you for this home and our fellowship in it. Thank you for your blessings upon us, help us always share them with each other and whoever you send to us in need. Amen."

Arabella finally raised her head and looked right at him. There was a shadow of fear in her eyes. What had he said or done to put it there? Would they ever get to a place where he didn't have to second guess his every word?

As he spooned green beans onto his plate, Arabella said, "They're the first beans from your garden. Leira and I picked them this morning."

Griff stabbed one with his fork and tasted it. "These are good. How did you cook them?"

While Arabella explained how to make green beans Amandine, Griff smeared garlic butter on two dinner rolls. He put one on his own plate, and one on Arabella's. He also filled her salad bowl. That's when he noticed her stillness.

She sat watching him. He studied the table and found nothing amiss. "What?"

There was almost a smile on her lips, but a shadow still lurked in her green eyes. She said, "You are a caretaker. It's so much a part of you, you don't even think about it, you just _do_."

"You didn't want the salad?"

She reached out and touched his hand. "I'm not complaining. I'm making an observation. You wouldn't sit down and be served. You had to help."

Griff wasn't quite sure where she was going with this. "What's your point?"

"I'm not trying to make a point. It's just—." She waved at the table. "You always, automatically serve me."

That did not clarify her meaning at all. "Is that bad?"

"No," Arabella said forcefully. "I don't think anyone has ever ... I ... you ..." she shook her head. "Never mind."

"I don't think I want to never mind," Griff said. "I've upset you."

"No," she repeated, but her eyes shimmered. She was definitely upset.

ARABELLA looked at Griff through a haze of tears. She knew she was making too big a deal out of what was for Griff probably nothing more than common courtesy. Still, it wasn't common for such courtesies to be extended to her. He didn't treat her like a place holder in his life. Someone here for a job and of no other importance. He saw her as a person, and his actions made it clear that he valued her. "I'm not upset." A tear rolled down her cheek.

Griff edged away from the table. "You're crying."

She blotted her eyes on her napkin. "Not all tears are bad."

"Your tears hurt here." He tapped himself on the chest.

That brought a fresh spate. "I'm sorry." Arabella reached for his hand.

Griff stood and pulled her into his embrace. He whispered into her hair, "Tell me what I did wrong."

She shook her head and tightened her arms around his waist. "Nothing. That's just it."

"I see," Griff buried his hand in her curls and tugged. He tried to get her to look at him, but she resisted and kept her forehead pressed to his sternum. "I'm supposed to believe you're crying because I didn't hurt you?" His baritone voice rumbled through her.

Arabella gave a little watery laugh. "Pretty much."

"You realize that doesn't make any sense?"

She nodded and relaxed, enjoying the press of his hand against her head and his heartbeat beneath her ear. His gentleness and kindness healed wounds she hadn't known existed. Finally, she said, "You're very different from the man I first met."

"Thank God," Griff answered. "You taught me a couple of pretty powerful lessons about snap judgments and regret."

"And in exchange, you've taught me how it feels to have a friend and be cared for. I'm used to fending for myself or looking after others, and when you just automatically do things for me, it heals. It's a good kind of ache, and it comes with tears."

Griff's hands moved to her shoulders, and this time she allowed the space. She looked up at him. He said, "Okay, that explains the tears. Tell me why I still see fear in your eyes."

She drew a shaky breath. "I already told you. I'm not used to people caring about me." She looked down at his shirt buttons. "What happens when it ends?" Her voice got smaller. "How am I going to feel then?"

"What makes you think our relationship will end?"

She tried to lean back into him, but he wouldn't let her, so she whispered toward their feet, "Because nothing lasts forever."

Griff stepped out of her arms and grabbed her by the hand. "Come with me!" She didn't have much choice. He towed her into the dining room and stopped at the window. "Look," he said, maneuvering her in front of him and pointing over her shoulder toward her cottage. "You live in the middle of a ranch that has been in my family for over one hundred thirty years. I have no intention of leaving here, ever, so any ending this side of death is completely under your control."

Arabella used her free hand to brush at the tears on her cheeks. Griff proffered his handkerchief. She unfolded the snowy white piece of cotton and remembered. "The last time you handed me your handkerchief, you said that when a woman cries, everything a man says only makes it worse."

"I remember."

She looked into Griff's serious indigo blue eyes and said, "It isn't true. Some things do make it better."

He cupped her cheek in his hand and leaned in. Flustered, she lowered her chin.

He kissed her on the forehead. "Come on," he said. "Let's go eat dinner."

Arabella followed him back to the dining room, berating herself for flinching. It almost seemed like Griff wanted to kiss her. She vowed not to shy away if it happened again.

Chapter Eighteen

Arabella knew that Griff was wrong. At some point, their relationship would end, or at the very least change drastically. There was no way he'd find a wife who was comfortable with him eating at least one meal a day with Arabella. He often held her hand or slipped his arm around her. Many evenings Griff walked her home. Sometimes they'd pause to look up at the night stars. And Griff would stand behind her with his arms around her waist. She'd lean back against him as he told her some story about his childhood and life on the ranch.

Having no history of her own, she loved those stories. What she loved even more was when Griff shared excerpts from the ranch journals.

One particular evening after they settled in the porch swing, he pulled out a journal and said, "This is the one I've been searching for. Come and see."

Arabella curled up on the swing and snuggled against Griff's shoulder as he read the journal entry detailing the gifting of her cottage and acreage to Elias Harper in partial payment for a herd of cattle, including one Brahma bull.

> *"Elias Harper rode in today with my new herd. After three months on the trail, they were sure a sight to see. More dust then men. That new bull is a beauty. He's going to help secure the future of Spitfire ranch. Although for a bit it looked like I wouldn't get him. I was a little short of money, but Harper took what cash I could spare and I deeded him five acres of land as an IOU."*

"IOU?" Arabella interrupted.

"Yeah." Griff pointed at the journals. "We'll likely come across that story a little further along in this journal, but I already know it. My great-great-grandfather, the first Griffin Blake—I'm number four, by the way—didn't have enough ready cash to settle his bill when Elias Harper arrived with the cattle. They haggled and came to the land grant compromise with the understanding that Griffin Sr. would buy the land back as soon as he could. In the meantime, Elias hired on as ranch foreman and married—" Griff stumbled to a stop.

"What?" Arabella shifted to face him.

"Nothing." Griff grinned. "Well, something, but it's a surprise."

"Surprise?" Arabella's eyes widened and her hands tightened around his arm. She was not used to surprises being good things. "What kind of surprise? Will I like it?"

Laughing, Griff lifted the journal and wiggled it. "I'm trying to tell you. It's a little bit more of your family history and yes, I think you're going to like it."

"Oh!" She nodded at the book. "My surprise is in there?"

"Yes. And after I read it, I'll explain what happened with the IOU." He flipped the journal open to a faded ribbon bookmark. "Are you ready?"

"Yes. Read! I always hoped—." She shook her head. "I grew up without any sense of family history. My great uncle was basically a checkbook that paid my school tuition, and my mother was a painting in the library. I've never met anybody with less family history than I have."

"Then I think you'll find this even more interesting. It's dated about a month after Elias moved into the cottage." Griff waited to make certain she was listening and continued,

"*Elias came home with a wife today. A pretty, little blonde named Arabella.*"

Arabella jerked to attention, jolting the porch swing. "That's where my name came from? I've always wondered." She motioned toward the journal. "May I see?"

Griff handed her the leather-bound journal and watched as she ran her fingertips over the words. "You do have a history," he said. "And it's right here."

He picked up a second journal and opened it to a place he'd book-marked with a scrap of paper.

> *"Elias Harper passed today. Went home to join his beloved Arabella. Jonas Harper, Elias's second son, inherited the Harper land."*

Griff added in his own words, "Jonas was grandfather to your great Uncle Tom."

Arabella counted the generations on her fingers. "So, he would have been my great-great-great grandfather, right? And what happened to his first-born son?"

"I don't remember. And I don't know which journal it's in. This says that Jonas was 47 when Elias died. Each journal covers a three- to five-year time-span. You'd probably have to search backward through seven or eight journals to find the relevant entry."

"Can I?" Arabella hugged the journal to her chest. "Will you let me?"

Griff blinked. "You're really interested in Spitfire Ranch history? I mean, sure there are births and deaths and marriages and feuds, but most of it, especially in the early journals, is about ranch maintenance and livestock purchases."

She bounced in her seat and set the swing wiggling. "Recorded by the people living it! Do you know how incredible that is? You have 125 years of history at your fingertips. I know it's mostly about your family, but there are bits and pieces of my family origins in them as well. Will you let me read them?"

As he studied her face, his lips slowly curved into a smile. "Yeah, Bella, you can read them. In fact, we should read them together. And while we're at it, why don't we index them as part of our contribution to continuing generations?"

"Yes!" If she helped with the project, then she would have a real place in the ranch's history, too. Just like her ancestors. Speaking of which ... "When can we start?"

"Not tonight." Griff laughed. He picked up a third journal and showed the cover to Arabella. "I made this entry just a few months after my parents died." He recited the date and then read:

> "*Tom Harper came to the house this morning and told me his grandfather, Jonas Harper, died during the early hours of the morning. Tom has already been living here with Jonas for the past several months. He's a good, quiet neighbor.*"

"What did you write when my uncle died?" Arabella swiveled to fsce him on the porch swing and tucked her bare toes under Griff's thigh for warmth.

He flipped several journal pages, then glanced up at her. "You want me to read it?"

She hugged her knees. "I don't know. Do I?"

"I knew I was recording history. It's just a report." He flipped to the right page, read the date, and continued.

> "*I found a message from the hospital on my cell phone informing me that Tom Harper passed away this afternoon. When I went in to see what arrangements needed to be made, they told me his next-of-kin had been in to take care of it. On the way home, I spotted an unknown car in Tom's driveway, so I stopped in. Tom has left the five-acre Harper parcel to his great-niece, Arabella Harper. I don't know that country life is going to agree with her.*"

Arabella snorted. "That last was quite an understatement, given your opinion of me at the time."

"I left that out on purpose—which is just as well since it turned out to be wrong," Griff lifted the journal. "There are three more entries about you, I think you'll appreciate them more."

"The day the bull got into my garden?"

"Yes, plus two earlier entries."

Arabella frowned. "Earlier?"

"Hmmm." Griff recited the date and looked at Arabella like he was asking her to remember. She shook her head, so he read:

> "I stopped at the Harper cottage today in connection with a stray dog I found on the highway. The inside of the cottage has been completely renovated. Arabella Harper is committed to staying. Aside from a couple minor incidents over fencing and her dog, she has been a good neighbor."

"Minor incidents?" Arabella tapped herself on the chest. "I remember some trauma."

He reached out and placed his hand over hers. "I would change that if I could."

"I know, and I really don't expect you to keep apologizing. We've come a long way since then."

"We have," he agreed. "The next entry is short."

> "It's time to find a wife. To that end, I've hired Bella Harper to update the main house."

Arabella nodded her head and sat up straighter. "I've been thinking about that—you're spending all this money. What happens if your future wife doesn't like what we've done and wants to change it?"

"I'm not too worried." He flashed his dimple. "I'll just take your advice and keep her in the master bathroom."

Arabella laughed. "You'd be better off finding someone who loves you more than they love your house."

Griff grinned. "I don't know. That might be a tall order."

"As far as I can tell, you haven't even tried. You spend all of your free time with me."

"What do you think I should be doing instead?"

"How should I know where to look for dates?" Arabella raised her hands and shrugged. "You could try a couple of online sites."

Griff crossed his arms. "I much prefer meeting someone the old-fashioned way and dating in person."

"How do you plan to do that when you never leave the ranch?" Arabella leaned forward. "At the bar, there was a woman you danced with. The tall brunette. You two looked pretty good together."

"I danced with you ...." Griff tipped his head and exclaimed, "Pamela? I've known her since kindergarten. We look good together because we've taken some of the same line dance classes, but since her husband is the instructor, I think I'll have to pass on dating her. And I'm pretty sure marrying her is even less likely."

"Well, there are plenty of nice, single women in church. Why don't you start there?"

"I'll keep that in mind," he said, sounding annoyed.

Arabella decided to change the subject. She pointed at the journal. "There should be one more entry. What did you write when the bull trashed my garden?"

Griff complied. He seemed eager to change the subject.

"Muerte Manchado got into Bella's garden today while she was working there. Mason Fremont bragged about deliberately moving MM into the buffer field in order to frighten her. Hale fired Fremont. I wanted to beat the man to a pulp, but Bella wouldn't let me."

"Wait!" Arabella held up her hand. "Why did you put that last part in there?"

"Why not? It's the truth."

"But it was over." She shook her head.

He set the journal aside and grabbed her hands. "Bella, if you had been harmed in any way, I would probably be in prison right now for murder."

Surprise jolted through Arabella. Not at Griff's words, but at the warmth that filled her chest. "Sometimes you can be a very scary man."

"Not with you, sweetheart. With you, I'm a marshmallow."

The look in his eyes gave flight to a million butterflies in her stomach. She fought the urge to crawl across the seat and into his arms. Sometimes she got the impression he wanted more from their relationship than handholding and hugs. On a number of occasions, she even thought he wanted to kiss her, but his lips always brushed her forehead, never her mouth. It wasn't like Griff was shy. She knew that if he wanted more than friendship, he'd say so.

ALMOST a week passed before Arabella remembered that Griff never had explained what happened to the Harper property IOU. They'd already decided how to organize the index for the journals. Arabella compiled the subject data on her laptop while Griff read. He opened the first journal and began:

> *"This is it. Idaho Territory. The 160 acres I claimed under The Desert Land Act is mine. My cattle will arrive in just over three months. I'd better get busy."*

"Wait." Arabella stopped typing. "Is that the same cattle that Elias Harper delivered?"

"Probably. I mean, it's the same journal." Griff flipped to the page he'd left marked with a small scrap of paper. "Yeah, I'd say it's the same cattle. There are only a dozen or so pages between the two entries."

"It is so cool that you have this history. I wish I knew what Elias was thinking. Wasn't this area still unsettled and pretty wild?"

"Probably not as wild as you might think. There were already missionaries here. At least one had brought his wife along." Griff shrugged. "The first peoples were friendly."

"Yeah, but Elias didn't come here planning to stay. He didn't know he'd get paid in land."

"That's true. Initially, he only accepted the land as collateral for the wages he didn't get paid."

Arabella nodded. "You said that before, but you never explained why the land is still in my family. What kept the first Griffin Blake from redeeming it?"

Griff grinned. "The woman you're named after. She was the daughter of one of the missionaries. Elias fell in love. His Arabella didn't want to move to Texas and leave her family, but her father wouldn't let her marry a hired-hand with no property."

"Oh. I see." Arabella sighed. "That's kind of a sweet story."

NEAR THE END OF JUNE, Griff went with Hale and Johnny to their monthly meeting with Johnny's parole officer and the social worker assigned to Johnny's case. Griff wanted to talk about Johnny's return to school in September, and to ask if Johnny could stay on the ranch.

Arabella tried to paint the family room baseboards while she waited for word, but she kept stopping to look out the window. Finally, the ranch pickup pulled into the yard. She ran to the dining room window in time to see Hale and Johnny heading toward the bunkhouse and Griff coming through the back gate. She met him at the kitchen door.

He barely had one foot in the house before she demanded, "What happened?"

Griff took off his hat and ran his fingers through his hair. "School starts the beginning of September. Johnny won't be sixteen until the middle of November. Since he has a job and a place to live, he can petition the court for emancipation after his birthday."

Arabella put her hands on her hips. "After his birthday? What's he supposed to do between now and then?"

"He's ours until August 31st no matter what, and I've got a hearing for family court a week before that. However, the social worker thinks our best bet is for Johnny to get permission from Roger to stay on the ranch even after school starts."

"Do you think Roger will agree?"

Griff shrugged. "Johnny doesn't, and he says we can't make him go back to his father. If we do, he'll just quit school and runaway."

"That would be pretty foolish. He wouldn't have a job then, and they'd never grant him emancipation without one."

"That's what I told him," Griff answered. He stood there, holding his hat at his side and looking at her. "I'm afraid I'm not going to be able to pull this one off."

She crossed the kitchen floor and put her hand on his arm. "Don't give up yet. We'll figure something out."

Griff pulled her in for a hug and sighed.

After Griff went back to work, Arabella cleaned up her paint supplies. She usually quit early on Wednesdays to go riding at Ty's, but about a half an hour before her usual arrival time, Ty sent a text saying he had a big buyer in. He asked that she hold off riding for a day, so Arabella decided to use the unexpected free time to get her weekly grocery shopping done.

On her way home, she passed Griff headed for town. They exchanged waves.

Two hours later, Griff's truck rolled past her kitchen window. Arabella grinned and pulled her hands from the dishwater, drying them on a towel as she walked toward the back door. Her smile died. Griff strode angrily toward her across the back deck. She squared her shoulders, raised her chin, and settled her fists on her hips. She voice was steady despite the sick feeling in the pit of her stomach. "Good-evening, Mr. Blake. What can I do for you?"

Griff stopped in his tracks. "Don't pull that ice princess crap on me. What in the world did you think you were doing?"

"I'd thank you not to yell at me." Her chin jutted higher. "And I'm afraid you're going to have to be more specific. I don't know what you're talking about."

He jerked his hat off and pointed it at her. "I'm talking about Roger Kilpatrick, dammit. Johnny's father. Why in tarnation did you go looking for him?"

Her chin thrust out. "First off, don't cuss at me. And secondly, I didn't go looking for him. I went into the grocery store. He just happened to be there."

"You confronted him!" Griff yelled.

Arabella crossed her arms and looked past him toward the side of her garage. "Actually, I had a rather civil conversation with him," she kept her voice smooth and low. Her gaze cut back to him. "Maybe you should try it sometime." She turned her back and went into the house, closing the door behind her. She crossed to the sink, reached into the dishwater and scrubbed her dinner plate.

She hadn't bothered to lock the door and wasn't surprised when it opened behind her. She heard Griff shucking out of his boots but didn't turn around. "Don't take those off if you plan on cussing at me. There's a reason you weren't allowed in my house the first ten months I knew you."

"I'm not going to cuss at you." His tone was measured. He crossed the floor and clasped her arms lightly just below her shoulders. "Roger is an unstable drunk," he bit off each word, his baritone voice low and vibrating.

"He was stone-cold sober in the *public* grocery store. It's not like we were alone." Arabella put the plate in the dish rack and attacked the silverware. "I take it you went to see him? What happened that made you come flying back here so hot under the collar?" She drained the sink, rinsed it, and dried her hands.

"He was drunk as a skunk and accused us of alienating his kid."

Griff tried to turn her to face him. Arabella resisted for a moment, then turned. She lifted her hand, put two fingers in the middle of his chest, and pushed. When Griff stepped backward, she shrugged out of his hold and went to the coffee pot. Opening the cupboard, she grabbed one mug.

"That's it?" She contemplated the cup in her hand and considered not offering him coffee. "You're far too angry for that to be all he said."

She heard Griff sigh. "Arabella, I'm sorry I yelled at you. Are you ever going to look at me again?"

Her mouth turned down. "Probably, but not for a while." Reaching up, she took down a second coffee mug. After filling them both, she turned toward him, her gaze landing on his clenched fists. "I'm not giving you this coffee cup if you're still angry."

His teeth clicked together. Griff unclenched his fists and ground out, "Just tell me why you confronted Roger."

"I told you." She stared at the coffee cups in her hands. "Roger was in the grocery store—sober, although there was a case of beer in his cart. *He* approached *me* and asked if I lived on Spitfire Ranch. I told him I lived near Spitfire Ranch. He asked if I knew Johnny, and was he okay." Arabella crossed to the table and put their coffee mugs down at their usual spots.

She glanced toward Griff. His fists were no longer clenched, but he kept working his hands open and closed. That caught her attention. She considered his stance. Before they'd become friends, whenever they'd argued, he'd always stayed loose. Fluid. What made this disagreement different from those other times?

Her refusal to look him in the face stemmed from her fear of seeing the old Griff, eyes blazing with contempt. What if he felt the same fear? He'd called her *'ice princess'* and *'Arabella.'* Did he feel the same way she did? Was he afraid their friendship was crumbling? She decided to find out.

Turning, she met his gaze. His eyes didn't hold contempt. He looked wary and maybe even sad. She held out her hand. "Please come and sit down."

Griff made a strangled noise and crossed the space between them in two steps. He pulled Arabella into his arms. "Bella. Why did you go all ice princess on me?"

She leaned back far enough to see his face. "Are you kidding? When you came across my deck, you were so angry sparks were shooting off you!"

"I wasn't angry at you!"

"How was I supposed to know that?"

Griff tightened his arms around her. "Kilpatrick said I'd better keep you away from him, or we'd both regret it."

She rested her forehead on his collarbone and pressed her right hand over his heart. "I guess something I said must have gotten to him."

Griff's hands moved to her waist. "What did you say?"

Arabella shrugged. "I was angry. I said quite a bit."

"Hmmm, did you go all ice princess on him?"

"Maybe." She shrugged again. "I told him Johnny was an excellent employee. I said that he loved his job and was hoping to keep working even after school started. Roger answered that his kid belonged at home with him. Then I said I had given Johnny his first driving lesson, and that you'd gotten him into a driver's ed class." Her indignation rose. "I also told him that you and Hale invested more time in Johnny in the last month than he'd bothered to spend with his son in the last year. I said I thought he should think about what kind of home he was offering Johnny. Then I told him he was a lousy role model, and I asked if he was raising Johnny the way his wife would have wanted him to."

Griff sucked air through his teeth. "You certainly didn't pull your punches."

Arabella shook her head. "Why should I have? It's the truth. I also reminded him that Johnny is almost sixteen years old, and that if he didn't want his son to leave home forever, he'd better get his act together."

Griff blew out his breath in a long sigh.

Indignation spent, Arabela wilted in his arms. "So, I suppose I've made things even worse?"

"I don't know that they're worse." Griff kissed the top of her head. "But they certainly aren't any better. Kilpatrick ordered me off his property and told me not to return."

AN older, beige, Chevy Suburban rolled into the barnyard the next afternoon as Griff and Arabella finished lunch. Johnny had just returned from the bunkhouse. He stepped out on the veranda, glaring toward the car and demanded, "What's my father doing here?"

Arabella and Griff rose to their feet. "I don't know," Griff answered.

The driver's door opened. Roger stepped out of the Suburban. He walked to the fence and stopped, looking at the trio on the porch.

Arabella and Johnny spoke at once.

"He looks sober."

"I don't wanna talk to him."

Griff responded, "Wait here." He vaulted over the porch rail and strode to the fence. The two men spoke for several minutes. Roger handed Griff an envelope, Griff opened it, read the papers inside, then tucked the whole thing into this shirt pocket. The men continued talking.

Their words didn't carry to the veranda, but their tone remained even and reasonable. Then Griff clasped Roger's right hand in his own. He placed his left hand on Roger's shoulder, and the two men bowed their heads.

"Are they praying?" Johnny whispered.

"Sure looks like it," Arabella answered.

A couple of moments later, Griff turned and walked back toward the house. Roger stood at the fence, looking at Johnny. He raised his hand offering a half wave, half salute.

Johnny shook his head.

Griff stopped at the rail and looked up at the boy. "Your father is checking himself into rehab this afternoon. He asked me to look out for you while he's there. He'll be gone at least one month, maybe as many as three. You might want to say good-bye to him, Johnny. Give him some hope."

Johnny crossed his arms. "Do I have to?"

"No—," Griff answered. Roger moved to the driver's door of the Suburban and looked back toward the house. "—but if you ever want to have a relationship with him, this would be a place to start." Griff tipped his head toward Roger. "He needs you."

Tugging his hat down over his eyes, Johnny answered, "Yeah? Well, where was he when I needed him?"

"I get it," Griff said. "And believe it or not, your dad does, too. He expected you to refuse."

Arabella reached out and put her hand on Johnny's shoulder. Roger stepped into the Suburban and closed the door. The engine rumbled, and the SUV reversed out of the lot, backing to face the access road. Seconds later, it shifted to drive and started away, Johnny vaulted the veranda rail and ran to the gate.

"Dad!" He wrenched the gate open and stumbled into the barn-yard. The Suburban stopped. Roger opened the driver's door. Father and son stared at each other, separated by twelve feet and more pain than either could express.

Griff's arms closed around Arabella. She leaned back against him, pressed her hands to her face, and watched the reunion through tear spangled eyes.

Roger stepped out of the rig, moving slowly as if he were afraid of frightening Johnny away. Arms out, he walked toward his son. Johnny caught his father's hand. They paused to look at one another again, then came together in an awkward, sideways hug.

Arabella sniffled as Roger held Johnny by the shoulders and talked. Johnny nodded repeatedly. Finally, Roger's hands dropped, they executed a complicated fist bump, then Roger climbed back into the Suburban and drove away.

Hip cocked, hands in his back pockets, Johnny watched the Suburban until it turned onto the access road and disappeared from sight. He looked toward Griff and Arabella, then turned on his heel and strode toward the corral. Arabella straightened away from Griff, who tightened his arms and said, "Let him go. He needs some time alone. He knows we're here for him."

Arabella turned in Griff's arms. "But what now? What happens come August 31st?"

Griff reached to tap the envelope in his shirt pocket. "I have temporary custody of Johnny for the next six months. At that point, he will be sixteen and can make his own decisions. The clinic Roger is signing into required him to make custody arrangements for 90 days. Roger filled it out for one hundred eighty days."

"So," Arabella counted on her fingers. "That means Johnny will still be in your custody when he turns sixteen."

"Yes. Roger wanted Johnny to know he wasn't going to force their relationship." Griff turned her to face him. "You did this. The things you said to Roger in the grocery store made him think."

"I am glad." Arabella leaned forward and rested on Griff's broad chest. "I guess I'm kind of touchy about parents who throw their kids away."

Griff rested his cheek on her head and hugged her a little tighter.

Chapter Nineteen

G radually, eating lunch together became a common occurrence. Griff would walk through the kitchen door sometime between noon and one o'clock and Arabella would have a meal waiting.

One day he teasingly asked what her catering services added to his bill. "Nothing!" She reached across the table and grabbed his hand. "It's already my lunchtime. Well, most of the produce comes from your garden, but—."

"I was teasing," he chided, then leaned over and placed a kiss on her forehead. Griff was easy with his affection. A gentle touch, a hug, an oc-casional chaste kiss, but he never asked for more or gave any indication he wanted those affections returned.

The following Friday morning, she was on the scaffold in the dining room painting window trim when the door opened far earlier than usual. Griff stepped into the kitchen. He wore his red and blue plaid shirt, only there was a lot more red than usual. Arabella came off the scaffold and was at his side in a matter of seconds.

"You're bleeding! What happened? Sit down!" She slipped under his arm on his uninjured side, bracing her right hand on his back and her left hand on his hard stomach.

"It's not as bad as it looks. Just a scratch." Griff draped his arm around her and gave her a hug. "It just hurts like the devil, and that'll help remind me not to be so stupid."

Given the spreading stain marring the right side of his shirt, he'd sustained more than 'just a scratch,' but he was walking and talking and had made it into the house under his own power. "What happened?" She guided him toward a chair.

"I turned my back on Muerte Manchado."

Her hands momentarily tightened on him. Arabella jerked her gaze to his, then she was all hands, unsnapping his shirt. "Let me see!"

Griff hissed. Her hands slowed, gentled, but her desperation remained. "How hard were you hit?" His shirt, tucked securely into his belt, wouldn't pull far enough away from his body to suit her. Griff stilled her hands by capturing them in his own. She tried to twist free. "I can't see!" What if he had internal injuries? She wouldn't be able to see them anyway, but he could die....

"The bull didn't get me." He said. "I did this to myself when I dove over the fence."

Relief rocked through her, followed by a rush of tears that clogged her throat. *Oh, sweet heaven, I could have lost him. That fast. I could have lost him, and he wouldn't even know that I ... love him.* Realization vibrated through her body like a shock wave. *I'm in love with him.* She closed her eyes and leaned forward, resting her forehead on his breastbone. She couldn't stop trembling.

Griff released her wrists and dropped his hands to her waist. Arabella lifted her fist and pounded three times on his left shoulder, not too hard because she didn't want to injure him further, but not lightly either because she needed the emotional release. "You just scared me half to death!" She wanted to kick him, too, but restrained herself.

He bent his head over hers. "I'm sorry," he murmured. "I guess I should have cleaned up in the barn some. I didn't really think it was that big a deal."

Arabella realized that he was comforting her and fought to pull herself together. She might feel like she'd taken the hit, but she wasn't the one battered and bloody. Wiping her face with her hands, she raised her chin and stepped away from him. "I'm sorry," she expelled a shaky breath and focused her gaze on Griff's shirt front. "Where's the first aid kit? Let's take a look at this."

GRIFF led the way to the utility room. Arabella wasn't looking at him again, but just for a moment, when she'd stepped into his arms, he'd totally thought that strand of barbed wire to the ribs was worth it. She had to care, or she wouldn't have reacted so violently, right? Although she was tenderhearted enough that she just might. How was he supposed to know?

He took the first-aid kit out of the cupboard above the sink and placed it on the counter. Then he unbuckled his belt and loosed the top button on his jeans. Arabella was there, brushing his hands away. She took hold of the left side of his shirt and gently tugged it from his jeans. She worked around him, pausing to free his left arm from his sleeve, then circling his back, removing his shirt by increments.

When she got to his wounded right side, Arabella moved more slowly. She freed the shirt from his waistband, reaching up and slipping it from his shoulder. She held the weight of the fabric so it wouldn't tug on his injury.

He hissed through his teeth as she peeled the torn and bloodied shirt from his rib cage, revealing three long, jagged, red welts. Blood beaded in some spots and oozed in others, but he was right. His life wasn't in jeopardy. He watched the tension ease from her shoulders.

She looked down at the cloth in her hands and murmured, "You know this was my favorite shirt, right?"

She had a favorite article of his clothing? Griff grinned. "Actually, I didn't. What was so special about that shirt?"

Extending her hand, she dropped the bloodied fabric into the wastebasket. She nodded at his ribcage and said, "Move your arm so I can get this cleaned up."

Griff extended his right arm and grabbed the clothes rod that hung above the drier. Obviously, Arabella had no intention of answering his question. A few seconds later, she pressed a gauze pad soaked in antiseptic to his side. He flinched, forgetting the question, how to breathe, and how to open his eyes.

He gripped the clothes bar and concentrated on standing still and not acting like a baby.

"Have you had your tetanus booster?" Arabella asked.

"Yes. That's all part of the ranch maintenance, too. Hale has spreadsheets on all of us. Shots, physicals, injuries—he says even people need to be maintained properly."

"Hmmm." Her voice was flat. "It's a pity he can't run you in for a common-sense checkup every now and again."

Griff studied Arabella's bent head as she examined and cleaned his side. She was there, moving around him, talking to him, touching him, but there was a remoteness to her as well. One minute she'd been concerned and compassionate, and in the next, she was cool, brisk and efficient. What prompted her change? Fear? Anger?

"These two cuts are pretty deep at the top of your ribs. They're still oozing blood. You may want to go into the clinic for a couple of stitches."

Griff grabbed the first aid kit. "Nah. Just use the butterfly bandages. I'll be fine."

Arabella's hands stopped. She stood immobile for several seconds, then said, "Right," and did as he'd asked.

Much too soon, her hands moved away from his side. She repacked the first aid kit and threw the trash away. "I've butterfly spliced the worst of the cuts, covered everything in antiseptic and gauze, and sealed it with waterproof tape. Feel free to shower. I'm going back to work."

She left the room without looking at him.

Griff went to his room to shower. When he returned, he wasn't at all surprised to discover Arabella had gone. He found her paintbrushes cleaned and put away rather than sealed in plastic for later use. She likely didn't plan to return to work before Monday.

She'd left him two ham and cheese sandwiches, a mound of potato salad, a chunk of lemon cake, and a note in the fridge. *Gone to town.* She hadn't even signed her name.

Every time he got too close, she ran.

Grabbing a can of soda, he carried it and his lunch platter to the master bedroom. Arabella came here every afternoon and sat on the window seat, but she'd yet to begin work. Lately, he'd begun to wonder why and that wondering gave him hope.

He knew Arabella cared for him. Her reaction to his injury provided further proof. But how much did she care? Could it be love, or would he sit in this barren room and stare out at her cottage for the rest of his life?

She insisted she wasn't afraid of him, but sometimes she still got tense, and he could see fear in her eyes. What exactly caused it? She touched him. She fought with him. She teased him. He raised his fingers to his left shoulder. She even thumped him from time-to-time. She trusted him not to hurt her, so what frightened her?

He stared at her cottage and sighed. There was only one way to find out.

It was time to stop letting her run.

That's why he stood at that same window Sunday morning, watching Arabella's house and waiting for her to leave. As soon as she pulled out of her driveway, he headed for his own truck. With the exception of Christmas Eve, he hadn't been to church since his parents died. When he walked into the sanctuary and sat down beside her, he figured Arabella would be the only one in the building who didn't know why he was there. He supposed that meant he was gambling in church and sure hoped the good Lord forgave him.

Chapter Twenty

Arabella took her usual seat on the right side of the church, second pew from the front. She put her Bible on her knees and opened her bulletin to preview the order of worship. Someone stepped past her and stopped.

She looked up as Griff sat down. Her eyes widened when he extended his arm along the pew behind her. "Morning." He smiled and her stomach flipped over. She slowly took in his black, western-cut suit, white shirt, and black leather, silver-tipped bolo tie. He looked delectable from his freshly cut ebony hair to his fancy grey snakeskin boots.

"Wha—"Her voice broke as his scent surrounded her. She swallowed and tried again, whispering urgently. "What are you doing here?"

A slow smile curved his lips. "You told me I should start coming to church."

"Yes, I did, but that doesn't explain why you're here." She pointed toward the pew between them.

"Worshipping the Lord?" His grin widened.

Her eyes narrowed. She clenched her teeth. "Not here," she said, twirling her index finger to encompass the church. "Here." Again, she pointed at the pew between them.

"Sitting with a pretty girl?"

"Move your arm! People are going to talk!"

Griff shrugged.

Her head came up and her chin jutted out. "If you—."

The music started, and the liturgist stepped to the pulpit. "All rise."

Arabella stood. Griff reached for the hymnal, flipped to the indicated page, and held the book in his big right hand. He turned slightly toward Arabella and used his left arm to pull her closer so they could share the hymnal. She resisted his embrace. He moved even closer. "Griff!" She hissed.

"Shhhh. Just sing."

Her throat had a lump in it too big to sing around. His scent and the heat of his body had her stomach in turmoil. His rich, wonderful baritone voice had her fighting the insane urge to put her head on his chest and bask in the rumble.

It was an impossibly long hymn. By the end of it, Anabella had developed a stitch in her side and stopped fighting Griff's hold. It was like trying to move a wall, anyway.

Arabella sat stiff and unbending, feet together, knees clamped, hands in her lap. Occasionally she tried to inch away. Griff just shifted with her. Soon she was trapped between the arm of the pew and his big body. Knowing she was sitting on his uninjured side, she dug her elbow into his ribs. He grunted, moved his arm from the back of the pew, and settled it firmly around her shoulders, pulling her even closer. She didn't have the leverage to jab him again.

He leaned down and whispered in her ear. "Stop. You're causing a scene."

"Me?" She hissed.

"Mm-hmm," he grinned at her.

Butterflies exploded in her stomach. She dropped her hand to Griff's knee and dug her fingernails into the inseam of his jeans. He tensed but did not move away. Arabella had intended to pinch the tender skin there but couldn't bring herself to actually hurt him. She loosened her grip. His right hand covered hers and held it in place.

She was causing a scene? Did the man have any idea what kind of impression his behavior was making on the rest of the congregation? How did he expect to find a wife with her in his arms?

Wait. Why did she care? She didn't want him marrying anyone else, anyway.

When the postlude began, Griff gathered up Arabella's purse and Bible, then offered her his hand. She didn't take it, but she did stand and reach for her belongings. "You do realize, don't you—. "

Griff shifted her purse and Bible out of her reach. "It's first Sunday," he said. "Do they still hold the monthly potluck?"

"Yes. Listen—"

"Are you staying?"

"Yes. I'm on the service committee. Would you please—"

"Help? I'd love to. Come on." He put his hand in the small of her back and nudged her toward the kitchen.

"Listen—."

By then, several other members of the congregation had stepped forward to welcome Griff back into their midst. Griff and Arabella had an escort all the way to the kitchen. Once there, Griff returned her possessions, kissed her on the cheek, and went to help the men set up tables and chairs in the Fellowship Hall.

"Oooh." Someone said as the ladies gathered around Arabella. "What's going on with you and Griff?"

"I don't know," Arabella said. "But certainly not what it looks like!"

Comments like, "*Oh, honey, that's too bad;*" "*He is fine;*" and "*Hey lady, you could do a lot worse,*" bounced around the kitchen. Arabella resolutely ignored them and Griff as she began organizing the covered dishes for the potluck table.

Griff was hard to ignore. As soon as the tables and chairs were in place, he was back at her side, lifting, carrying, fetching—and insisting she take a break and fix her own plate.

He ate beside her, chatting companionably with everyone at the table, something about second-cut haying and impossibly long, hot days. Near the end of the meal, he picked up her empty coffee cup and left, only to return moments later with a refill and five of her own pecan-chocolate chip cookies. He put the plate in front of her without a word, then proceeded to eat three of the cookies himself.

The ladies were all giving her knowing looks, except there was nothing to know. Arabella planned a few choice words for Griff.

Finally, the food was eaten, the tables and chairs put away, the dishes done, the kitchen cleaned, and the floors mopped. Griff walked Arabella to the parking lot. Beside her pickup, away from listening ears, she rounded on him. "What is wrong with you? Do you know what kind of impression you're making? You're giving people the wrong idea."

Griff took her key fob from her hand and unlocked her pickup door. "I don't think so," he said. "You worry too much." Then he dropped a chaste kiss on her stunned lips, curled her keys into her palm, and added, "Bye. Drive safely. Haying starts tomorrow. I'll be busy the next few days, but I promise I'll make time to see you," and he left.

Short of chasing him or yelling after him—and she wasn't providing any more entertainment for the congregation—their conversation was over. Arabella stood in the parking lot and watched him saunter away.

She was ready for him Monday morning—except he was out in the field before she arrived at work and didn't return for lunch. It was unusual for him to stay away without texting her. And even more unusual for him to miss lunch. He said he'd see her, so he would. Although, as the afternoon wore on, she had to remind herself of that fact every twenty minutes or so.

She checked her phone frequently and kept one eye on the door. While painting the dining room trim, she resolved to set firmer boundaries and stop all of the touching and kissing. It had to end before she did something foolish like declaring her undying love for him.

She lectured herself about that as well. She couldn't love Griff. Where was her self-preservation? He'd said they'd be together for as long as she lived on Spitfire Ranch; however, the first ten months of their relationship was proof that living side by side didn't mean they'd remain friends. It was probably already too late, but she needed to establish firmer boundaries.

Tomorrow she would pull the tarps and masking tape out of the dining room. Wednesday, the new downstairs furniture would be delivered. Once she completed the master suite, the house would be finished. Then the two of them could naturally return to being next-door neighbors who saw each other every now and then. She would start eating at her own house again. There would be a lot less touching.

But she still had to face the master suite.

Arabella climbed the stairs. She stepped through the double doors of the master bedroom and latched them behind her. Over the last couple of weeks, she'd ended every day in this room, unable to start the renovation.

Now she understood why.

Everyday Arabella had expected Griff to ask about the master bedroom. Even though the door always remained closed, it seemed odd he hadn't noticed the room had yet to be prepped, especially since the remainder of the upstairs was finished. Most afternoons, she came to sit on the window seat and wish. She knew exactly what she'd do with the room if it were hers, but it wasn't, and she couldn't create her dream for Griff to share with another woman.

The huge, multifaceted window drew her. Beyond it, heavy machinery moved across the field, compacting the hay into big round bales. A semi pulled a trailer with an extension arm that collected the round bales and rolled them onto its contoured deck.

She watched the busy-ness in the field for a while, then looked over at her own little cottage. What would happen when Griff did eventually find a wife? Arabella wondered how she'd survive living so close. She couldn't bear to think of him loving someone else. How could she stand watching his house, seeing the lights in this room go out every night?

The only way to ensure her emotional survival was to start now. First, she'd insist that there be no more kissing. None. Not on the forehead. Not on the cheek. Definitely not on the lips. Why had he done that anyway? Sunday had made everything so much worse. He'd treated her with enough care that people actually thought they were a couple. It all needed to stop while she was still strong enough to survive.

And where was Griff anyway? He was hours late. She needed him to be here now, which was ridiculous since once he arrived, she planned to insist they not see each other anymore. Or maybe it would be better if she just left and didn't see him at all today? Yes, not seeing him seemed a wise place to start.

She rose to her feet.

The door opened and Griff stepped into the room. Even though she'd been practicing all afternoon, Arabella hadn't prepared to have the conversation in the room consecrated for his marriage. But she needed this talk behind them. She needed boundaries cemented in place and the dread and uncertainty of their future to end. Clasping her hands to keep them from trembling, she squared her shoulders and faced him.

"Hey." He focused on her, not the room. "You've been sitting in that window for at least an hour. Are you all right?"

Arabella hugged herself. "R-really?" Her voice cracked. She drew in a breath and tried again. "An hour? Are you sure?"

Griff walked further into the room. "I could see you pretty clearly from the field. You usually come in here about four o'clock every afternoon and stay for a while."

She turned, hiding the shock on her face. She had no idea he knew.

"The rest of the house looks fabulous, but this room seems to be giving you some trouble." His hands cupped her shoulders. The scents of freshly mown hay and hard-working man enveloped her.

As his calloused hands slid down her arms, he murmured, "Why?"

She closed her eyes and sought for words to explain, but her breath left her as his arms slid around her waist. Dropping her hands to his wrists, she swallowed. Tried to shrug. "I can't ...." She shook her head and tried again. "I don't ...." No matter what she said, he was going to know. And then what? She'd go back to sitting in her cottage all alone.

No. Not even that. She suddenly realized that she'd leave Yellow Pine if Griff ever married someone else.

He pulled her back against his chest. She let her head drop back onto his shoulder. Would they ever stand like this again? How could he have become so dear to her without her realizing it?

He murmured, "You didn't have any trouble remodeling the other bedrooms."

"They're generic." She forced the words out. "I can't work on this room for the same reason you don't sleep here." Please let him accept that answer without embellishment.

"You don't want to be in the room alone?" He smoothed his right hand up her arm. A slow slide that ignited every nerve ending in her body. Her lungs malfunctioned. She couldn't seem to draw a breath. She needed out of his arms. Out of this room.

"Please." She tugged on his wrist. "I need to go."

"In a minute." His breath heated her face as his lips feathered against her ear. "Something about this room upsets you. Tell me what it is."

I want to share it with you! But she couldn't very well say that, could she? She shook her head and felt her hair snag the beard stubble on his chin. She strained her body away from his, but he held her tight, his muscled left arm around her waist.

"Don't!" She closed her eyes. Too late. A tear splashed on his wrist. A sob followed, and she tried to twist away. He let her turn but held her lightly in his embrace. "Let me go!" She cried. "Can't you see? I can't do this! I can't create a room for you to share with someone else!"

His hold loosened. She stumbled backward. The window seat behind her brought her up short. *What have I done?* She hung her head and clasped her arms across her middle where his had been. Tears splashed the floor at her feet.

Griff reached out and cupped her shoulders in his hands. "Oh, sweetheart, don't cry." He pulled her against his hard chest and cradled her head in his hand, gently tugging her hair, tilting her face to his.

She splayed her hands on his chest, intending to push him away, but made the mistake of opening her eyes. Their gazes locked. Suddenly she was drowning in indigo, unable to move. Unable to breathe.

His head descended slowly. "No," she whispered, but her gaze snapped to his lips. She'd wanted to kiss him so badly for so long now. What difference would it make? She'd already ruined everything anyway. Why couldn't she have a memory to take with her? Something to sustain her through the long, lonely years. She pushed up on her tiptoes, twined her arms around his neck, and pulled his head down.

As their lips met, he made a rough sound in his throat. His arms tightened and her feet left the floor. The room tilted crazily as Griff spun her away from the window. She clutched him tighter as he pressed her back against the wall. Nothing mattered but their kiss.

Too soon, he braced his arms on either side of her, letting her feet slide to the floor. He lifted his head. Unable to look him in the eyes, Arabella focused on the shirt snap at his throat. She pressed her hands to his chest, searching for something to say. She felt the pounding of his heart, then realized he was trembling, too. He rested his forehead on hers and whispered, "Honey, you'd better finish this room soon, because if you kiss me like that again before it's done, we may just have our honeymoon before our wedding."

Her hands fisted his shirt. "Griff?"

He raised his head and looked into her eyes. "I love you, Bella." He smoothed his thumbs across her wet cheeks and gave her a lopsided grin. "I love you. And this empty room was my greatest hope that you cared." He dipped his head and kissed her again.

This time when their lips parted, she lifted a trembling hand and cupped his beard-stubbled cheek. "You love me?" Her voice came out a whisper of hope.

"Oh, honey, I started falling in love with you the night you got the flat tire. Maybe even before that. Most everything I've done since our first kiss has been to show you how much I love you."

Fresh tears filled her eyes. "Why didn't you just tell me?"

"Because we started out all wrong. I decided to take it slow and romance you, but every time I'd get close, you'd shut down." He traced her kiss swollen lips with his index finger. His hand shook. "I couldn't risk losing you all together, so I went along with it. Changed my tactics. I tried so hard to get you to see me as a lover, but you persisted in keeping me at arm's length. Discovering you hadn't touched this room gave me hope. You came in here every afternoon to sit, but you never did any work."

"I couldn't."

"I saw that. I prayed I knew why, but I was afraid to say anything and chase you away altogether." His lips quirked in that half-smile she loved.

They stared at each other in silence. His eyes clouded. "What?" Arabella whispered.

"You think you could tell me?" His Adam's apple bobbed.

Her eyes widened in surprise. Did he need the words as badly as she did? Arabella touched her thumbs to his lips and held his face. "I love you," she said. "I love you."

Griff reached up, covered her fingers with his own, and froze. He studied her face carefully, then shifted his hands to her shoulders. "Stay right here. Hold this thought." Releasing her, he took a step backward.

"What?" She reached for him. "Where are you going?"

Griff grabbed her hand and kissed her fingers. "To shave."

THE next day, as lunchtime neared, Arabella sealed her paintbrush in a plastic bag, popped the lid on the paint can and went to wash up. She tossed her baseball cap on the floor and let her French braid fall down her back. It wasn't free, the way Griff preferred, but as close as she could get to free while working.

She'd started on the master bedroom that morning. Despite quite a bit of passionate kissing, they hadn't anticipated their honeymoon. Griff w as d etermined t hey h ave a t raditional w hite w edding i n the formal dining room, and their honeymoon night in the master suite. They'd decided to marry on his grandparents' anniversary, which left them only thirty-seven days to prepare both the room and the wedding.

Arabella fairly skipped to the refrigerator. She loved the kitchen but surely would have enjoyed creating it a whole lot more if she'd known she was designing it for herself.

That thought stopped her. She stared blankly into the fully stocked fridge as she realized, she had designed it for herself. Standing in the middle of the kitchen, she made a slow 360-degree turn.

Next, she studied the dining room and living room in much the same way, remembering that Griff initially suggested she make the decor decisions without him. The kitchen table had been the only furniture item he'd chosen without soliciting her opinion, which he'd already heeded when they'd selected the materials for the cabinets and countertops.

As she moved through the house, she replayed the thoughts she'd had while working in each room. He'd agreed to the removal of the batwing doors between the dining room and the kitchen. He'd told her to go ahead and pick the closet organizers she thought would most efficiently store personal items. She'd made the final decisions on the couch and rocking chair in his study. For every selection, he'd deferred to her. Was that because of her expertise, or because he wanted his home to suit her?

She stood in the study with her hands on the back of the rocking chair and remembered. That day when Griff first told her how he want-ed the study furnished—that he wanted a love seat and chair for his wife —even then, he was planning that she would be his wife.

All their dinners on the veranda, the time they'd spent rocking on the porch swing, the nights he'd walked her home, last Sunday in church ... he'd been courting her, and she hadn't even realized. She considered his patience, the disruption of his house, the expense! When she'd initially presented her prospectus, he'd chosen column three, all the way down, the dream column. He'd even agreed to help her promote her business while refusing a price discount. He had done it all for her. It was more than she could take in.

She turned and ran through the house, down the back steps, and all the way to the equipment shed where Griff said he'd be working on the tractor. She didn't stop until she stepped through the door and paused to let her eyes adjust to the dark.

He was in front of her before her vision cleared, catching her hands and pulling her toward him. "Bella, love, are you okay?" He tugged off his gloves. His calloused hands skimmed up her arms, paused on her shoulders, and then cupped her face. "What is it, honey?"

She pressed her hands to his chest and felt his heartbeat. "Did you plan it? Did you hire me to renovate your house for *me*? Did you know then that you wanted me to be your wife?"

Griff studied her face. His Adam's apple bobbed. "Yes," he barely whispered his answer.

"Why?" Arabella cried.

"Ah, honey, I already told you, because I love you." His thumbs caressed her shoulder.

"But Griff ...." She felt tears burn her eyes and floundered for words. "I've never—" She shook her head. "I don't—" How could she explain? Her feelings were too big for words. "Not even my family loved me," she burst out.

"Sweetheart," Griff tucked her to his chest. "I don't know what was wrong with your relatives, but their inability to love has nothing to do with you."

"How do you know that?" She tipped her head back and looked up at him.

Griff traced his finger down a blond corkscrew curl at her temple. "God knew you before you were born. He wanted you. He shaped your life. And while it might not have made sense to you as a kid, look what it's done for you as an adult. Your love has helped Johnny and possibly even his father."

"No way." Arabella shook her head. "I was way too angry with Roger for that to be love."

He kissed her nose. "It was love for Johnny, and it did have a positive impact on Kilpatrick. It's up to him to change his life, but God used you to get his attention. There's also your friendship with Tyner. You changed my opinion of him for the better. There's the care and compassion you showed Katy." Griff tightened his arms around Arabella. "And then there's me. You have softened my heart and changed me more than you realize. I wouldn't have given Johnny the support he needed if you hadn't led the way. But more than that, you taught me that I need to look at people as individuals and not make snap judgments."

"But—"

Griff didn't let her form her argument. "Somethings do last, Bella. And we've already proven our relationship is important. We know how to work together to make it strong."

"I think you did most of the work." Arabella rested her forehead on his collarbone. "As I walked through the house this morning, I realized just how much. Your perseverance is a little intimidating. Sometimes you're a very scary man."

Griff chuckled. "There were days I despaired that you'd never see me as more than a friend, but with you, Bella, I'm a marshmallow." He bent his head and covered her lips with his. Arabella rose to her tiptoes and twined her arms around his neck.

When their kiss ended, she said, "Mmm, I love kissing you. So many times you touched me, and held me, and I hoped you would kiss me, but you never did."

"You'd go all tense and stiff. I thought if I kissed you, you'd run."

She rested her forehead on his breast-bone and puffed out a rueful laugh. "Anticipation. Fear of wanting more than I could have. If I weren't so insecure, we could have been here a lot sooner."

Griff raised her face and looked into her eyes. "I have prayed for you every single day since that night in your kitchen. I think we did this exactly the way God wanted us to. First, we learned to communicate. Through that we become friends. Next, we'll get married and learn how to be lovers. Everything we've gone through has helped us build a firm foundation for the rest of our lives."

Slightly more than an hour later, Griff climbed the back steps and entered the kitchen. Arabella looked up from the Reuben sandwiches she had ready to grill and smiled at him.

Griff pulled her near. "In case you're still wondering what's in this relationship for me, I get to come home to this every day for the rest of my life."

With a butter knife in one hand and a spatula in the other, Arabella stood on her tiptoes to kiss him. "I don't know, sandwiches might get boring after a while."

"Not the food." Griff grinned and shook his head. "Your smile. It tells me you're happy to see me." He leaned in for another kiss. "Before we eat, there's something I want to share."

"Okay." She stepped back, prepared to listen.

He took the knife and spatula out of her hands and said, "Come with me to the study."

Arabella's gaze sharpened. "This sounds serious."

He smiled at her. "I'm hoping you'll find it a nice serious."

In the study, Griff directed her to the couch. He took a small box from inside his desk, turned and knelt in front of her. Arabella pressed her hands to her cheeks and stared at him through wide, luminous eyes.

His dimple flashed. "Are you going to cry on me again?"

She nodded her head as the first tear beaded on her eyelashes. Griff reached up and collected it on his finger. "Maybe you should wait to see if this is worth crying over." He indicated the black velvet box. "This is pretty much as old as the house. Griffin One had it made for his wife somewhere around their fifteenth wedding anniversary. If it doesn't fit, we can have it resized. Or, if you want something more modern or fancy, we can do that, too. But, I wanted to propose with this ring because our marriage will continue the legacy they started when they built Spitfire."

Arabella answered with a nod, a sniffle, and more tears.

Griff opened the box. A wedding set nestled inside. The engagement ring was a simple gold band with a one-carat, radiant-cut sapphire. The wedding ring featured five small, baguette-cut stones, three sapphires spaced by two white agates, all set in gold.

"Oh," Arabella took a shuddering breath. "They're beautiful."

Lifting the engagement ring from the box, Griff said, "The Montana state gemstone is the blue sapphire. According to the ranch journals, my great-whatever-grandmother didn't realize what the geode was and used it as a doorstop. Then one day she knocked it down the back steps and it broke open."

Arabella laughed.

Griff stopped and shook his head. "Drat me. I seem to be doing this wrong. I'm supposed to be proposing, and instead, I'm giving you ranch history lessons."

She leaned forward, took his face in her hands, and kissed him sweetly. "It's perfect."

When their kiss ended, he proffered the sapphire ring between his thumb and forefinger. "My darling, Bella, will you marry me? Will you let me, and Spitfire Ranch, always and forever be your home?"

Arabella slipped off the couch and into his arms. "There's nothing I want more."

Epilogue

Arabella dialed Katy's number. She leaned against Griff on the porch swing as they listened to the phone ring.

"Hi," Katy answered. "I'm glad you called. I have to cancel our lunch date. Something came up."

"No worries." Arabella answered. "We can reschedule. That's not why I'm calling though. Griff is here with me and you're on speaker phone. We have big news." Arabella tipped her head back and grinned at Griff.

After a moment of silence, Katy gasped. "You're getting married? Oh my gosh! You're getting married, aren't you?"

Griff laughed. "Yes, Katy-Bug. We're getting married in just a little over a month."

"I knew there was something going on with you two!"

Arabella laughed. "Yeah, well, then you knew it before I did."

"I'm really glad for you," Katy said.

"Thank you," Arabella answered. "I want you to be my maid of honor."

Silence.

Arabella sat up and stared at her phone. "Katy?"

"I don't know," Katy said.

"You don't know if you want to be my maid of honor? I guess I could ask Ty, but he'd look pretty comical in a bridesmaid dress."

Katy laughed. "You've got to know that I'd say 'no' just so I could see that."

Griff laughed. "Don't be mean, Katy-Bug."

"I don't think I can be in your wedding. I planned to share this to-morrow, after my first successful night, but I guess now is good. I got a job in Missoula. I'm managing a bar here."

"Wait! You're driving back and forth?" Griff asked.

"No." Katy said. "I moved here last week."

Griff stood up and lifted the phone from Arabella's hand. "How could you move without telling me?"

"Look, it was kind of sudden. Gar and I—" Katy huffed. "Never mind. The thing is, this job came up and I took it. And, well, I'm going to be pretty busy here learning the ropes."

"Surely you can take one day off for our wedding?" Griff asked.

More silence from Katy.

"You won't have to help me plan or anything," Arabella said. "We're keeping it simple. Around 20 people. Tank is making bar-b-que so, you know, it's really informal. I don't even care what you wear."

Katy sniffed. "Look, I just—" A sigh sounded over the phone. "I just can't."

"Are you all right?" Arabella interrupted as Griff demanded, "Are you crying?"

Katy sniffed. "I—I have to go—"

Arabella reached up and took the phone back. "You married him, didn't you? You married Gar to help him claim his inheritance even though you said you weren't going to."

"Yes." Katy answered.

"What on earth—" Griff exclaimed.

Arabella held up her hand to shush him and asked Katy, "When did you get married? Why didn't you tell me? And why have you moved to Missoula? I thought this was so Gar could inherit the farm?"

"It was. He did." Katy sounded tired. "Look, I had to help him. The farm has been in his family for 90 years. I couldn't let him lose it."

"But why get married?" Griff sounded frustrated. "And why keep it a secret?"

"The marriage was a trust fund condition," Katy answered. "And we didn't tell anybody so it wouldn't be awkward when we divorced."

"You lied to your friends and now you've moved to Missoula," Griff said. "I'd dang-well say that's awkward."

Arabella waved her hands in the universal gesture for 'no' and shook her head. "Katy? Are you okay? Do you need anything?"

"I'm fine," Katy answered. "Gar and I planned this from the beginning. Well, not my being offered this job. That was serendipity."

"You didn't leave Yellow Pine because of Gar?" Arabella questioned.

"I moved to Missoula for this job." Katy answered decisively. "And I really have to get back to it. I'm glad the two of you worked your relationship out. I'm sorry I can't be there for your wedding. It's just won't work out."

"But Katy—"

"Bye. See you later." The call disconnected.

"She hung up." Arabella stared at her cellphone screen. "I still have questions."

"I have a few, too," Griff answered. "You knew about this?"

"No," Shaking her head, Arabella shoved her cell phone in her back pocket. "I knew about the marriage-inheritance thing. I had no idea Katy married him. Before she left my house that morning, she told me there was no way that was going to happen. Since then, I've talked to her on the phone at least once a week and we've been out to lunch together twice. She never said a word."

"Why would they get married and keep it a secret?"

"I get that part." Arabella scooted around until she could lean back against Griff's chest. "It wasn't a real marriage, so why get their friends caught up in it? But if everything worked out the way they'd planned, then why did Katy leave town?"

Charlene Amsden

Thank you for reading my story. If you enjoyed this novel, please consider leaving a review on Amazon[1] or GoodReads[2].

IF YOU WANT TO KNOW why Katy left town, stay tuned for, *Conceived For Love*[3], book #2 in *The Yellow Pine Series*[4]. Soon to be available for preorder on Amazon.com.

AND IF YOU'RE INTERESTED in my real-life romance, come visit me at: http://www.charlene-amsden.com/.

---

1. https://amzn.to/2FAW7jp

2. https://www.goodreads.com/author/show/20670627.Charlene_Amsden

3. *https://smile.amazon.com/dp/B08HXGR7X4/*

4. *https://amazon.com/dp/B08HJ1F93H?ref_=dbs_s_ks_series_rwt*